SOME EXPERIENCES
OF AN IRISH R.M.

Country Races of a Typical Sort

E.Œ. SOMERVILLE AND
MARTIN ROSS

SOME EXPERIENCES
OF AN IRISH R.M.

With Illustrations by Edith Somerville

J.S. SANDERS & COMPANY

NASHVILLE

1998

The stories in this collection were first published in book form in London by Longmans, Green, 1899.

First J.S. Sanders & Company edition, 1998.

Library of Congress Cataloging-in-Publication Data

Somerville, E. Œ. (Edith Œnone), 1858-1949.
    Some Experiences of an Irish R.M. / by E. Œ.
Somerville and Martin Ross.
        p.   cm.
    ISBN 1-879941-40-6 (pbk. : alk. paper)
        1. Ireland—Social life and customs—19th century—
Fiction.   2. Humorous stories, English—Irish authors.
3. Justices of the peace—Ireland—Fiction.   4. British—Ireland—
Fiction.   I. Ross, Martin, 1862-1915.   II. Title.
PR6037.06S5   1998   98-34554
823′.8—dc21   CIP

Published in the United States by:

J.S. Sanders & Company, Inc.
Post Office Box 50331
Nashville, Tennessee 37205

Printed in the United States

1   3   5   7   9   10   8   6   4   2

CONTENTS

One

GREAT-UNCLE McCARTHY

A RESIDENT Magistracy in Ireland is not an easy thing to come by nowadays; neither is it a very attractive job; yet on the evening when I first propounded the idea to the young lady who had recently consented to become Mrs. Sinclair Yeates, it seemed glittering with possibilities. There was, on that occasion, a sunset, and a string band playing "The Gondoliers," and there was also an ingenuous belief in the omnipotence of a godfather of Philippa's—(Philippa was the young lady)—who had once been a member of the Government.

I was then climbing the steep ascent of the Captains towards my Majority. I have no fault to find with Philippa's godfather; he did all and more than even Philippa had expected; nevertheless, I had attained to the dignity of mud major, and had spent a good deal on postage stamps, and on railway fares to interview people of influence, before I found myself in the hotel at Skebawn, opening long envelopes addressed to "Major Yeates, R.M."

My most immediate concern, as any one who has spent nine weeks at Mrs. Raverty's hotel will readily believe, was to leave it at the earliest opportunity; but in those nine weeks I had learned, amongst other painful things, a little, a very little, of the methods of the artisan in the West of Ireland. Finding a house had been easy enough. I had had my choice of several, each with some hundreds of acres of shooting, thoroughly poached, and a considerable portion of the roof intact. I had selected one; the one that had the largest extent of roof in proportion to the shooting, and had been assured by my landlord that in a fortnight or so it would be fit for occupation.

"There's a few little odd things to be done," he said easily; "a lick of paint here and there, and a slap of plaster——"

I am short-sighted; I am also of Irish extraction; both facts that make for toleration—but even I thought he was understating the case. So did the contractor.

At the end of three weeks the latter reported progress, which mainly consisted of the facts that the plumber had accused the carpenter of stealing sixteen feet of his inch-pipe to run a bell wire through, and that the carpenter had replied that he wished the divil might run the plumber through a wran's quill. The plumber having reflected upon the carpenter's parentage, the work of renovation had merged in battle, and at the next Petty Sessions I was reluctantly compelled to allot to each combatant seven days, without the option of a fine.

These and kindred difficulties extended in an unbroken chain through the summer months, until a certain wet and windy day in October, when, with my baggage, I drove over to establish myself at Shreelane. It was a tall, ugly house of three storeys high, its walls faced with weather-beaten slates, its windows staring, narrow, and vacant. Round the house ran an area, in which grew some laurustinus and holly bushes among ash heaps, and nettles, and broken bottles. I stood on the steps, waiting for the door to be opened, while the rain sluiced upon me from a broken eaveshoot that had, amongst many other things, escaped the notice of my landlord. I thought of Philippa, and of her plan, broached in to-day's letter, of having the hall done up as a sitting-room.

The door opened, and revealed the hall. It struck me that I had perhaps overestimated its possibilities. Among them I had certainly not included a flagged floor, sweating with damp, and a reek of cabbage from the adjacent kitchen stairs. A large elderly woman, with a red face, and a cap worn helmet-wise on her forehead, swept me a magnificent curtsey as I crossed the threshold.

"Your honour's welcome——" she began, and then every door in the house slammed in obedience to the gust that drove through it. With something that sounded like "Mend ye for a back door!" Mrs. Cadogan abandoned her opening speech and made for the kitchen stairs. (Improbable as it may appear, my housekeeper was called Cadogan, a name made locally possible by being pronounced Caydogawn.)

Only those who have been through a similar experience can know what manner of afternoon I spent. I am a martyr to colds in the head, and I felt one coming on. I made a laager in front of the dining-room fire, with a tattered leather screen and the dinner table, and gradually, with cigarettes and strong tea, baffled the smell of must and cats, and fervently trusted that the rain might avert a threatened visit from my landlord. I was then but superficially acquainted with Mr. Florence McCarthy Knox and his habits.

At about 4.30, when the room had warmed up, and my cold was yielding to treatment, Mrs. Cadogan entered and informed me that "Mr. Flurry" was in the yard, and would be thankful if I'd go out to him, for he couldn't come in. Many are the privileges of the female sex; had I been a woman I should unhesitatingly have said that I had a cold in my head. Being a man, I huddled on a mackintosh, and went out into the yard.

My landlord was there on horseback, and with him there was a man standing at the head of a stout grey animal. I recognised with despair that I was about to be compelled to buy a horse.

"Good afternoon, Major," said Mr. Knox in his slow,

sing-song brogue; "it's rather soon to be paying you a visit, but I thought you might be in a hurry to see the horse I was telling you of."

I could have laughed. As if I were ever in a hurry to see a horse! I thanked him, and suggested that it was rather wet for horse-dealing.

"Oh, it's nothing when you're used to it," replied Mr. Knox. His gloveless hands were red and wet, the rain ran down his nose, and his covert coat was soaked to a sodden brown. I thought that I did not want to become used to it. My relations with horses have been of a purely military character. I have endured the Sandhurst riding-school, I have galloped for an impetuous general, I have been steward at regimental races, but none of these feats have altered my opinion that the horse, as a means of locomotion, is obsolete. Nevertheless, the man who accepts a resident magistracy in the south-west of Ireland voluntarily retires into the prehistoric age; to institute a stable became inevitable.

"You ought to throw a leg over him," said Mr. Knox, "and you're welcome to take him over a fence or two if you like. He's a nice flippant jumper."

Even to my unexacting eye the grey horse did not seem to promise flippancy, nor did I at all desire to find that quality in him. I explained that I wanted something to drive, and not to ride.

"Well, that's a fine raking horse in harness," said Mr. Knox, looking at me with his serious grey eyes, "and you'd drive him with a sop of hay in his mouth. Bring him up here, Michael."

Michael abandoned his efforts to kick the grey horse's forelegs into a becoming position, and led him up to me.

I regarded him from under my umbrella with a quite unreasonable disfavour. He had the dreadful beauty of a horse in a toy-shop, as chubby, as wooden, and as conscientiously dappled, but it was unreasonable to urge this as an objection, and I was incapable of finding any more technical drawback. Yielding to circumstance, I "threw my leg" over the brute, and after pacing gravely round the quadrangle that formed the yard, and jolting to my entrance gate and back, I decided that as he had neither fallen down nor kicked me off, it was worth paying twenty-five pounds for him, if only to get in out of the rain.

Mr. Knox accompanied me into the house and had a drink. He was a fair, spare young man, who looked like a stable boy among gentlemen, and a gentleman among stable boys. He belonged to a clan that cropped up in every grade of society in the county, from Sir Valentine Knox of Castle Knox down to the auctioneer Knox, who bore the attractive title of Larry the Liar. So far as I could judge, Florence McCarthy of that ilk occupied a shifting position about midway in the tribe. I had met him at dinner at Sir Valentine's, I had heard of him at an illicit auction, held by Larry the Liar, of brandy stolen from a wreck. They were "Black Protestants," all of them, in virtue of their descent from a godly soldier of Cromwell, and all were prepared at any moment of the day or night to sell a horse.

"You'll be apt to find this place a bit lonesome after the hotel," remarked Mr. Flurry, sympathetically, as he placed his foot in its steaming boot on the hob, "but it's a fine sound house anyway, and lots of rooms in it, though indeed, to tell you the truth, I never was through the whole of them since the time my great-uncle, Denis McCarthy, died here. The dear knows I had enough of it that time." He paused, and lit a cigarette—one of my best, and quite thrown away upon him. "Those top floors, now," he resumed, "I wouldn't make too free with them. There's some of them would jump under you like a spring bed. Many's the night I was in and out of those attics, following my poor uncle when he had a bad turn on him—the horrors, y' know—there were nights he never stopped walking through the house. Good Lord! will I ever forget the morning he said he saw the devil coming up the avenue! "Look at the two horns on him," says he, and he out with his gun and shot him, and, begad, it was his own donkey!"

Mr. Knox gave a couple of short laughs. He seldom laughed,

having in unusual perfection the gravity of manner that is bred by horse-dealing, probably from the habitual repression of all emotion save disparagement.

The autumn evening, grey with rain, was darkening in the tall windows, and the wind was beginning to make bullying rushes among the shrubs in the area; a shower of soot rattled down the chimney and fell on the hearthrug.

"More rain coming," said Mr. Knox, rising composedly; "you'll have to put a goose down these chimneys some day soon, it's the only way in the world to clean them. Well, I'm for the road. You'll come out on the grey next week, I hope; the hounds'll be meeting here. Give a roar at him coming in at his jumps." He threw his cigarette into the fire and extended a hand to me. "Good-bye, Major, you'll see plenty of me and my hounds before you're done. There's a power of foxes in the plantations here."

This was scarcely reassuring for a man who hoped to shoot woodcock, and I hinted as much.

"Oh, is it the cock?" said Mr. Flurry; "b'leeve me, there never was a woodcock yet that minded hounds, now, no more than they'd mind rabbits! The best shoots ever I had here, the hounds were in it the day before."

When Mr. Knox had gone, I began to picture myself going across country roaring, like a man on a fire-engine, while Philippa put the goose down the chimney; but when I sat down to write to her I did not feel equal to being humorous about it. I dilated ponderously on my cold, my hard work, and my loneliness, and eventually went to bed at ten o'clock full of cold shivers and hot whiskey-and-water.

After a couple of hours of feverish dozing, I began to understand what had driven Great-Uncle McCarthy to perambulate the house by night. Mrs. Cadogan had assured me that the Pope of Rome hadn't a betther bed undher him than myself; wasn't I down on the new flog mattherass the old masther bought in Father Scanlan's auction? By the smell I recognised that "flog" meant flock, otherwise I should have said my couch was stuffed with old boots. I have seldom spent a more wretched night. The rain drummed with soft fingers on my window panes; the house was full of noises. I seemed to see Great-Uncle McCarthy ranging the passages with Flurry at his heels; several times I thought I heard him. Whisperings seemed borne on the wind through my keyhole, boards creaked in the room overhead, and once I could have sworn that a hand passed, groping, over the panels of my door. I am, I may admit, a believer in ghosts; I even take in a paper that deals with their culture, but I cannot pretend that on that night I looked forward to a manifestation of Great-Uncle McCarthy with any enthusiasm.

The morning broke stormily, and I woke to find Mrs. Cadogan's understudy, a grimy nephew of about eighteen, standing by my bedside, with a black bottle in his hand.

"There's no bath in the house, sir," was his reply to my command; "but me A'nt said, would ye like a taggeen?"

This alternative proved to be a glass of raw whisky. I declined it.

I look back to that first week of housekeeping at Shreelane as to a comedy excessively badly staged, and striped with lurid melodrama. Towards its close I was positively home-sick for Mrs. Raverty's, and I had not a single clean pair of boots. I am not one of those who hold the convention that in Ireland the rain never ceases, day or night, but I must say that my first November at Shreelane was composed of weather of which my friend Flurry Knox remarked that you wouldn't meet a Christian out of doors, unless it was a snipe or a dispensary doctor. To this lamentable category might be added a resident magistrate. Daily, shrouded in mackintosh, I set forth for the Petty Sessions Courts of my wide district; daily, in the inevitable atmosphere of wet frieze and perjury, I listened to indictments of old women who plucked geese alive, of publicans whose hospitality to their friends broke forth uncontrollably on Sunday afternoon, of "parties" who, in the language of the police sergeant, were subtly defined as "not to say dhrunk, but in good fighting thrim."

I got used to it all in time—I suppose one can get used to anything—I even became callous to the surprises of Mrs. Cadogan's cooking. As the weather hardened and the woodcock came in, and one by one I discovered and nailed up the rat holes, I began to find life endurable, and even to feel some remote sensation of home-coming when the grey horse turned in at the gate of Shreelane.

The one feature of my establishment to which I could not become inured was the pervading sub-presence of some thing or things which, for my own convenience, I summarised as Great-Uncle McCarthy. There were nights on which I was certain that I heard the inebriate shuffle of his foot overhead, the touch of his fumbling hand against the walls. There were dark times before the dawn when sounds went to and fro, the moving of weights, the creaking of doors, a far-away rapping in which was a workmanlike suggestion of the undertaker, a rumble of wheels on the avenue. Once I was impelled to the perhaps imprudent measure of cross-examining Mrs. Cadogan. Mrs. Cadogan, taking the preliminary precaution of crossing herself, asked me fatefully what day of the week it was.

"Friday!" she repeated after me. "Friday! The Lord save us! 'Twas a Friday the old masther was buried!"

At this point a saucepan opportunely boiled over, and Mrs. Cadogan fled with it to the scullery, and was seen no more.

In the process of time I brought Great-Uncle McCarthy down to a fine point. On Friday nights he made coffins and drove hearses; during the rest of the week he rarely did more than patter and shuffle in the attics over my head.

One night, about the middle of December, I awoke, suddenly aware that some noise had fallen like a heavy stone into my dreams. As I felt for the matches it came again, the long, grudging groan and the uncompromising bang of the cross door at the head of the kitchen stairs. I told myself that it was a draught that had done it, but it was a perfectly still night.

Even as I listened, a sound of wheels on the avenue shook the stillness. The thing was getting past a joke. In a few minutes I was stealthily groping my way down my own staircase, with a box of matches in my hand, enforced by scientific curiosity, but none the less armed with a stick. I stood in the dark at the top of the back stairs and listened; the snores of Mrs. Cadogan and her nephew Peter rose tranquilly from their respective lairs. I descended to the kitchen and lit a candle; there was nothing unusual there, except a great portion of the Cadogan wearing apparel, which was arranged at the fire, and was being serenaded by two crickets. Whatever had opened the door, my household was blameless.

The kitchen was not attractive, yet I felt indisposed to leave it. None the less, it appeared to be my duty to inspect the yard. I put the candle on the table and went forth into the outer darkness. Not a sound was to be heard. The night was very cold, and so dark, that I could scarcely distinguish the roofs of the stables against the sky; the house loomed tall and oppressive above me; I was conscious of how lonely it stood in the dumb and barren country. Spirits were certainly futile creatures, childish in their manifestations, stupidly content with the old machinery of raps and rumbles. I thought how fine a scene might be played on a stage like this; if I were a ghost, how bluely I would glimmer at the windows, how whimperingly chatter in the wind. Something whirled out of the darkness above me, and fell with a flop on the ground, just at my feet. I jumped backwards, in point of fact I made for the kitchen door, and, with my hand on the latch, stood still and waited. Nothing further happened; the thing that lay there did not stir. I struck a match. The moment of tension turned to bathos as the light flickered on nothing more fateful than a dead crow.

Dead it certainly was. I could have told that without looking at it; but why should it, at some considerable period after its death, fall from the clouds at my feet. But did it fall from the clouds? I struck another match, and stared up at the impenetrable face of the house. There was no hint of solution in the dark windows, but I determined to go up and search the rooms that gave upon the yard.

How cold it was! I can feel now the frozen musty air of those attics, with their rat-eaten floors and wall-papers furred with damp. I went softly from one to another, feeling like a burglar in my own house, and found nothing in elucidation of the mystery. The windows were hermetically shut, and sealed with cobwebs. There was no furniture, except in the end room, where a wardrobe without doors stood in a corner, empty save for the solemn presence of a monstrous tall hat. I went back to bed, cursing those powers of darkness that had got me out of it, and heard no more.

My landlord had not failed of his promise to visit my coverts with his hounds; in fact, he fulfilled it rather more conscientiously than seemed to me quite wholesome for the cock-shooting. I maintained a silence which I felt to be magnanimous on the part of a man who cared nothing for hunting and a great deal for shooting, and wished the hounds more success in the slaughter of my foxes than seemed to be granted to them. I met them all, one red frosty evening, as I drove down the long hill to my demesne gates, Flurry at their head, in his shabby pink coat and dingy breeches, the hounds trailing dejectedly behind him and his half-dozen companions.

"What luck?" I called out, drawing rein as I met them.

"None," said Mr. Flurry briefly. He did not stop, neither did he remove his pipe from the down-twisted corner of his mouth; his eye at me was cold and sour. The other members of the hunt passed me with equal hauteur; I thought they took their ill luck very badly.

On foot, among the last of the straggling hounds, cracking a carman's whip, and swearing comprehensively at them all, slouched my friend Slipper. Our friendship had begun in Court, the relative positions of the dock and the judgment-seat forming no obstacle to its progress, and had been cemented during several days' tramping after snipe. He was, as usual, a little drunk, and he hailed me as though I were a ship.

"Ahoy, Major Yeates!" he shouted, bringing himself up with a lurch against my cart; "it's hunting you should be, in place of sending poor divils to gaol!"

My friend Slipper

"But I hear you had no hunting," I said.

"Ye heard that, did ye?" Slipper rolled upon me an eye like that of a profligate pug. "Well, begor, ye heard no more than the thruth."

"But where are all the foxes?" said I.

"Begor, I don't know no more than your honour. And Shreelane—that there used to be as many foxes in it as there's crosses in a yard of check! Well, well, I'll say nothin' for it, only that it's quare! Here, Vaynus! Naygress!" Slipper uttered a yell, hoarse with whisky, in adjuration of two elderly ladies of the pack who had profited by our conversation to stray away into an adjacent cottage. "Well, good-night, Major. Mr. Flurry's as cross as briars, and he'll have me ate!"

He set off at a surprisingly steady run, cracking his whip, and whooping like a madman. I hope that when I also am fifty I shall be able to run like Slipper.

That frosty evening was followed by three others like unto it, and a flight of woodcock came in. I calculated that I could do with five guns, and I despatched invitations to shoot and dine on the following day to four of the local sportsmen, among whom was, of course, my landlord. I remember that in my letter to the latter I expressed a facetious hope that my bag of cock would be more successful than his of foxes had been.

The answers to my invitations were not what I expected. All, without so much as a conventional regret, declined my invitation; Mr. Knox added that he hoped the bag of cock would be to my liking, and that I need not be "affraid" that the hounds would trouble my coverts any more. Here was war! I gazed in stupefaction at the crooked scrawl in which my landlord had declared it. It was wholly and entirely inexplicable, and instead of going to sleep comfortably over the fire and my newspaper as a gentleman should, I spent the evening in irritated ponderings over this bewildering and exasperating change of front on the part of my friendly squireens.

My shoot the next day was scarcely a success. I shot the woods in company with my game-keeper, Tim Connor, a gentleman whose duties mainly consisted in limiting the poaching privileges to his personal friends, and whatever my offence might have been, Mr. Knox could have wished me no bitterer punishment than hearing the unavailing shouts of "Mark cock!" and seeing my birds winging their way from the coverts, far out of shot. Tim Connor and I got ten couple between us; it might have been thirty if my neighbours had not boycotted me, for what I could only suppose was the slackness of their hounds.

I was dog-tired that night, having walked enough for three men, and I slept the deep, insatiable sleep that I had earned. It was somewhere about 3 A.M. that I was gradually awakened by a continuous knocking, interspersed with muffled calls. Great-Uncle McCarthy had never before given tongue, and I freed one ear from blankets to listen. Then I remembered that Peter had told me the sweep had promised to arrive that morning, and to arrive early. Blind with sleep and fury I went to the passage window, and thence desired the sweep to go to the devil. It availed me little. For the remainder of the night I could hear him pacing round the house, trying the windows, banging at the doors, and calling upon Peter Cadogan as the priests of Baal called upon their god. At six o'clock I had fallen into a troubled doze, when Mrs. Cadogan knocked at my door and imparted the information that the sweep had arrived. My answer need not be recorded, but in spite of it the door opened, and my housekeeper, in a weird *déshabille*, effectively lighted by the orange beams of her candle, entered my room.

"God forgive me, I never seen one I'd hate as much as that sweep!" she began; "he's these three hours—arrah, what, three hours!—no, but all night, raising tallywack and tandem round the house to get at the chimbleys."

"Well, for Heaven's sake let him get at the chimneys and let me go to sleep," I answered, goaded to desperation, "and you may tell him from me that if I hear his voice again I'll shoot him!"

Mrs. Cadogan silently left my bedside, and as she closed the door she said to herself, "The Lord save us!"

Subsequent events may be briefly summarised. At 7.30 I was wakened anew by a thunderous sound in the chimney, and a brick crashed into the fireplace, followed at a short interval by two dead jackdaws and their nests. At eight, I was informed by Peter that there was no hot water, and that he wished the divil would roast the same sweep. At 9.30, when I came down to breakfast, there was no fire anywhere, and my coffee, made in the coach-house, tasted of soot. I put on an overcoat and opened my letters. About fourth or fifth in the uninteresting heap came one in an egregiously disguised hand.

"Sir," it began, "this is to inform you your unsportsmanlike conduct has been discovered. You have been suspected this good while of shooting the Shreelane foxes, it is known now you do worse. Parties have seen your gamekeeper going regular to meet the Saturday early train at Salters Hill Station, with your grey horse under a cart, and your labels on the boxes, and we know as well as *your agent in Cork* what it is you have in those boxes. Be warned in time.—Your Wellwisher."

I read this through twice before its drift became apparent, and I realised that I was accused of improving my shooting and my finances by the simple expedient of selling my foxes. That is to say, I was in a worse position than if I had stolen a horse, or murdered Mrs. Cadogan, or got drunk three times a week in Skebawn.

For a few moments I fell into wild laughter, and then, aware that it was rather a bad business to let a lie of this kind get a start, I sat down to demolish the preposterous charge in a letter to Flurry Knox. Somehow, as I selected my sentences, it was borne in upon me that, if the letter spoke the truth, circumstantial evidence was rather against me. Mere lofty repudiation would be unavailing, and by my infernal facetiousness about the woodcock I had effectively filled in the case against myself. At all events, the first thing to do was to establish a basis, and have it out with Tim Connor. I rang the bell.

"Peter, is Tim Connor about the place?"

"He is not, sir. I heard him say he was going west the hill to mend the bounds fence." Peter's face was covered with soot, his eyes were red, and he coughed ostentatiously. "The sweep's after breaking one of his brushes within in yer bedroom chimney, sir," he went on, with all the satisfaction of his class in announcing domestic calamity; "he's above on the roof now, and he'd be thankful to you to go up to him."

I followed him upstairs in that state of simmering patience that any employer of Irish labour must know and sympathise with. I climbed the rickety ladder and squeezed through the dirty trapdoor involved in the ascent to the roof, and was confronted by the hideous face of the sweep, black against the frosty blue sky. He had encamped with all his paraphernalia on the flat top of the roof, and was good enough to rise and put his pipe in his pocket on my arrival.

"Good morning, Major. That's a grand view you have up here," said the sweep. He was evidently far too well-bred to talk shop. "I thravelled every roof in this counthry, and there isn't one where you'd get as handsome a prospect!"

Theoretically he was right, but I had not come up to the roof to discuss scenery, and demanded brutally why he had sent for me. The explanation involved a recital of the special genius required to sweep the Shreelane chimneys; of the fact that the sweep had in infancy been sent up and down every one of them by Great-Uncle McCarthy; of the three ass-loads of soot that by his peculiar skill he had this morning taken from the kitchen chimney; of its present purity, the draught being such that it would "dhraw up a young cat with it." Finally—realising that I could endure no more—he explained that my bedroom chimney had got what he called "a wynd" in it, and he proposed to climb down a little way in the stack to try "would he get to come at the brush." The sweep was very small, the chimney very large. I stipulated that he should have a rope round his waist, and despite the illegality, I let him go. He went down like a monkey, digging his toes and fingers into the niches made for the purpose in the old chimney; Peter held the rope. I lit a cigarette and waited.

Certainly the view from the roof was worth coming up to look at. It was rough, heathery country on one side, with a string of little blue lakes running like a turquoise necklet round the base of a firry hill, and patches of pale green pasture were set amidst the rocks and heather. A silvery flash behind the undulations of the hills told where the Atlantic lay in immense plains of sunlight. I turned to survey with an owner's eye my own grey woods and straggling plantations of larch, and espied a man coming out of the western wood. He had something on his back, and he was walking very fast; a rabbit poacher no doubt. As he passed out of sight into the back avenue he was beginning to run. At the same instant I saw on the hill beyond my western boundaries half-a-dozen horsemen scrambling by zigzag ways down towards the wood. There was one red coat among them; it came first at the gap in the fence that Tim Connor had gone out to mend, and with the others was lot to sight in the covert, from which, in another instant, came clearly through the frosty air a shout of "Gone to ground!" Tremendous horn blowings followed, then, all in the same moment, I saw the hounds break in full cry from the wood, and come stringing over the grass and up the back avenue towards the yard gate. Were they running a fresh fox into the stables?

I do not profess to be a hunting-man, but I am an Irishman, and so, it is perhaps superfluous to state, is Peter. We forgot the sweep as if he had never existed, and precipitated ourselves down the ladder, down the stairs, and out into the yard. One side of the yard is formed by the coach-house and a long stable, with a range of lofts above them, planned on the heroic scale in such matters that obtained in Ireland formerly. These join the house at the corner by the back door. A long flight of stone steps leads to the lofts, and up these, as Peter and I emerged from the back door, the hounds were struggling helter-skelter. Almost simultaneously there was a confused clatter of hoofs in the back avenue, and Flurry Knox came stooping at a gallop under the archway followed by three or four other riders. They flung themselves from their horses and made for the steps of the loft; more hounds pressed, yelling, on their heels, the din was indescribable, and justified Mrs. Cadogan's subsequent remark that "when she heard the noise she thought 'twas the end of the world and the divil collecting his own!"

I jostled in the wake of the party, and found myself in the loft, wading in hay, and nearly deafened by the clamour that was bandied about the high roof and walls. At the farther end of the loft the hounds were raging in the hay, encouraged thereto by the whoops and screeches of Flurry and his friends. High up in the gable of the loft, where it joined the main wall of the house, there was a small door, and I noted with a transient surprise that there was a long ladder leading up to it. Even as it caught my eye a hound fought his way out of a drift of hay and began to jump at the ladder, throwing his tongue vociferously, and even clambering up a few rungs in his excitement.

"There's the way he's gone!" roared Flurry, striving through hounds and hay towards the ladder, "Trumpeter has him! What's up there, back of the door, Major? I don't remember it at all."

My crimes had evidently been forgotten in the supremacy of the moment. While I was futilely asserting that had the fox gone up the ladder he could not possibly have opened the door and shut it after him, even if the door led anywhere, which, to the best of my belief, it did not, the door in question opened, and to my amazement the sweep appeared at it. He gesticulated violently, and over the tumult was heard to asseverate that there was nothing above there, only a way into the flue, and any one would be destroyed with the soot——

"Ah, go to blazes with your soot!" interrupted Flurry, already half-way up the ladder.

I followed him, the other men pressing up behind me. That Trumpeter had made no mistake was instantly brought home to our noses by the reek of fox that met us at the door. Instead of a chimney, we found ourselves in a dilapidated bedroom, full of people. Tim Connor was there, the sweep was there, and a squalid elderly man and woman on whom I had never set eyes before. There was a large open fireplace, black with the soot the sweep had brought down with him, and on the table stood a bottle of my own special Scotch whisky. In one corner of the room was a pile of broken packing-cases, and beside these on the floor lay a bag in which something kicked.

Flurry, looking more uncomfortable and nonplussed than I could have believed possible, listened in silence to the ceaseless harangue of the elderly woman. The hounds were yelling like lost spirits in the loft below, but her voice pierced the uproar like a bagpipe. It was an unspeakably vulgar voice, yet it was not the voice of a countrywoman, and there were frowzy remnants of respectability about her general aspect.

"And is it you, Flurry Knox, that's calling me a disgrace! Disgrace, indeed, am I? Me that was your poor mother's own uncle's daughter, and as good a McCarthy as ever stood in Shreelane!"

What followed I could not comprehend, owing to the fact that the sweep kept up a perpetual under-current of explanation to me as to how he had got down the wrong chimney. I noticed that his breath stand of whisky—Scotch, not the native variety.

Never, as long as Flurry Knox lives to blow a horn, will he hear the last of the day that he ran his mother's first cousin to ground in the attic. Never, while Mrs. Cadogan can hold a basting spoon, will she cease to recount how, on the same occasion, she plucked and roasted ten couple of woodcock in one torrid hour to provide luncheon for the hunt. In the glory of this achievement her confederacy with the stowaways in the attic is wholly slurred over, in much the same manner as the startling outburst of summons for trespass, brought by Tim Connor during the remainder of the shooting season, obscured the unfortunate episode of the bagged fox. It was, of course, zeal for my shooting that induced him to assist Mr. Knox's disreputable relations in the deportation of my foxes; and I have allowed it to remain at that.

In fact, the only things not allowed to remain were Mr. and Mrs. McCarthy Gannon. They, as my landlord informed me, in the midst of vast apologies, had been permitted to squat at

Shreelane until my tenancy began, and having then ostentatiously and abusively left the house, they had, with the connivance of the Cadogans, secretly returned to roost in the corner attic, to sell foxes under the ægis of my name, and to make inroads on my belongings. They retained connection with the outer world by means of the ladder and the loft, and with the house in general, and my whisky in particular, by a door into the other attics—a door concealed by the wardrobe in which reposed Great-Uncle McCarthy's tall hat.

It is with the greatest regret that I relinquish the prospect of writing a monograph on Great-Uncle McCarthy for a Spiritualistic Journal, but with the departure of his relations he ceased to manifest himself, and neither the nailing up of packing-cases, nor the rumble of the cart that took them to the station, disturbed my sleep for the future.

I understand that the task of clearing out the McCarthy Gannon's effects was of a nature that necessitated two glasses of whisky per man; and if the remnants of rabbit and jackdaw disinterred in the process were anything like the crow that was thrown out of the window at my feet, I do not grudge the restorative.

As Mrs. Cadogan remarked to the sweep, "A Turk couldn't stand it."

Two

————⇒●⇐————

IN THE CURRANHILTY COUNTRY

IT is hardly credible that I should have been induced to depart from my usual walk of life by a creature so uninspiring as the grey horse that I bought from Flurry Knox for £25.

Perhaps it was the monotony of being questioned by every other person with whom I had five minutes' conversation, as to when I was coming out with the hounds, and being further informed that in the days when Captain Browne, the late Coastguard officer, had owned the grey, there was not a fence between this and Mallow big enough to please them. At all events, there came an epoch-making day when I mounted the Quaker and presented myself at a meet of Mr. Knox's hounds. It is my belief that six out of every dozen people who go out hunting are disagreeably conscious of a nervous system, and two out of the six are in what is brutally called "a blue funk." I was not in a blue funk, but I was conscious not only of a nervous system, but of the anatomical fact that I possessed large, round legs, handsome in their way, even admirable in their proper sphere, but singularly ill adapted for adhering to the slippery surfaces of a saddle. By a fatal intervention of Providence, the sport, on this my first day in the hunting-field, was such as I could have enjoyed from a bath-chair. The hunting-field was, on this occasion, a relative term, implying long stretches of unfenced moorland and bog, anything, in fact, save a field; the hunt itself might also have been termed a relative one, being mainly composed of Mr. Knox's relations in all degrees of cousinhood. It was a day when frost and sunshine combined went to one's head like iced champagne; the distant sea looked like the Mediterranean, and for four sunny hours the Knox relatives and I followed nine couple of hounds at a tranquil footpace along the hills, our progress mildly enlivened by one or two scrambles in the shape of jumps. At three o'clock I jogged home, and felt within me the newborn desire to brag to Peter Cadogan of the Quaker's doings, as I dismounted rather stiffly in my own yard.

I little thought that the result would be that three weeks later I should find myself in a railway carriage at an early house of a December morning, in company with Flurry Knox and four or five of his clan, journeying towards an unknown town, named Drumcurran, with an appropriate number of horses in boxes behind us and a van full of hounds in front. Mr. Knox's hounds were on their way, by invitation, to have a day in the country of their neighbours, the Curranhilty Harriers, and with amazing fatuity I had allowed myself to be cajoled into joining the party. A northerly shower was striking in long spikes on the glass of the window, the atmosphere of the carriage was blue with tobacco smoke, and my feet, in a pair of new butcher boots, had sunk into a species of Arctic sleep.

"Well, you got my letter about the dance at the hotel to-night?" said Flurry Knox, breaking off a whispered conversation with his amateur whip, Dr. Jerome Hickey, and sitting down beside me. "And we're to go out with the Harriers to-day, and they've a sure fox for our hounds to-morrow. I tell you you'll have the best fun ever you had. It's a great country to ride. Fine honest banks, that you can come racing at anywhere you like."

Dr. Hickey, a saturnine young man, with a long nose and a

black torpedo beard, returned to his pocket the lancet with which he had been trimming his nails.

"They're like the Tipperary banks," he said; "you climb down nine feet and you fall the rest."

It occurred to me that the Quaker and I would most probably fall all the way, but I said nothing.

"I hear Tomsy Flood has a good horse this season," resumed Flurry.

"Then it's not the one you sold him," said the Doctor.

"I'll take my oath it's not," said Flurry with a grin. "I believe he has it in for me still over that one."

Dr. Jerome's moustache went up under his nose and showed his white teeth.

"Small blame to him! when you sold him a mare that was wrong of both her hind-legs. Do you know what he did, Major Yeates? The mare was lame going into the fair, and he took the two hind-shoes off her and told poor Flood she kicked them off in the box, and that was why she was going tender, and he was so drunk he believed him."

The conversation here deepened into trackless obscurities of horse-dealing. I took out my stylograph pen, and finished a letter to Philippa, with a feeling that it would probably be my last.

The next step in the day's enjoyment consisted in trotting in cavalcade through the streets of Drumcurran, with another northerly shower descending upon us, the mud splashing in my face, and my feet coming torturingly to life. Every man and boy in the town ran with us; the Harriers were somewhere in the tumult ahead, and the Quaker began to pull and hump his back ominously. I arrived at the meet considerably heated, and found myself one of some thirty or forty riders, who, with traps and bicycles and footpeople, were jammed in a narrow, muddy road. We were late, and a move was immediately made across a series of grass fields, all considerably furnished with gates. There was a glacial gleam of sunshine, and people began to turn down the collars of their coats. As they spread over the field I observed that Mr. Knox was no longer riding with old Captain Handcock, the Master of the Harriers, but had attached himself to a square-shouldered young lady with effective coils of dark hair and a grey habit. She was riding a fidgety black mare with great decision and a not disagreeable swagger.

It was at about this moment that the hounds began to run, fast and silently, and every one began to canter.

"This is nothing at all," said Dr. Hickey, thundering alongside of me on a huge young chestnut; "there might have been a hare here last week, or a red herring this morning. I wouldn't care if we only got what'd warm us. For the matter of that, I'd as soon hunt a cat as a hare."

I was already getting quite enough to warm me The Quaker's respectable grey head had twice disappeared between his forelegs in a brace of most unsettling bucks, and all my experiences at the riding-school at Sandhurst did not prepare me for the sensation of jumping a briary wall with a heavy drop into a lane so narrow that each horse had to turn at right angles as he landed. I did not so turn, but saved myself from entire disgrace by a timely clutch at the mane. We scrambled out of the lane over a pile of stones and furze bushes, and at the end of the next field were confronted by a tall, stone-faced bank. Every one, always excepting myself, was riding with that furious valour which is so conspicuous when neighbouring hunts meet, and the leading half-dozen charged the obstacle at steeplechase speed. I caught a glimpse of the young lady in the grey habit, sitting square and strong as her mare topped the bank, with Flurry and the redoubtable Mr. Tomsy Flood riding on either hand; I followed in their wake, with a blind confidence in the Quaker, and none at all in myself. He refused it. I suppose it was in token of affection and gratitude that I fell upon his neck: at all events, I had reason to respect his judgment, as, before I had recovered myself, the hounds were straggling back into the field by a gap lower down.

It finally appeared that the hounds could do no more with

the line they had been hunting, and we proceeded to jog interminably, I knew not whither. During this unpleasant process Flurry Knox bestowed on me many items of information, chiefly as to the pangs of jealousy he was inflicting on Mr. Flood by his attentions to the lady in the grey habit, Miss "Bobbie" Bennett.

"She'll have all old Handcock's money one of these days—she's his niece, y' know—and she's a good girl to ride, but she's not as young as she was ten years ago. You'd be looking at a chicken a long time before you thought of her! She might take Tomsy some day if she can't do any better." He stopped and looked at me with a gleam in his eye. "Come on, and I'll introduce you to her!"

Before, however, this privilege could be mine, the whole cavalcade was stopped by a series of distant yells, which apparently conveyed information to the hunt, though to me they only suggested a Red Indian scalping his enemy. The yells travelled rapidly nearer, and a young man with a scarlet face and a long stick sprang upon the fence, and explained that he and Patsy Lorry were after chasing a hare two miles down out of the hill above, and ne'er a dog nor a one with them but themselves, and she was lying, beat out, under a bush, and Patsy Lorry was minding her until the hounds would come. I had a vision of the humane Patsy Lorry fanning the hare with his hat, but apparently nobody else found the fact unusual. The hounds were hurried into the fields, the hare was again spurred into action, and I was again confronted with the responsibilities of the chase. After the first five minutes I had discovered several facts about the Quaker. If the bank was above a certain height he refused it irrevocably, if it accorded with his ideas he got his forelegs over and ploughed through the rest of it on his stifle-joints, or, if a gripe made this inexpedient, he remained poised on top till the fabric crumbled under his weight. In the case of walls he butted them down with his knees, or squandered them with his hind-legs. These operations took time, and the leaders of the hunt streamed farther and farther away over the crest of a hill, while the Quaker pursued at the equable gallop of a horse in the Bayeux Tapestry.

I began to perceive that I had been adopted as a pioneer by a small band of followers, who, as one of their number candidly explained, "liked to have some one ahead of them to soften the banks," and accordingly waited respectfully till the Quaker had made the rough places smooth, and taken the raw edge off the walls. They, in their turn, showed me alternative routes when the obstacle proved above the Quaker's limit; thus, in ignoble confederacy, I and the offscourings of the Curranhilty hunt pursued our way across some four miles of country. When at length we parted it was with extreme regret on both sides. A river crossed our course, with boggy banks pitted deep with the hoof-marks of our forerunners; I suggested it to the Quaker, and discovered that Nature had not in vain endued him with the hindquarters of the hippopotamus. I presume the others had jumped it; the Quaker, with abysmal flounderings, walked through and heaved himself to safety on the farther bank. It was the dividing of the ways. My friendly company turned aside as one man, and I was left with the world before me, and no guide save the hoof-marks in the grass. These presently led me to a road, on the other side of which was a bank, that was at once added to the Quaker's black list. The rain had again begun to fall heavily, and was soaking in about my elbows; I suddenly asked myself why, in Heaven's name, I should go any farther. No adequate reason occurred to me, and I turned in what I believed to be the direction of Drumcurran.

I rode on for possibly two or three miles without seeing a human being, until, from the top of a hill I descried a solitary lady rider. I started in pursuit. The rain kept blurring my eye-glass, but it seemed to me that the rider was a schoolgirl with hair hanging down her back, and that her horse was a trifle lame. I pressed on to ask my way, and discovered that I had been privileged to overtake no less a person than Miss Bobbie Bennett.

My question as to the route led to information of a varied character. Miss Bennett was going that way herself; her mare had given her what she called "a toss and a half," whereby she had strained her arm and the mare her shoulder, her habit had been torn, and she had lost all her hairpins.

"I'm an awful object," she concluded; "my hair's the plague of my life out hunting! I declare I wish to goodness I was bald!"

I struggled to the level of the occasion with an appropriate protest. She had really very brilliant grey eyes, and her complexion was undeniable. Philippa has since explained to me that it is a mere male fallacy that any woman can look well with her hair down her back, but I have always maintained that Miss Bobbie Bennett, with the rain glistening on her dark tresses, looked uncommonly well.

"I shall never get it dry for the dance to-night," she complained.

"I wish I could help you," said I.

"Perhaps you've got a hairpin or two about you!" said she, with a glance that had certainly done great execution before now.

I disclaimed the possession of any such tokens, but volunteered to go and look for some at a neighbouring cottage.

The cottage door was shut, and my knockings were answered by a stupefied-looking elderly man. Conscious of my own absurdity, I asked him if he had any hairpins.

"I didn't see a hare this week!" he responded in a slow bellow.

"Hairpins!" I roared; "has your wife any hairpins?"

"She has not." Then, as an after-thought, "She's dead these ten years."

At this point a young woman emerged from the cottage, and, with many coy grins, plucked from her own head some half-dozen hairpins, crooked, and grey with age, but still hairpins, and as such well worth my shilling. I returned with my spoil to Miss Bennett, only to be confronted with a fresh difficulty. The arm that she had strained was too stiff to raise to her head.

Miss Bobbie turned her handsome eyes upon me. "It's no use," she said plaintively, "I can't do it!"

I looked up and down the road; there was no one in sight. I offered to do it for her.

Miss Bennett's hair was long, thick, and soft; it was also slippery with rain. I twisted it conscientiously, as if it were a hay rope, until Miss Bennett, with an irrepressible shriek, told me it would break off. I coiled the rope with some success, and proceeded to nail it to her head with the hairpins. At all the most critical points one, if not both, of the horses moved, hairpins were driven home into Miss Bennett's skull, and were with difficulty plucked forth again; in fact, a more harrowing performance can hardly be imagined, but Miss Bennett bore it with the heroism of a pin-cushion.

I was putting the finishing touches to the coiffure when some sound made me look round, and I beheld at a distance of some fifty yards the entire hunt approaching us at a foot-pace. I lost my head, and, instead of continuing my task, I dropped the last hairpin as if it were red-hot, and kicked the Quaker away to the far side of the road, thus, if it were possible, giving the position away a shade more generously.

There were fifteen riders in the group that overtook us, and fourteen of them, including the Whip, were grinning from ear to ear; the fifteenth was Mr. Tomsy Flood, and he showed no sign of appreciation. He shoved his horse past me and up to Miss Bennett, his red moustache bristling, truculence in every outline of his heavy shoulders. His green coat was muddy, and his hat had a cave in it. Things had apparently gone ill with him.

Flurry's witticisms held out for about two miles and a half; I do not give them, because they were not amusing, but they all dealt ultimately with the animosity that I, in common with himself, should henceforth have to fear from Mr. Flood.

"Oh, he's a holy terror!" he said conclusively; "he was riding the tails off the hounds to-day to best me. He was near killing me twice. We had some words about it, I can tell you. I very near took my whip to him. Such a bull-rider of a fellow I never saw! He wouldn't so much as stop to catch Bobbie Bennett's horse when I picked her up, he was riding so jealous. His own girl, mind you! And such a crumpler as she got too! I declare she knocked a groan out of the road when she struck it!"

"She doesn't seem so much hurt?" I said.

"Hurt!" said Flurry, flicking casually at a hound. " You couldn't hurt that one unless you took a hatchet to her!"

The rain had reached a pitch that put further hunting out of the question, and we bumped home at that intolerable pace known as a "hounds' jog." I spent the remainder of the afternoon over a fire in my bedroom in the Royal Hotel, Drumcurran, official letters to write having mercifully provided me with an excuse for seclusion, while the bar and the billiard-room hummed below, and the Quaker's three-cornered gallop wreaked its inevitable revenge upon my person. As this process continued, and I became proportionately embittered, I asked myself, not for the first time, what Philippa would say when introduced to my present circle of acquaintances.

I have already mentioned that a dance was to take place at the hotel, given, as far as I could gather, by the leading lights of the Curranhilty Hunt. A less jocund guest than the wreck who at the pastoral hour of nine crept stiffly down to "chase the glowing hours with flying feet" could hardly have been encountered. The dance was held in the coffee-room, and a conspicuous object outside the door was a saucer bath full of something that looked like flour.

"Rub your feet in that," said Flurry; "that's French chalk! They hadn't time to do the floor, so they hit on this dodge."

I complied with this encouraging direction, and followed

him into the room. Dancing had already begun, and the first sight that met my eyes was Miss Bennett, in a yellow dress, waltzing with Mr. Tomsy Flood. She looked very handsome, and, in spite of her accident, she was getting round the sticky floor and her still more sticky partner with the swing of a racing cutter. Her eye caught mine immediately, and with confidence. Clearly our acquaintance that, in the space of twenty minutes, had blossomed tropically into hair-dressing, was not to be allowed to wither. Nor was I myself allowed to wither. Men, known and unknown, plied me with partners, till my shirt cuff was black with names, and the number of dances stretched away into the blue distance of to-morrow morning. The music was supplied by the organist of the church, who played with religious unction and at the pace of a processional hymn. I put forth into the mêlée with a junior Bennett, inferior in calibre to Miss Bobbie, but a strong goer, and, I fear, made but a sorry début in the eyes of Drumcurran. At every other moment I bumped into the unforeseen orbits of those who reversed, and of those who walked their partners backwards down the room with faces of ineffable supremacy. Being unskilled in these intricacies of an elder civilisation, the younger Miss Bennett fared but ingloriously at my hands; the music pounded interminably on, until the heel of Mr. Flood put a period to our sufferings.

"The nasty dirty filthy brute!" shrieked the younger Miss Bennett in a single breath; "he's torn the gown off my back!"

She whirled me to the cloak-room; we parted, mutually unregretted, at its door, and by, I fear, common consent, evaded our second dance together.

Many, many times during the evening I asked myself why I did not go to bed. Perhaps it was the remembrance that my bed was situated some ten feet above the piano in a direct line; but, whatever was the reason, the night wore on and found me still working my way down my shirt cuff. I sat out as much as possible, and found my partners to be, as a body, pretty, talkative, and ill dressed, and during the evening I had many and varied opportunities of observing the rapid progress of Mr. Knox's flirtation with Miss Bobbie Bennett. From No. 4 to No. 8 they were invisible; that they were behind a screen in the commercial-room might be inferred from Mr. Flood's thunder-cloud presence in the passage outside.

At No. 9 the young lady emerged for one of her dances with me; it was a barn dance, and particularly trying to my momently stiffening muscles; but Miss Bobbie, whether in dancing or sitting out, went in for "the rigour of the game." She was in as hard condition as one of her uncle's hounds, and for a full fifteen minutes I capered and swooped beside her, larding the lean earth as I went, and replying but spasmodically to her even flow of conversation.

*Mr. Flood's thundercloud
presence*

"That'll take the stiffness out of you!" she exclaimed, as the organist slowed down reverentially to a conclusion. "I had a bet with Flurry Knox over that dance. He said you weren't up to my weight at the pace!"

I led her forth to the refreshment table, and was watching with awe her fearless consumption of claret cup that I would not have touched for a sovereign, when Flurry, with a partner on his arm, strolled past us.

"Well, you won the gloves, Miss Bobbie!" he said. "Don't you wish you may get them!"

"Gloves without the *g*, Mr. Knox!" replied Miss Bennett, in a voice loud enough to reach the end of the passage, where Mr. Thomas Flood was burying his nose in a very brown whisky-and-soda.

"Your hair's coming down!" retorted Flurry. "Ask Major Yeates if he can spare you a few hairpins!"

Swifter than lightning Miss Bennett hurled a macaroon at her retreating foe, missed him, and subsided laughing on to a sofa. I mopped my brow and took my seat beside her, wondering how much longer I could live up to the social exigencies of Drumcurran. Miss Bennett, however, proved excellent company. She told me artfully, and inch by inch, all that Mr. Flood had said to her on the subject of my hair-dressing; she admitted that she had, as a punishment, cut him out of three dances and given them to Flurry Knox. When I remarked that in fairness they should have been given to me, she darted a very attractive glance at me, and pertinently observed that I had not asked for them.

As steals the dawn into a fevered room,
And says "Be of good cheer, the day is born!"

so did the rumour of supper pass among the chaperons, male and female. It was obviously due to a sense of the fitness of things that Mrs. Bennett was apportioned to me, and I found myself in the gratifying position of heading with her the procession to supper. My impressions of Mrs. Bennett are few but salient. She wore an apple-green satin dress and filled it tightly; wisely mistrusting the hotel supper, she had imported sandwiches and cake in a pocket-handkerchief, and, warmed by two glasses of sherry, she made me the recipient of the remarkable confidence that she had but two back teeth in her head, but, thank God, they met. When, with the other starving men, I fell upon the remains of the feast, I regretted that I had declined her offer of a sandwich.

Of the remainder of the evening I am unable to give a detailed account. Let it not for one instant be imagined that I had looked upon the wine of the Royal Hotel when it was red, or, indeed, any other colour; as a matter of fact, I had espied an inconspicuous corner in the entrance hall, and there I first smoked a cigarette, and subsequently sank into uneasy sleep. Through my dreams I was aware of the measured pounding of the piano, of the clatter of glasses at the bar, of wheels in the street, and then, more clearly, of Flurry's voice assuring Miss Bennett that if she'd only wait for another dance he'd get the R.M. out of bed to do her hair for her—then again oblivion.

At some later period I was dropping down a chasm on the Quaker's back, and landing with a shock; I was twisting his mane into a chignon, when he turned round his head and caught my arm in his teeth. I awoke with the dew of terror on my forehead, to find Miss Bennett leaning over me in a scarlet cloak with a hood over her head, and shaking me by my coat sleeve.

"Major Yeates," she began at once in a hurried whisper, "I want you to find Flurry Knox, and tell him there's a plan to feed his hounds at six o'clock this morning so as to spoil their hunting!"

"How do you know?" I asked, jumping up.

"My little brother told me. He came in with us to-night to see the dance, and he was hanging round in the stables, and he heard one of the men telling another there was a dead mule in an out-house in Bride's Alley, all cut up ready to give to Mr. Knox's hounds."

"But why shouldn't they get it?" I asked in sleepy stupidity.

"Is it fill them up with an old mule just before they're going out hunting?" flashed Miss Bennett. "Hurry and tell Mr. Knox; don't let Tomsy Flood see you telling him—or any one else."

"Oh, then it's Mr. Flood's game?" I said, grasping the situation at length.

"It is," said Miss Bennett, suddenly turning scarlet; "he's a disgrace! I'm ashamed of him! I'm done with him!"

I resisted a strong disposition to shake Miss Bennett by the hand.

"I can't wait," she continued. "I made my mother drive back a mile—she doesn't know a thing about it—I said I'd left my purse in the cloak-room. Good-night! Don't tell a soul but Flurry!"

She was off, and upon my incapable shoulders rested the responsibility of the enterprise.

It was past four o'clock, and the last bars of the last waltz were being played. At the bar a knot of men, with Flurry in their midst, were tossing "Odd man out" for a bottle of champagne. Flurry was not in the least drunk, a circumstance worthy of remark in his present company, and I got him out into the hall and unfolded my tidings. The light of battle lit in his eye as he listened.

"I knew by Tomsy he was shaping for mischief," he said coolly; "he's taken as much liquor as'd stiffen a tinker, and he's only half-drunk this minute. Hold on till I get Jerome Hickey and Charlie Knox—they're sober; I'll be back in a minute."

I was not present at the council of war thus hurriedly convened; I was merely informed when they returned that we were all to "hurry on." My best evening pumps have never recovered the subsequent proceedings. They, with my swelled and aching feet inside them, were raced down one filthy lane after another, until, somewhere on the outskirts of Drumcurran, Flurry pushed open the gate of a yard and went in. It was nearly five o'clock on that raw December morning; low down in the sky a hazy moon shed a diffused light; all the surrounding houses were still and dark. At our footsteps an angry bark or two came from inside the stable.

"Whisht!" said Flurry, "I'll say a word to them before I open the door."

At his voice a chorus of hysterical welcome arose; without more delay he flung open the stable door, and instantly we were all knee-deep in a rush of hounds. There was not a moment lost. Flurry started at a quick run out of the yard with the whole pack pattering at his heels. Charley Knox vanished; Dr. Hickey and I followed the hounds, splashing into puddles and hobbling over patches of broken stones, till we left the town behind and hedges arose on either hand.

"Here's the house!" said Flurry, stopping short at a low entrance gate; "many's the time I've been here when his father had it; it'll be a queer thing if I can't find a window I can manage, and the old cook he has is as deaf as the dead."

He and Doctor Hickey went in at the gate with the hounds; I hesitated ignobly in the mud.

"This isn't an R.M.'s. job," said Flurry in a whisper, closing the gate in my face; "you'd best keep clear of house-breaking."

I accepted his advice, but I may admit that before I turned for home a sash was gently raised, a light had sprung up in one of the lower windows, and I heard Flurry's voice saying, "Over, over, over!" to his hounds.

There seemed to me to be no interval at all between these events and the moment when I woke in bright sunlight to find Dr. Hickey standing by my bedside in a red coat with a tall glass in his hand.

"It's nine o'clock," he said. "I'm just after waking Flurry Knox. There wasn't one stirring in the hotel till I went down and pulled the 'boots' from under the kitchen table! It's well for us the meet's in the town; and, by-the-bye, your grey horse has four legs on him the size of bolsters this morning; he won't be fit to go out, I'm afraid. Drink this anyway, you're in the want of it."

Dr. Hickey's eyelids were rather pink, but his hand was as steady as a rock. The whisky-and-soda was singularly untempting.

"What happened last night?" I asked eagerly as I gulped it.

"Oh, it all went off very nicely, thank you," said Hickey, twisting his black beard to a point. "We benched as many of the hounds in Flood's bed as'd fit, and we shut the lot into the room. We had them just comfortable when we heard his latchkey below at the door." He broke off and began to snigger.

"Well?" I said, sitting bolt upright.

"Well, he got in at last, and he lit a candle then. That took him five minutes. He was pretty tight. We were looking at him over the banisters until he started to come up, and according as he came up, we went on up the top flight. He stood admiring his candle for a while on the landing, and we wondered he didn't hear the hounds snuffing under the door. He opened it then, and, on the minute, three of them bolted out between his legs." Dr. Hickey again paused to indulge in Mephistophelian laughter. "Well, you know," he went on, "when a man in poor Tomsy's condition sees six dogs jumping out of his bed he's apt to make a wrong diagnosis. He gave a roar, and pitched the candlestick at them, and ran for his life downstairs, and all the hounds after him. 'Gone away!' screeches that devil Flurry, pelting downstairs on top of them in the dark. I believe I screeched too."

"Good heavens!" I gasped, "I was well out of that!"

"Well, you were," admitted the Doctor. "However, Tomsy bested them in the dark, and he got to ground in the pantry. I heard the cups and saucers go as he slammed the door on the hounds' noses, and the minute he was in Flurry turned the key on him. 'They're real dogs, Tomsy, my buck!' says Flurry, just to quiet him; and there we left him."

"Was he hurt?" I asked, conscious of the triviality of the question.

"Well, he lost his brush," replied Dr. Hickey. "Old Merrylegs tore the coat-tails off him; we got them on the floor when we struck a light; Flurry has them to nail on his kennel door. Charley Knox had a pleasant time too," he went on, "with the man that brought the barrow-load of meat to the stable. We picked out the tastiest bits and arranged them round Flood's breakfast table for him. They smelt very nice. Well, I'm delaying you with my talking——"

Flurry's hounds had the run of the season that day. I saw it admirably throughout—from Miss Bennett's pony cart. She drove extremely well, in spite of her strained arm.

Three

TRINKET'S COLT

I T was petty sessions day in Skebawn, a cold, grey day of February. A case of trespass had dragged its burden of cross summonses and cross swearing far into the afternoon, and when I left the bench my head was singing from the bellowings of the attorneys, and the smell of their clients was heavy upon my palate.

The streets still testified to the fact that it was market day, and I evaded with difficulty the sinuous course of carts full of soddenly screwed people, and steered an equally devious one for myself among the groups anchored round the doors of the public-houses. Skebawn possesses, among its legion of public-houses, one establishment which timorously, and almost imperceptibly, proffers tea to the thirsty. I turned in there, as was my custom on court days, and found the little dingy den, known as the Ladies' Coffee-Room, in the occupancy of my friend Mr. Florence McCarthy Knox, who was drinking strong tea and eating buns with serious simplicity. It was a first and quite unexpected glimpse of that domesticity that has now become a marked feature in his character.

"You're the very man I wanted to see," I said as I sat down

beside him at the oilcloth-covered table; "a man I know in England who is not much of a judge of character has asked me to buy him a four-year-old down here, and as I should rather be stuck by a friend than a dealer, I wish you'd take over the job."

Drinking strong tea and eating buns with serious simplicity

Flurry poured himself out another cup of tea, and dropped three lumps of sugar into it in silence.

Finally he said, "There isn't a four-year-old in this country that I'd be seen dead with at a pig fair."

This was discouraging, from the premier authority on horse-flesh in the district.

"But it isn't six weeks since you told me you had the finest filly in your stables that was ever foaled in the County Cork," I protested; "what's wrong with her?"

"Oh, is it that filly?" said Mr. Knox with a lenient smile; "she's gone these three weeks from me. I swapped her and £6 for a three-year-old Ironmonger colt, and after that I swapped the colt and £19 for that Bandon horse I rode last week at your place, and after that again I sold the Bandon horse for £75 to old Welply, and I had to give him back a couple of sovereigns luck-money. You see I did pretty well with the filly after all."

"Yes, yes—oh rather," I assented, as one dizzily accepts the propositions of a bimetallist; "and you don't know of anything else——?"

The room in which we were seated was closely screened from the shop by a door with a muslin-curtained window in it; several of the panes were broken, and at this juncture two voices that had for some time carried on a discussion forced themselves upon our attention.

"Begging your pardon for contradicting you, ma'am," said the voice of Mrs. McDonald, proprietress of the tea-shop, and a leading light in Skebawn Dissenting circles, shrilly tremulous with indignation, "if the servants I recommend you won't stop with you, it's no fault of mine. If respectable young girls are set picking grass out of your gravel, in place of their proper work, certainly they will give warning!"

The voice that replied struck me as being a notable one, well-bred and imperious.

"When I take a barefooted slut out of a cabin, I don't expect her to dictate to me what her duties are!"

Flurry jerked up his chin in a noiseless laugh. "It's my grandmother!" he whispered. "I bet you Mrs. McDonald don't get much change out of her!"

"If I set her to clean the pig-sty I expect her to obey me," continued the voice in accents that would have made me clean forty pig-stys had she desired me to do so.

"Very well, ma'am," retorted Mrs. McDonald, "if that's the way you treat your servants, you needn't come here again looking for them. I consider your conduct is neither that of a lady nor a Christian!"

"Don't you, indeed?" replied Flurry's grandmother. "Well, your opinion doesn't greatly distress me, for, to tell you the truth, I don't think you're much of a judge."

"Didn't I tell you she'd score?" murmured Flurry, who was by this time applying his eye to a hole in the muslin curtain. "She's off," he went on, returning to his tea. "She's a great character! She's eighty-three if she's a day, and she's as sound on her legs as a three-year-old! Did you see that old shandry-dan of hers in the street a while ago, and a fellow on the box with a red beard on him like Robinson Crusoe? That old mare that was on the near side—Trinket her name is—is mighty near clean bred. I can tell you her foals are worth a bit of money."

I had heard of old Mrs. Knox of Aussolas; indeed, I had seldom dined out in the neighbourhood without hearing some new story of her and her remarkable ménage, but it had not yet been my privilege to meet her.

"Well, now," went on Flurry in his slow voice, "I'll tell you a thing that's just come into my head. My grandmother promised me a foal of Trinket's the day I was one-and-twenty, and that's five years ago, and deuce a one I've got from her yet. You never were at Aussolas? No, you were not. Well, I tell you the place there is like a circus with horses. She has a couple of score of them running wild in the woods, like deer."

"Oh come," I said, "I'm a bit of a liar myself—"

"Well, she has a dozen of them anyhow, rattling good colts too, some of them, but they might as well be donkeys for all the good they are to me or any one. It's not once in three years she sells one, and there she has them walking after her for bits of sugar, like a lot of dirty lapdogs," ended Flurry with disgust.

"Well, what's your plan? Do you want me to make her a bid for one of the lapdogs?"

"I was thinking," replied Flurry, with great deliberation, "that my birthday's this week, and maybe I could work a four-year-old colt of Trinket's she has out of her in honour of the occasion."

"And sell your grandmother's birthday present to me?"

"Just that, I suppose," answered Flurry with a slow wink.

A few days afterwards a letter from Mr. Knox informed me that he had "squared the old lady, and it would be all right about the colt." He further told me that Mrs. Knox had been good enough to offer me, with him, a day's snipe shooting on

the celebrated Aussolas bogs, and he proposed to drive me
there the following Monday, if convenient. Most people found
it convenient to shoot the Aussolas snipe bog when they got
the chance. Eight o'clock on the following Monday morning
saw Flurry, myself, and a groom packed into a dogcart, with
portmanteaus, gun-cases, and two rampant red setters.

It was a long drive, twelve miles at least, and a very cold one.
We passed through long tracts of pasture country, fraught, for
Flurry, with memories of runs, which were recorded for me,
fence by fence, in every one of which the biggest dog-fox in
the country had gone to ground, with not two feet—measured
accurately on the handle of the whip—between him and the
leading hound; through bogs that imperceptibly melted into
lakes, and finally down and down into a valley, where the
fir-trees of Aussolas clustered darkly round a glittering lake,
and all but hid the grey roofs and pointed gables of Aussolas
Castle.

"There's a nice stretch of a demesne for you," remarked
Flurry, pointing downwards with the whip, "and one little
old woman holding it all in the heel of her fist. Well able to
hold it she is, too, and always was, and she'll live twenty years
yet, if it's only to spite the whole lot of us, and when all's said
and done goodness knows how she'll leave it!"

"It strikes me you were lucky to keep her up to her promise
about the colt," I said.

Flurry administered a composing kick to the ceaseless
strivings of the red setters under the seat.

"I used to be rather a pet with her," he said, after a pause;
"but mind you, I haven't got him yet, and if she gets any
notion I want to sell him I'll never get him, so say nothing
about the business to her."

The tall gates of Aussolas shrieked on their hinges as they
admitted us, and shut with a clang behind us, in the faces of an
old mare and a couple of young horses, who, foiled in their
break for the excitements of the outer world, turned and

galloped defiantly on either side of us. Flurry's admirable cob hammered on, regardless of all things save his duty.

"He's the only one I have that I'd trust myself here with," said his master, flicking him approvingly with the whip; "there are plenty of people afraid to come here at all, and when my grandmother goes out driving she has a boy on the box with a basket full of stones to peg at them. Talk of the dickens, here she is herself!"

A short, upright old woman was approaching, preceded by a white woolly dog with sore eyes and a bark like a tin trumpet; we both got out of the trap and advanced to meet the lady of the manor.

I may summarise her attire by saying that she looked as if she had robbed a scarecrow; her face was small and incongruously refined, the skinny hand that she extended to me had the grubby tan that bespoke the professional gardener, and was decorated with a magnificent diamond ring. On her head was a massive purple velvet bonnet.

"I am very glad to meet you, Major Yeates," she said with an old-fashioned precision of utterance; "your grandfather was a dancing partner of mine in old days at the Castle, when he was a handsome young aide-de-camp there, and I was—you may judge for yourself what I was."

She ended with a startling little hoot of laughter, and I was aware that she quite realised the world's opinion of her, and was indifferent to it.

Our way to the bogs took us across Mrs. Knox's home farm, and through a large field in which several young horses were grazing.

"There now, that's my fellow," said Flurry, pointing to a fine-looking colt, "the chestnut with the white diamond on his forehead. He'll run into three figures before he's done, but we'll not tell that to the old lady!"

The famous Aussolas bogs were as full of snipe as usual, and a good deal fuller of water than any bogs I had ever shot before. I was on my day, and Flurry was not, and as he is ordinarily an infinitely better snipe shot than I, I felt at peace with the world and all men as we walked back, wet through, at five o'clock.

The sunset had waned, and a big white moon was making the eastern tower of Aussolas look like a thing in a fairy tale or a play when we arrived at the hall door. An individual, whom I recognised as the Robinson Crusoe coachman, admitted us to a hall, the like of which one does not often see. The walls were panelled with dark oak up to the gallery that ran round three sides of it, the balusters of the wide staircase were heavily carved, and blackened portraits of Flurry's ancestors on the spindle side stared sourly down on their descendant as he tramped upstairs with the bog mould on his hobnailed boots.

We had just changed into dry clothes when Robinson Crusoe shoved his red beard round the corner of the door, with the information that the mistress said we were to stay for dinner. My heart sank. It was then barely half-past five. I said something about having no evening clothes and having to get home early.

"Sure the dinner'll be in another half-hour," said Robinson Crusoe, joining hospitably in the conversation; "and as for evening clothes—God bless ye!"

The door closed behind him.

"Never mind," said Flurry, "I dare say you'll be glad enough to eat another dinner by the time you get home." He laughed. "Poor Slipper!" he added inconsequently, and only laughed again when I asked for an explanation.

Old Mrs. Knox received us in the library, where she was seated by a roaring turf fire, which lit the room a good deal more effectively than the pair of candles that stood beside her in tall silver candlesticks. Ceaseless and implacable growls from under her chair indicated the presence of the woolly dog. She talked with confounding culture of the books that rose all round her to the ceiling; her evening dress was accomplished by means of an additional white shawl, rather dirtier than its congeners; as I took her in to dinner she quoted Virgil to me, and in the same breath screeched an objurgation at a being whose matted head rose suddenly into view from behind an ancient Chinese screen, as I have seen the head of a Zulu woman peer over a bush.

Dinner was as incongruous as everything else. Detestable soup in a splendid old silver tureen that was nearly as dark in hue as Robinson Crusoe's thumb; a perfect salmon, perfectly cooked, on a chipped kitchen dish; such cut glass as is not easy to find nowadays; sherry that, as Flurry subsequently remarked, would burn the shell off an egg; and a bottle of port, draped in immemorial cobwebs, wan with age, and probably priceless. Throughout the vicissitudes of the meal Mrs. Knox's conversation flowed on undismayed, directed sometimes at me—she had installed me in the position of friend of her youth, and talked to me as if I were my own grandfather— sometimes at Crusoe, with whom she had several heated arguments, and sometimes she would make a statement of remarkable frankness on the subject of her horse-farming affairs to Flurry, who, very much on his best behaviour, agreed with all she said, and risked no original remark. As I listened to them both, I remembered with infinite amusement how he had told me once that "a pet name she had for him was 'Tony Lumpkin,' and no one but herself knew what she meant by it." It seemed strange that she made no allusion to Trinket's colt or to Flurry's birthday, but, mindful of my instructions, I held my peace.

As, at about half-past eight, we drove away in the moonlight, Flurry congratulated me solemnly on my success with his grandmother. He was good enough to tell me that she would marry me to-morrow if I asked her, and he wished I would, even if it were only to see what a nice grandson he'd be for me. A sympathetic giggle behind me told me that Michael, on the back seat, had heard and relished the jest.

We had left the gates of Aussolas about half a mile behind when, at the corner of a by-road, Flurry pulled up. A short squat figure arose from the black shadow of a furze bush and came out into the moonlight, swinging its arms like a cabman and cursing audibly.

"Oh murdher, oh murdher, Misther Flurry! What kept ye at all? 'Twould perish the crows to be waiting here the way I am these two hours—"

"Ah, shut your mouth, Slipper!" said Flurry, who, to my surprise, had turned back the rug and was taking off his driving coat, "I couldn't help it. Come on, Yeates, we've got to get out here."

"What for?" I asked, in not unnatural bewilderment.

"It's all right. I'll tell you as we go along," replied my companion, who was already turning to follow Slipper up the by-road. "Take the trap on, Michael, and wait at the River's Cross." He waited for me to come up with him, and then put his hand on my arm. "You see, Major, this is the way it is. My grandmother's given me that colt right enough, but if I waited for her to send him over to me I'd never see a hair of his tail. So I just thought that as we were over here we might as well take him back with us, and maybe you'll give us a help with him; he'll not be altogether too handy for a first go off."

I was staggered. An infant in arms could scarcely have failed to discern the fishiness of the transaction, and I begged Mr. Knox not to put himself to this trouble on my account, as I had no doubt I could find a horse for my friend elsewhere. Mr. Knox assured me that it was no trouble at all, quite the contrary, and that, since his grandmother had given him the colt, he saw no reason why he should not take him when he wanted him; also, that I didn't want him he'd be glad enough to keep him himself; and finally, that I wasn't the chap to go back on a friend, but I was welcome to drive back to Shreelane with Michael this minute if I liked.

Of course I yielded in the end. I told Flurry I should lose my job over the business, and he said I could then marry his grandmother, and the discussion was abruptly closed by the necessity of following Slipper over a locked five-barred gate.

Our pioneer took us over about half a mile of country,

knocking down stone gaps where practicable and scrambling over tall banks in the deceptive moonlight. We found ourselves at length in a field with a shed in one corner of it; in a dim group of farm buildings a little way off a light was shining.

"Wait here," said Flurry to me in a whisper; "the less noise the better. It's an open shed, and we'll just slip in and coax him out."

Slipper unwound from his waist a halter, and my colleagues glided like spectres into the shadow of the shed, leaving me to meditate on my duties as Resident Magistrate, and on the questions that would be asked in the House by our local member when Slipper had given away the adventure in his cups.

In less than a minute three shadows emerged from the shed, where two had gone in They had got the colt.

"He came out as quiet as a calf when he winded the sugar," said Flurry; "it was well for me I filled my pockets from grandmamma's sugar basin."

He and Slipper had a rope from each side of the colt's head; they took him quickly across a field towards a gate. The colt stepped daintily between them over the moonlit grass; he snorted occasionally, but appeared on the whole amenable.

The trouble began later, and was due, as trouble often is, to the beguilements of a short cut. Against the maturer judgment of Slipper, Flurry insisted on following a route that he assured us he knew as well as his own pocket, and the consequence was that in about five minutes I found myself standing on top of a bank hanging on to a rope, on the other end of which the colt dangled and danced, while Flurry, with the other rope, lay prone in the ditch, and Slipper administered to the bewildered colt's hindquarters such chastisement as could be ventured on.

I have no space to narrate in detail the atrocious difficulties and disasters of the short cut. How the colt set to work to buck, and went away across a field, dragging the faithful Slipper, literally *ventre-à-terre*, after him, while I picked myself in ignominy out of a briar patch, and Flurry cursed himself black in the face. How we were attacked by ferocious cur dogs, and I lost my eyeglass; and how, as we neared the River's Cross, Flurry espied the police patrol on the road, and we all hid behind a rick of turf, while I realised in fulness what an exceptional ass I was, to have been beguiled into an enterprise that involved hiding with Slipper from the Royal Irish Constabulary.

Let it suffice to say that Trinket's infernal offspring was finally handed over on the highroad to Michael and Slipper, and Flurry drove me home in a state of mental and physical overthrow.

I saw nothing of my friend Mr. Knox for the next couple of days, by the end of which time I had worked up a high polish on my misgivings, and had determined to tell him that under no circumstances would I have anything to say to his grandmother's birthday present. It was like my usual luck that, instead of writing a note to this effect, I thought it would be good for my liver to walk across the hills to Tory Cottage and tell Flurry so in person.

It was a bright, blustery morning, after a muggy day. The feeling of spring was in the air, the daffodils were already in bud, and crocuses showed purple in the grass on either side of the avenue. It was only a couple of miles to Tory Cottage by the way across the hills; I walked fast, and it was barely twelve o'clock when I saw its pink walls and clumps of evergreens below me. As I looked down at it the chiming of Flurry's hounds in the kennels came to me on the wind; I stood still to listen, and could almost have sworn that I was hearing again the clash of Magdalen bells, hard at work on May morning.

The path that I was following led downwards through a larch plantation to Flurry's back gate. Hot wafts from some hideous caldron at the other side of a wall apprised me of the vicinity of the kennels and their cuisine, and the fir-trees round were hung with gruesome and unknown joints. I thanked Heaven that I was not a master of hounds, and passed on as quickly as might be to the hall door.

I rang two or three times without response; then the door opened a couple of inches and was instantly slammed in my face. I heard the hurried paddling of bare feet on oilcloth, and a voice, "Hurry, Bridgie, hurry! There's quality at the door!"

Bridgie, holding a dirty cap on with one hand, presently arrived and informed me that she believed Mr. Knox was out about the place. She seemed perturbed, and she cast scared glances down the drive while speaking to me.

I knew enough of Flurry's habits to shape a tolerably direct course for his whereabouts. He was, as I had expected, in the training paddock, a field behind the stable-yard, in which he had put up practice jumps for his horses. It was a good-sized field with clumps of furze in it, and Flurry was standing near one of these with his hands in his pockets, singularly unoccupied. I supposed that he was prospecting for a place to put up another jump. He did not see me coming, and turned with a start as I spoke to him. There was a queer expression of mingled guilt and what I can only describe as divilment in his grey eyes as he greeted me. In my dealings with Flurry Knox, I have since formed the habit of sitting tight, in a general way, when I see that expression.

"Well, who's coming next, I wonder!" he said, as he shook hands with me; "it's not ten minutes since I had two of your d—d peelers here searching the whole place for my grandmother's colt!"

"What!" I exclaimed, feeling cold all down my back; "do you mean the police have got hold of it?"

"They haven't got hold of the colt anyway," said Flurry, looking sideways at me from under the peak of his cap, with the glint of the sun in his eye. "I got word in time before they came."

"What do you mean?" I demanded; "where is he? For Heaven's sake don't tell me you've sent the brute over to my place!"

"It's a good job for you I didn't," replied Flurry, "as the police are on their way to Shreelane this minute to consult you about it. *You!*" He gave utterance to one of his short diabolical fits of laughter. "He's where they'll not find him, anyhow. Ho! ho! It's the funniest hand I ever played!"

"Oh yes, it's devilish funny, I've no doubt," I retorted, beginning to lose my temper, as is the manner of many people when they are frightened; "but I give you fair warning that if Mrs. Knox asks me any questions about it, I shall tell her the whole story."

"All right," responded Flurry; "and when you do, don't forget to tell her how you flogged the colt out on the road over her own bounds ditch."

"Very well," I said hotly, "I may as well go home and send in my papers. They'll break me over this—"

"Ah, hold on, Major," said Flurry soothingly, "it'll be all right. No one knows anything. It's only on spec the old lady sent the bobbies here. If you'll keep quiet it'll all blow over."

"I don't care," I said, struggling hopelessly in the toils; "if I meet your grandmother, and she asks me about it, I shall tell her all I know."

"Please God you'll not meet her! After all, it's not once in a blue moon that she—" began Flurry. Even as he said the words his face changed. "Holy fly!" he ejaculated, "isn't that her dog coming into the field? Look at her bonnet over the wall! Hide, hide for your life!" He caught me by the shoulder and shoved me down among the furze bushes before I realised what had happened.

"Get in there! I'll talk to her."

I may as well confess that at the mere sight of Mrs. Knox's purple bonnet my heart had turned to water. In that moment I knew what it would be like to tell her how I, having eaten her salmon, and capped her quotations, and drunk her best port, had gone forth and helped to steal her horse. I abandoned my dignity, my sense of honour; I took the furze prickles to my breast and wallowed in them.

Mrs. Knox had advanced with vengeful speed; already she was in high altercation with Flurry at no great distance from where I lay; varying sounds of battle reached me, and I gathered that Flurry was not—to put it mildly—shrinking from that economy of truth that the situation required.

"Is it that curby, long-backed brute? You promised him to me long ago, but I wouldn't be bothered with him!"

The old lady uttered a laugh of shrill derision. "Is it likely I'd promise you my best colt! And still more, is it likely that you'd refuse him if I did?"

"Very well, ma'am." Flurry's voice was admirably indignant. "Then I suppose I'm a liar and a thief."

"I'd be more obliged to you for the information if I hadn't known it before," responded his grandmother with lightening speed; "if you swore to me on a stack of Bibles you knew nothing about my colt I wouldn't believe you! I shall go straight to Major Yeates and ask his advice. I believe *him* to be a gentleman, in spite of the company he keeps!"

I writhed deeper into the furze bushes, and thereby discovered a sandy rabbit run, along which I crawled, with my cap well over my eyes, and the furze needles stabbing me through my stockings. The ground shelved a little, promising profounder concealment, but the bushes were very thick, and I laid hold of the bare stem of one to help my progress. It lifted out of the ground in my hand, revealing a freshly-cut stump. Something snorted, not a yard away; I glared through the opening, and was confronted by the long, horrified face of Mrs. Knox's colt, mysteriously on a level with my own.

Even without the white diamond on his forehead I should have divined the truth; but how in the name of wonder had Flurry persuaded him to couch like a woodcock in the heart of a furze brake? For a full minute I lay as still as death for fear of frightening him, while the voices of Flurry and his grandmother raged on alarmingly close to me. The colt snorted, and blew long breaths through his wide nostrils, but he did not move. I crawled an inch or two nearer, and after a few seconds of cautious peering I grasped the position. They had buried him.

A small sandpit among the furze had been utilised as a grave; they had filled him in up to his withers with sand, and a few furze bushes, artistically disposed round the pit, had done the rest. As the depth of Flurry's guile was revealed, laughter came upon me like a flood; I gurgled and shook apoplectically, and the colt gazed at me with serious surprise, until a sudden outburst of barking close to my elbow administered a fresh shock to my tottering nerves.

Mrs. Knox's woolly dog had tracked me into the furze, and was now baying the colt and me with mingled terror and indignation. I addressed him in a whisper, with perfidious endearments, advancing a crafty hand towards him the while,

I advanced a crafty hand

made a snatch for the back of his neck, missed it badly, and got him by the ragged fleece of his hind-quarters as he tried to flee. If I had flayed him alive he could hardly have uttered a more deafening series of yells, but, like a fool, instead of letting him go, I dragged him towards me, and tried to stifle the noise by holding his muzzle. The tussle lasted engrossingly for a few seconds, and then the climax of the nightmare arrived.

Mrs. Knox's voice, close behind me, said, "Let go my dog this instant, sir! Who are you—"

Her voice faded away, and I knew that she also had seen the colt's head.

I positively felt sorry for her. At her age there was no knowing what effect the shock might have on her. I scrambled to my feet and confronted her.

"Major Yeates!" she said. There was a deathly pause. "Will you kindly tell me," said Mrs. Knox slowly, "am I in Bedlam, or are you? And *what is that?*"

She pointed to the colt, and that unfortunate animal, recognising the voice of his mistress, uttered a hoarse and lamentable whinny. Mrs. Knox felt around her for support, found only furze prickles, gazed speechlessly at me, and then, to her eternal honour, fell into wild cackles of laughter.

So, I may say, did Flurry and I. I embarked on my explanations and broke down; Flurry followed suit and broke down too. Overwhelming laughter held us all three, disintegrating our very souls. Mrs. Knox pulled herself together first.

"I acquit you, Major Yeates, I acquit you, though appearances are against you. It's clear enough to me you've fallen among thieves." She stopped and glowered at Flurry. Her purple bonnet was over one eye. "I'll thank you, sir," she said, "to dig out that horse before I leave this place. And when you've dug him out you may keep him. I'll be no receiver of stolen goods!"

She broke off and shook her fist at him. "Upon my conscience, Tony, I'd give a guinea to have thought of it myself!"

Four

THE WATERS OF STRIFE

I KNEW Bat Callaghan's face long before I was able to put a name to it. There was seldom a court day in Skebawn that I was not aware of his level brows and superfluously intense expression somewhere among the knot of corner-boys who patronised the weekly sittings of the bench of magistrates. His social position appeared to fluctuate: I have seen him driving a car; he sometimes had my horse for me—this is to say, he sat on the counter of a public-house while the Quaker slumbered in the gutter; and, on one occasion, he retired, at my bidding, to Cork gaol, there to meditate upon the inadvisability of defending a friend from the attentions of the police with the tailboard of a cart.

He next obtained prominence in my regard at a regatta held under the auspices of "The Sons of Liberty," a local football club that justified its title by the patriot green of its jerseys and its free interpretation of the rules of the game. The announcement of my name on the posters as a patron—a privilege acquired at the cost of a reluctant half-sovereign—made it incumbent on me to put in an appearance, even though the festival coincided with my Petty Sessions day at Skebawn; and at some five of the clock on a brilliant September afternoon I found myself driving down the stony road that dropped in zigzags to the borders of the lake on which the races were to come off.

I believe that the selection of Lough Lonen as the scene of the regatta was not unconnected with the fact that the secretary of the club owned a public-house at the cross roads at one end of it; none the less, the president of the Royal Academy could scarcely have chosen more picturesque surroundings. A mountain towered steeply up from the lake's

The bandmaster of "The Sons of Liberty"

edge, dark with the sad green of beech-trees in September; fir woods followed the curve of the shore, and leaned far over the answering darkness of the water; and above the trees rose the toppling steepnesses of the hill, painted with a purple glow of heather. The lake was about a mile long, and, tumbling from its farther end, a fierce and narrow river fled away west to the sea, some four or five miles off.

I had not seen a boat race since I was at Oxford, and the words still called up before my eyes a vision of smart parasols, of gorgeous barges, of snowy-clad youths, and of low slim out-riggers, winged with the level flight of oars, slitting the water to the sway of the line of flat backs. Certainly undreamed-of possibilities in aquatics were revealed to me as I reined in the Quaker on the outskirts of the crowd, and saw below me the festival of the Sons of Liberty in full swing. Boats of all shapes and sizes, outrageously overladen, moved about the lake, with oars flourishing to the strains of concertinas. Black swarms of people seethed along the water's edge, congesting here and there round the dingy tents and stalls of green apples; and the club's celebrated brass band, enthroned in a wagonette, and stimulated by the presence of a barrel of porter on the box-seat, was belching forth "The Boys of Wexford," under the guidance of a disreputable ex-militia drummer, in a series of crashing discords.

Almost as I arrived a pistol-shot set the echoes clattering round the lake, and three boats burst out abreast from the throng into the open water. Two of the crews were in shirt-sleeves, the third wore the green jerseys of the football club; the boats were of the heavy sea-going build, and pulled six oars apiece, oars of which the looms were scarcely narrower than the blades, and were, of the two, but a shade heavier. None the less the rowers started dauntlessly at thirty-five strokes a minute, quickening up, incredible as it may seem, as they rounded the mark boat in the first lap of the two-mile course. The rowing was, in general style, more akin to the action of beating up eggs with a fork than to any other form of athletic exercise; but in its unorthodox way it kicked the heavy boats along at a surprising pace. The oars squeaked and grunted against the thole-pins, the coxswains kept up an unceasing flow of oratory, and superfluous little boys in punts contrived to intervene at all the more critical turning-points of the race, only evading the flail of the oncoming oars by performing prodigies of "waggling" with a single oar at the stern. I took out my watch and counted the strokes when they were passing the mark boat for the second time; they were pulling a fraction over forty; one of the shirt-sleeved crews was obviously in trouble, the other, with humped backs and jerking oars, was holding its own against the green jerseys amid the blended yells of friends and foes. When for the last time they rounded the green flag there were but two boats in the race, and the foul that had been imminent throughout was at length achieved with a rattle of oars and a storm of curses. They were clear again in a moment, the shirt-sleeved crew getting away with a distinct lead, and it was at about this juncture that I became aware that the coxswains had abandoned their long handled tillers, and were standing over their respective "strokes," showing frantically at their oars, and maintaining the while a ceaseless bawl of encouragement and defiance. It looked like a foregone conclusion for the leaders, and the war of cheers rose to frenzy. The word "cheering," indeed, is but an euphuism, and in no way expresses the serrated yell, composed of epithets, advice, and imprecations, that was flung like a live thing at the oncoming boats. The green jerseys answered to this stimulant with a wild spurt that drove the bow of their boat within a measurable distance of their opponents' stroke oar. In another second a thoroughly successful foul would have been effected, but the cox of the leading boat proved himself equal to the emergency by upshipping his tiller, and with it dealing "bow" of the green jerseys such a blow over the head as effectually dismissed him from the sphere of practical politics.

A great roar of laughter greeted this feat of arms, and a voice at my dogcart's wheel pierced the clamour—

"More power to ye, Larry, me owld darlin'!"

I looked down and saw Bat Callaghan, with shining eyes, and a face white with excitement, poising himself on one foot on the box of my wheel in order to get a better view of the race. Almost before I had time to recognise him, a man in a green jersey caught him round the legs and jerked him down. Callaghan fell into the throng, recovered himself in an instant, and rushed, white and dangerous, at his assailant. The Son of Liberty was no less ready for the fray, and what is known in Ireland as "the father and mother of a row" was imminent. Already, however, one of those unequalled judges of the moral temperature of a crowd, a sergeant of the R.I.C., had quietly interposed his bulky person between the combatants, and the coming trouble was averted.

Elsewhere battle was raging. The race was over, and the committee boat was hemmed in by the rival crews, supplemented by craft of all kinds. The "objection" was being lodged, and in its turn objected to, and I can only liken the process to the screaming warfare of seagulls round a piece of carrion. The tumult was still at its height when out of its very heart two four-oared boats broke forth, and a pistol shot proclaimed that another race had begun, the public interest in which was specially keen, owing to the fact that the rowers were stalwart country girls, who made up in energy what they lacked in skill. It was a short race, once round the mark boat only, and, like the successful farce, it "went with a roar" from start to finish. Foul after foul, each followed by a healing interval of calm, during which the crews, who had all caught crabs, were recovering themselves and their oars, marked its progress; and when the two boats, locked in an inextricable embrace, at length passed the winning flag, and the crews, oblivious of judges and public, fell to untrammelled personal abuse and to doing up their hair, I decided that I had seen the best of the fun, and prepared to go home.

It was, as it happened, the last race of the day, and nothing remained in the way of excitement save the greased pole with the pig slung in a bag at the end of it. My final impression of the Lough Lonen Regatta was of Callaghan's lithe figure, sleek and dripping, against the yellow sky, as he poised on the swaying pole with the broken gold of the water beneath him.

Limited as was my experience of the South-west of Ireland,
I was in no way surprised to hear on the following afternoon
from Peter Cadogan that there had been "sthrokes" the night
before, when the boys were going home from the regatta, and
that the police were searching for one Jimmy Foley.

"What do they want him for?" I asked.

"Sure it's according as a man that was bringing a car of
bogwood was tellin' me, sir," answered Peter, pursuing his
occupation of washing the dogcart with unabated industry;
"they say Jimmy's wife went roaring to the police, saying she
could get no account of her husband."

"I suppose he's beaten some fellow and is hiding," I
suggested.

"Well, that might be, sir," asserted Peter respectfully. He
plied his mop vigorously in intricate places about the springs,
which would, I knew, have never been explored save for my
presence.

"It's what John Hennessy was saying, that he was hard set to
get his horse past Cluin Cross, the way the blood was sthrewn
about the road," resumed Peter; "sure they were fighting like
wasps in it half the night."

"Who were fighting?"

"I couldn't say, indeed, sir. Some o' thim low rakish lads
from the town, I suppose," replied Peter with virtuous respectability.

When Peter Cadogan was quietly and intelligently candid,
to pursue an inquiry was seldom of much avail.

Next day in Skebawn I met little Murray, the district
inspector, very alert and smart in his rifle-green uniform,
going forth to collect evidence about the fight. He told me
that the police were pretty certain that one of the Sons of
Liberty, named Foley, had been murdered, but, as usual, the
difficulty was to get any one to give information; all that was
known was that he was gone and that his wife had identified
his cap, which had been found, drenched with blood, by the
roadside. Murray gave it as his opinion that the whole business

had arisen out of the row over the disputed race, and that there must have been a dozen people looking on when the murder was done; but so far no evidence was forthcoming, and after a day and a night of search the police had not been able to find the body.

"No," said Flurry Knox, who had joined us, "and if it was any of those mountainy men did away with him you might scrape Ireland with a small-tooth comb and you'll not get him!"

That evening I smoked an after-dinner cigarette out of doors in the mild starlight, strolling about the rudimentary paths of what would, I hoped, some day be Philippa's garden. The bats came stooping at the red end of my cigarette, and from the covert behind the house I heard once or twice the delicate bark of a fox. Civilisation seemed a thousand miles off, as far away as the falling star that had just drawn a line of pale fire half-way down the northern sky. I had been nearly a year at Shreelane House by myself now, and the time seemed very long to me. It was slow work putting by money, even under the austerities of Mrs. Cadogan's *régime*, and though I had warned Philippa I meant to marry her after Christmas, there were moments, and this was one of them, when it seemed an idle threat.

"Pether!" the strident voice of Mrs. Cadogan intruded upon my meditations. "Go tell the Major his coffee is waitin' on him!"

I went gloomily into the house, and, with a resignation born of adversity, swallowed the mixture of chicory and liquorice which my housekeeper possessed the secret of distilling from the best and most expensive coffee. My theory about it was that it added to the illusion that I had dined, and moreover that it kept me awake, and I generally had a good deal of writing to do after dinner.

Having swallowed it I went downstairs and out past the kitchen regions to my office, a hideous whitewashed room, in which I interviewed policemen, and took affidavits, and did most of my official writing. It had a door that opened into the yard, and a window that looked out in the other direction, among lanky laurels and scrubby hollies, where lay the cats' main thoroughfare from the scullery window to the rabbit holes in the wood. I had a good deal of work to do, and the time passed quickly. It was Friday night, and from the kitchen at the end of the passage came the gabbling murmur, in two alternate keys, that I had learned to recognise as the recital of a litany by my housekeeper and her nephew Peter. This performance was followed by some of those dreary and heart-rending yawns that are, I think, peculiar to Irish kitchens, then such of the cats as had returned from the chase were loudly shepherded into the back scullery, the kitchen door shut with a slam, and my retainers retired to repose.

It was nearly half-an-hour afterwards when I finished the notes I had been making on an adjourned case of "stroke-hauling" salmon in the Lonen River. I leaned back in my chair and lighted a cigarette preparatory to turning in; my thoughts had again wandered on a sentimental journey across the Irish Channel, when I heard a slight stir of some kind outside the open window. In the wilds of Ireland no one troubles themselves about burglars; "more cats," I thought, "I must shut the window before I go to bed."

Almost immediately there followed a faint tap on the window, and then a voice said in a hoarse and hurried whisper, "Them that wants Jim Foley, let them look in the river!"

If I had kept my head I should have sat still and encouraged a further confidence, but unfortunately I acted on the impulse of the natural man, and was at the window in a jump, knocking down my chair, and making noise enough to scare a far less shy bird than an Irish informer. Of course there was no one there. I listened, with every nerve as taunt as a violin string. It was quite dark; there was just breeze enough to make a rustling in the evergreens, so that a man might brush through them without being heard; and while I debated on a plan of action there came from beyond the shrubbery the jar and twang of a loose strand of wire in the palling by the wood. My informant, whoever he might be, had vanished into the darkness from which he had come as irrecoverably as had the falling star that had written its brief message across the sky, and gone out again into infinity.

I got up very early next morning and drove to Skebawn to see Murray, and offer him my mysterious information for what it was worth. Personally I did not think it worth much, and was disposed to regard it as a red herring drawn across the trail. Murray, however, was not in a mood to despise anything that had a suggestion to make, having been out till nine o'clock the night before without being able to find any clue to the hiding-place of James Foley.

"The river's a good mile from the place where the fight was," he said, straddling his compasses over the Ordnance Survey map, "and there's no sort of a road they could have taken him along, but a tip like this is always worth trying. I remember in the Land League time how a man came one Saturday night to my window and told me there were holes drilled in the chapel door to shoot a boycotted man through while he was at mass. The holes were there right enough, and you may be quite sure that chap found excellent reasons for having family prayers at home next day!"

I had sessions to attend on the extreme outskirts of my district, and could not wait, as Murray suggested, to see the thing out. I did not get home till the following day, and when I arrived I found a letter from Murray awaiting me.

"Your pal was right. We found Foley's body in the river, knocking about against the posts of the weir. The head was wrapped in his own green jersey, and had been smashed in by a stone. We suspect a fellow named Bat Callaghan, who has bolted, but there were a lot of them in it. Possibly it was Callaghan himself who gave you the tip; you never can tell how superstition is going to take them next. The inquest will be held to-morrow."

The coroner's jury took a cautious view of the cause of the

catastrophe, and brought in a verdict of "death by misadventure," and I presently found it to be my duty to call a magisterial inquiry to further investigate the matter. A few days before this was to take place, I was engaged in the delicate task of displaying to my landlord, Mr. Flurry Knox, the defects of the pantry sink, when Mrs. Cadogan advanced upon us with the information that the Widow Callaghan from Cluin would be thankful to speak to me, and had brought me a present of "a fine young goose."

"Is she come over here looking for Bat?" said Flurry, withdrawing his arm and the longest kitchen-ladle from the pipe that he had been probing; "she knows you're handy at hiding your friends, Mary; maybe it's he that's stopping the drain!"

Mrs. Cadogan turned her large red face upon her late employer.

"God knows I wish yerself was stuck in it, Master Flurry, the way ye'd hear Pether cursin' the full o' the house when he's striving to wash the things in that unnatural little trough."

"Are you sure it's Peter does all the cursing?" retorted Flurry. "I hear Father Scanlan has it in for you this long time for not going to confession."

"And how can I walk two miles to the chapel with God's burden on me feet?" demanded Mrs. Cadogan in purple indignation; "the Blessed Virgin and Docthor Hickey knows well the hardship I gets from them. If it wasn't for a pair of the Major's boots he gave me, I'd be hard set to thravel the house itself!"

The contest might have been continued indefinitely, had I not struck up the swords with a request that Mrs. Callaghan might be sent round to the hall door. There we found a tall, grey-haired countrywoman waiting for us at the foot of the steps, in the hooded blue cloak that is peculiar to the south of Ireland; from the fact that she clutched a pocket-handkerchief in her right hand I augured a stormy interview, but nothing could have been more self-restrained and even imposing than the reverence with which she greeted Flurry and me.

"Good-morning to your honours," she began, with a dignified and extremely imminent snuffle. "I ask your pardon for troubling you, Major Yeates, but I haven't a one in the country to give me an adwice, and I have no confidence only in your honour's experiments."

"Experience, she means," prompted Flurry. "Didn't you get advice enough out of Mr. Murray yesterday?" he went on aloud. "I heard he was at Cluin to see you."

"And if he was itself, it's little adwantage any one'd get out of that little whipper-shnapper of a shnap-dhragon!" responded Mrs. Callaghan tartly; "he was with me for a half-hour giving me every big rock of English till I had a reel in my head. I declare to ye, Mr. Flurry, after he had gone out o' the house, ye wouldn't throw three farthings for me!"

The pocket-handkerchief was here utilised, after which, with a heavy groan, Mrs. Callaghan again took up her parable.

"I towld him first and last I'd lose me life if I had to go into the coort, and if I did itself sure th' attorneys could rip no more out o' me than what he did himself."

"Did you tell him where was Bat?" inquired Flurry casually.

At this Mrs. Callaghan immediately dissolved into tears.

"Is it Bat?" she howled. "If the twelve Apostles came down from heaven asking me where was Bat, I could give them no satisfaction. The divil a know I know what's happened him. He came home with me sober and good-natured from the rogatta, and the next morning he axed a fresh egg for his breakfast, and God forgive me, I wouldn't break the score I was taking to the hotel, and with that he slapped the cup o' tay into the fire and went out the door, and I never got a word of him since, good nor bad. God knows 'tis I got throuble with that poor boy, and he the only one I have to look to in the world!"

I cut the matter short by asking her what she wanted me to do for her, and sifted out from amongst much extraneous detail the fact that she relied upon my renowned wisdom and clemency to preserve her from being called as a witness at the coming inquiry. The gift of the goose served its intended purpose of embarrassing my position, but in spite of it I broke to the Widow Callaghan my inability to help her. She did not, of course, believe me, but she was too well-bred to say so. In Ireland one becomes accustomed to this attitude.

As it turned out, however, Bat Callaghan's mother had nothing to fear from the inquiry. She was by turns deaf, imbecile, garrulously candid, and furiously abusive of Murray's principal witness, a frightened lad of seventeen, who had sworn to having seen Bat Callaghan and Jimmy Foley "shaping at one another to fight," at an hour when, according to Mrs. Callaghan, Bat was "lying shtretched on the beddeen with a sick shtomach" in consequence of the malignant character of the porter supplied by the last witness's father. It all ended, as such cases so often do in Ireland, in complete and moral certainty in the minds of all concerned as to the guilt of the accused, and entire impotence on the part of the law to prove it. A warrant was issued for the arrest of Bartholomew Callaghan; and the clans of Callaghan and Foley fought rather more bloodily than usual, as occasion served; and at intervals during the next few months Murray used to ask me if my friend the murderer had dropped in lately, to which I was wont to reply with condolences on the failure of the R.I.C. to find the Widow Callaghan's only son for her; and that was about all that came of it.

Events with which the present story has no concern took me to England towards the end of the following March. It so happened that my old regiment, the——th Fusiliers, was quartered at Whincastle, within a couple of hours by rail of Philippa's home, where I was staying, and, since my wedding was now within measurable distance, my former brothers-in-arms invited me over to dine and sleep, and to receive a valedictory silver claret jug that they were magnanimous enough to bestow upon a backslider. I enjoyed the dinner as much as any man can enjoy his dinner when he knows he has to make a speech at the end of it; through much and varied conversation I strove, like a nervous mother who cannot trust her offspring out of her sight, to keep before my mind's eye the opening sentences that I had composed in the train; I felt that I could only "get away" satisfactorily I might trust the Ayala ('89) to do the rest, and of that fount of inspiration there was no lack. As it turned out, I got away all right, though the sight of the double line of expectant faces and red mess jackets nearly scattered those precious opening sentences, and I am afraid that so far as the various subsequent points went that I had intended to make, I stayed away; however, neither Demosthenes, nor a Nationalist member at a Cork election, could have been listened to with more gratifying attention, and I sat down, hot and happy, to be confronted with my own flushed visage, hideously reflected in the glittering paunch of the claret jug.

Once safely over the presentation, the evening mellowed into frivolity, and it was pretty late before I found myself settled down to whist, at sixpenny points, in the ancient familiar way, while most of the others fell to playing pool in the billiard-room next door. I have played whist from my youth up; with the preternatural seriousness of a subaltern, with the self-assurance of a senior captain, with the privileged irascibility of a major; and my eighteen months of abstinence at Shreelane had only whetted my appetite for what I consider the best of games. After the long lonely evenings there, with the rats for company, and, for relaxation, a "deck" of that specially demoniacal American variety of patience known as "Fooly Ann," it was wondrous agreeable to sit again among my fellows, and "lay the longs" on a severely scientific rubber of whist, as though Mrs. Cadogan and the Skebawn Bench of Magistrates had never existed.

We were in the first game of the second rubber, and I was holding a very nice playing hand; I had early in the game moved forth my trumps to battle, and I was now in the ineffable position of scoring with the small cards of my long suit. The cards fell and fell in silence, and Ballantyne, my partner, raked in the tricks like a machine. The concentrated quiet of the game was suddenly arrested by a sharp, unmistakable sound from the barrack yard outside, the snap of a Lee-Metford rifle.

"What was that?" exclaimed Moffat, the senior major.

Before he had finished speaking there was a second shot.

"By Jove, those were rifle-shots! Perhaps I'd better go and see what's up," said Ballantyne, who was captain of the week, throwing down his cards and making a bolt for the door.

He had hardly got out of the room when the first long high note of the "assembly" sang out, sudden and clear. We all sprang to our feet, and as the bugle-call went shrilly on, the other men came pouring in from the billiard-room, and stampeded to their quarters to get their swords. At the same moment the mess sergeant appeared at the outer door with a face as white as his shirtfront.

"The sentry on the magazine guard has been shot, sir!" he said excitedly to Moffat. "They say he's dead!"

We were all out in the barrack square in an instant; it was clear moonlight, and the square was already alive with hurrying figures cramming on clothes and caps as they ran to fall in. I was a free agent these times, and I followed the mess sergeant across the square towards the distant corner where the magazine stands. As we doubled round the end of the men's quarters, we nearly ran into a small party of men who were advancing slowly and heavily in our direction.

"Ere he is, sir!" said the mess sergeant, stopping himself abruptly.

They were carrying the sentry to the hospital. His busby had fallen off; the moon shone mildly on his pale, convulsed face, and foam and strange inhuman sounds came from his lips. His head was rolling from side to side on the arm of one of the men who was carrying him; as it turned towards me I was struck by something disturbingly familiar in the face, and I wondered if he had been in my old company.

"What's his name, sergeant?" I asked to the mess sergeant.

"Private Harris, sir," replied the sergeant; "he's only lately come up from the depôt, and this was his first time on sentry by himself."

I went back to the mess, and in process of time the others straggled in, thirsting for whiskies-and-sodas, and full of such information as there was to give. Private Harris was not wounded; both the shots had been fired by him, as was testified by the state of his rifle and the fact that two of the cartridges were missing from the packet in his pouch.

"I hear he was a queer, sulky sort of chap always," said Tomkinson, the subaltern of the day, "but if he was having a try at suicide he made a bally bad fist of it."

"He made as good a fist of it as you did of putting on your sword, Tommy," remarked Ballantyne, indicating a dangling white strap of webbing, that hung down like a tail below Mr. Tomkinson's mess jacket. "Nerves, obviously, in both cases!"

The exquisite satisfaction afforded by this discovery to Mr. Tomkinson's brother officers found its natural outlet in a bear fight that threatened to become more or less general, and in the course of which I slid away unostentatiously to bed in Ballantyne's quarters and took the precaution of barricading my door.

Next morning, when I got down to breakfast, I found Ballantyne and two or three others in the mess room, and my first inquiry was for Private Harris.

"Oh, the poor chap's dead," said Ballantyne; "it's a very queer business altogether. I think he must have been wrong in the top storey. The doctor was with him when he came to out of the fit, or whatever it was, and O'Reilly—that's the doctor y' know, Irish of course, and, by the way, poor Harris was an Irishman too—says that he could only jibber at first, but then he got better, and he got out of him that when he had been on sentry-go for about half-an-hour, he happened to look up at the angle of the barrack wall near where it joins the magazine tower, and saw a face looking at him over it. He challenged and got no answer, but the face stuck there staring at him; he challenged again, and then, as O'Reilly said, he 'just oop with his royfle and blazed at it.'" Ballantyne was not above the common English delusion that he could imitate an Irish brogue.

"Well, what happened then?"

"Well, according to the poor devil's own story, the face just kept on looking at him and he had another shot at it, and 'My God Almighty,' he said to O'Reilly, 'it was there always!' While he was saying that to O'Reilly he began to chuck another fit, and apparently went on chucking them till he died a couple of hours ago."

"One result of it is," said another man, "that they couldn't get a man to go on sentry there alone last night. I expect we shall have to double the sentries there every night as long as we're here."

"Silly asses!" remarked Tomkinson, but he said it without conviction.

After breakfast we went out to look at the wall by the magazine. It was about eleven feet high, with a coped top, and they told me there was a deep and wide dry ditch on the outside. A ladder was brought, and we examined the angle of the wall at which Harris said the face had appeared. He had made a beautiful shot, one of his bullets having flicked a piece off the ridge of the coping exactly at the corner.

"It's not the kind of shot a man would make if he had been drinking," said Moffat, regretfully abandoning his first simple hypothesis; "he must have been mad."

"I wish I could find out who his people are," said Brownlow, the adjutant, who had joined us; "they found in his box a letter to him from his mother, but we can't make out the name of the place. By Jove, Yeates, you're an Irishman, perhaps you can help us."

He handed me a letter in a dirty envelope. There was no

address given, the contents were very short, and I may be forgiven if I transcribe them:—

"My dear Son, I hope you are well as this leaves me at present, thanks be to God for it. I am very much unaisy about the cow. She swelled up this morning, she ran in and was frauding and I did not do but to run up for tom sweeney in the minute. We are thinking it is too much lairels or an eirub she took. I do not know what I will do with her. God help one that's alone with himself I had not a days luck since ye went away. I am thinkin' them that wants ye is tired lookin' for ye. And so I remain,

"YOUR FOND MOTHER."

"Well, you don't get much of a lead from the cow do you? And what the deuce is an eirub?" said Brownlow.

"It's another way of spelling herb," I said, turning over the envelope abstractedly. The postmark was almost obliterated, but it struck me it might be construed into the word Skebawn.

"Look here," I said suddenly, "let me see Harris. It's just possible I may know something about him."

The sentry's body had been laid in the dead-house near the hospital, and Brownlow fetched the key. It was a grim little whitewashed building, without windows, save a small one of lancet shape, high up in one gable, through which a streak of April sunlight fell sharp and slender on the whitewashed wall. The long figure of the sentry lay sheeted on a stone slab, and Brownlow, with his cap in his hand, gently uncovered the face.

I leaned over and looked at it—at the heavy brows, the short nose, the small moustache lying black above the pale mouth, the deep-set eyes sealed in appalling peacefulness. There rose before me the wild dark face of the young man who had hung on my wheel and yelled encouragement to the winning coxswain at the Lough Lonen Regatta.

"I know him," I said, "his name is Callaghan."

Five

⟫●⟪

LISHEEN RACES, SECOND-HAND

IT may or may not be agreeable to have attained the age of thirty-eight, but, judging from old photographs, the privilege of being nineteen has also its drawbacks. I turned over page after page of an ancient book in which were enshrined portraits of the friends of my youth, singly, in David and Jonathan couples, and in groups in which I, as it seemed to my mature and possibly jaundiced perception, always contrived to look the most immeasurable young bounder of the lot. Our faces were fat, and yet I cannot remember ever having been considered fat in my life; we indulged in low-necked shirts, in "Jemima" ties with diagonal stripes; we wore coats that seemed three sizes too small, and trousers that were three sizes too big; we also wore small whiskers.

I stopped at last at one of the David and Jonathan memorial portraits. Yes, here was the object of my researches; this stout and earnestly romantic youth was Leigh Kelway, and that fatuous and chubby young person seated on the arm of his chair was myself. Leigh Kelway was a young man ardently believed in by a large circle of admirers, headed by himself and seconded by me, and for some time after I had left Magdalen

for Sandhurst, I maintained a correspondence with him on
large and abstract subjects. This phase of our friendship did
not survive; I went soldiering to India, and Leigh Kelway took
honours and moved suitably on into politics, as is the duty of
an earnest young Radical with useful family connections and
an independent income. Since then I had at intervals seen in
the papers the name of the Honourable Basil Leigh Kelway
mentioned as a speaker at elections, as a writer of thoughtful
articles in the reviews, but we had never met, and nothing
could have been less expected by me than the letter, written
from Mrs. Raverty's Hotel, Skebawn, in which he told me he
was making a tour in Ireland with Lord Waterbury, to whom
he was private secretary. Lord Waterbury was at present
having a few days' fishing near Killarney, and he himself, not
being a fisherman, was collecting statistics for his chief on
various points connected with the Liquor Question in Ireland.
He had heard that I was in the neighbourhood, and was kind
enough to add that it would give him much pleasure to meet
me again.

With a stir of the old enthusiasm I wrote begging him to be
my guest for as long as it suited him, and the following
afternoon he arrived at Shreelane. The stout young friend of
my youth had changed considerably. His important nose and
slightly prominent teeth remained, but his wavy hair had
withdrawn intellectually from his temples; his eyes had acquired a statesmanlike absence of expression, and his neck had
grown long and birdlike. It was his first visit to Ireland, as he
lost no time in telling me, and he and his chief had already
collected much valuable information on the subject to which
they had dedicated the Easter recess. He further informed
me that he thought of popularising the subject in a novel, and
therefore intended to, as he put it, "master the brogue" before
his return.

During the next few days I did my best for Leigh Kelway. I
turned him loose on Father Scanlan; I showed him Mohona,
our champion village, that boasts fifteen public-houses out of

twenty buildings of sorts and a railway station; I took him to hear the prosecution of a publican for selling drink on a Sunday, which gave him an opportunity of studying perjury as a fine art, and of hearing a lady, on whom police suspicion justly rested, profoundly summed up by the sergeant as "a woman who had th' appairance of having knocked at a back door."

The net result of these experiences has not yet been given to the world by Leigh Kelway. For my own part, I had at the end of three days arrived at the conclusion that his society, when combined with a note-book and a thirst for statistics, was not what I used to find it at Oxford. I therefore welcomed a suggestion from Mr. Flurry Knox that we should accompany him to some typical country races, got up by the farmers at a place called Lisheen, some twelve miles away. It was the worst road in the district, the races of the most grossly unorthodox character; in fact, it was the very place for Leigh Kelway to collect impressions of Irish life, and in any case it was a blessed opportunity of disposing of him for the day.

In my guest's attire next morning I discerned an unbending from the rôle of cabinet minister towards that of sportsman; the outlines of the note-book might be traced in his breast pocket, but traversing it was the strap of a pair of field-glasses, and his light grey suit was smart enough for Goodwood.

Flurry was to drive us to the races at one o'clock, and we walked to Tory Cottage by the short cut over the hill, in the sunny beauty of an April morning. Up to the present the weather had kept me in a more or less apologetic condition; any one who has entertained a guest in the country knows the unjust weight of responsibility that rests on the shoulders of the host in the matter of climate, and Leigh Kelway, after two drenchings, had become sarcastically resigned to what I felt he regarded as my mismanagement.

Flurry took us into the house for a drink and a biscuit, to keep us going, as he said, till "we lifted some luncheon out of the Castle Knox people at the races," and it was while we were thus engaged that the first disaster of the day occurred. The dining-room door was open, so also was the window of the little staircase just outside it, and through the window travelled sounds that told of the close proximity of the stable-yard; the clattering of hoofs on cobble stones, and voices uplifted in loud conversation. Suddenly from this region there arose a screech of the laughter peculiar to kitchen flirtation, followed by the clank of a bucket, the plunging of a horse, and then an uproar of wheels and galloping hoofs. An instant afterwards Flurry's chestnut cob, in a dogcart, dashed at full gallop into view, with the reins streaming behind him, and two men in hot pursuit. Almost before I had time to realise what had happened, Flurry jumped through the half-opened window of the dining-room like a clown at a pantomime, and joined in the chase, but the cob was resolved to make the most of his chance, and went away down the drive and out of sight at a pace that distanced every one save the kennel terrier, who sped in shrieking ecstasy beside him.

"Oh merciful hour!" exclaimed a female voice behind me. Leigh Kelway and I were by this time watching the progress of events from the gravel, in company with the remainder of Flurry's household. "The horse is desthroyed! Wasn't that the quare start he took! And all in the world I done was to slap a bucket of wather at Michael out the windy, and 'twas himself got it in place of Michael!"

"Ye'll never ate another bit, Bridgie Dunnigan," replied the cook, with the exulting pessimism of her kind. "The Master'll have your life!"

Both speakers shouted at the top of their voices, probably because in spirit they still followed afar the flight of the cob.

Leigh Kelway looked serious as we walked on down the drive. I almost dared to hope that a note on the degrading oppression of Irish retainers was shaping itself. Before we reached the bend of the drive the rescue party was returning with the fugitive, all, with the exception of the kennel terrier, looking extremely gloomy. The cob had been confronted by a wooden gate, which he had unhesitatingly taken in his stride, landing on his head on the farther side with the gate and the cart on top of him, and had arisen with a lame foreleg, a cut on his nose, and several other minor wounds.

"You'd think the brute had been fighting the cats, with all the scratches and scrapes he has on him!" said Flurry, casting a vengeful eye at Michael, "and one shaft's broken and so is the dashboard. I haven't another horse in the place; they're all out at grass, and so there's an end of the races!"

We all three stood blankly on the hall-door steps and watched the wreck of the trap being trundled up the avenue.

"I'm very sorry you're done out of your sport," said Flurry to Leigh Kelway, in tones of deplorable sincerity; "perhaps, as there's nothing else to do, you'd like to see the hounds——?"

I felt for Flurry, but of the two I felt more for Leigh Kelway as he accepted this alleviation. He disliked dogs, and held the newest views on sanitation, and I knew what Flurry's kennels could smell like. I was lighting a precautionary cigarette, when we caught sight of an old man riding up the drive. Flurry stopped short.

"Hold on a minute," he said; "here's an old chap that often brings me horses for the kennels; I must see what he wants."

The man dismounted and approached Mr. Knox, hat in hand, towing after him a gaunt and ancient black mare with a big knee.

"Well, Barrett," began Flurry, surveying the mare with his hands in his pockets, "I'm not giving the hounds meat this month, or only very little."

"Ah, Master Flurry," answered Barrett, "it's you that's pleasant! Is it give the like o' this one for the dogs to ate! She's a vallyble strong young mare, no more than shixteen years of age, and ye'd sooner be lookin' at her goin' under a side-car than eatin' your dinner."

"There isn't as much meat on her as 'd fatten a jackdaw," said Flurry, clinking the silver in his pockets as he searched for a matchbox. "What are you asking for her?"

The old man drew cautiously up to him.

"Master Flurry," he said solemnly, "I'll sell her to *your* honour for five pounds, and she'll be worth ten after you give her a month's grass."

Flurry lit his cigarette; then he said imperturbably, "I'll give you seven shillings for her."

Old Barrett put on his hat in silence, and in silence buttoned his coat and took hold of the stirrup leather. Flurry remained immovable.

"Master Flurry," said old Barrett suddenly, with tears in his voice, "you must make it eight, sir!"

"Michael!" called out Flurry with apparent irrelevance, "run up to your father's and ask him would he lend me a loan of his side-car."

Half-an-hour later we were, improbable as it may seem, on our way to Lisheen races. We were seated upon an outside-car of immemorial age, whose joints seemed to open and close again as it swung in and out of the ruts, whose tattered cushions stank of rats and mildew, whose wheels staggered and rocked like the legs of a drunken man. Between the shafts jogged the latest addition to the kennel larder, the eight-shilling mare. Flurry sat on one side, and kept her going at a rate of not less than four miles an hour; Leigh Kelway and I held on to the other.

"She'll get us as far as Lynch's anyway," said Flurry, abandoning his first contention that she could do the whole distance, as he pulled her on to her legs after her fifteenth stumble, "and he'll lend us some sort of a horse, if it was only a mule."

"Do you notice that these cushions are very damp?" said Leigh Kelway to me, in a hollow undertone.

"Small blame to them if they are!" replied Flurry. "I've no doubt but they were out under the rain all day yesterday at Mrs. Hurly's funeral."

Leigh Kelway made no reply, but he took his note-book out of his pocket and sat on it.

We arrived at Lynch's at a little past three, and were there confronted by the next disappointment of this disastrous day. The door of Lynch's farmhouse was locked, and nothing replied to our knocking except a puppy, who barked hysterically from within.

"All gone to the races," said Flurry philosophically, picking his way round the manure heap. "No matter, here's the filly in the shed here. I know he's had her under a car."

An agitating ten minutes ensued, during which Leigh Kelway and I got the eight-shilling mare out of the shafts and the harness, and Flurry, with our inefficient help, crammed the young mare into them. As Flurry had stated that she had been driven before, I was bound to believe him, but the difficulty of getting the bit into her mouth was remarkable, and so also was the crab-like manner in which she sidled out of the yard, with Flurry and myself at her head, and Leigh Kelway hanging on to the back of the car to keep it from jamming in the gateway.

"Sit up on the car now," said Flurry when we got out on to the road; "I'll lead her on a bit. She's been ploughed anyway; one side of her mouth's as tough as a gad!"

Leigh Kelway threw away the wisp of grass with which he had been cleaning his hands, and mopped his intellectual forehead; he was very silent. We both mounted the car, and Flurry, with the reins in his hand, walked beside the filly, who, with her tail clasped in, moved onward in a succession of short jerks.

"Oh, she's all right!" said Flurry, beginning to run, and dragging the filly into a trot; "once she gets started—" Here the filly spied a pig in a neighbouring field, and despite the fact that she had probably eaten out of the same trough with it, she gave a violent side spring, and broke into a gallop.

"Now we're off!" shouted Flurry, making a jump at the car and clambering on; "if the traces hold we'll do!"

The English language is powerless to suggest the view-halloo with which Mr. Knox ended his speech, or to do more than indicate the rigid anxiety of Leigh Kelway's face as he regained his balance after the preliminary jerk, and clutched the back rail. It must be said for Lynch's filly that she did not kick; she merely fled, like a dog with a kettle tied to its tail, from the pursuing rattle and jingle behind her, with the shafts buffeting her dusty sides as the car swung to and fro. Whenever she showed any signs of slackening, Flurry loosed another yell at her that renewed her panic, and thus we precariously covered another two or three miles of our journey.

Had it not been for a large stone lying on the road, and had the filly not chosen to swerve so as to bring the wheel on top of it, I dare say we might have got to the races; but by an unfortunate coincidence both these things occurred, and when we recovered from the consequent shock, the tire of one of the wheels had come off, and was trundling with cumbrous gaiety into the ditch. Flurry stopped the filly and began to laugh; Leigh Kelway said something startlingly unparliamentary under his breath.

"Well, it might be worse," Flurry said consolingly as he lifted the tire on to the car; "we're not half a mile from a forge."

We walked that half-mile in funereal procession behind the car; the glory had departed from the weather, and an ugly wall of cloud was rising up out of the west to meet the sun; the hills had darkened and lost colour, and the white bog cotton shivered in a cold wind that smelt of rain.

By a miracle the smith was not at the races, owing, as he explained, to his having "the toothaches," the two facts combined producing in him a morosity only equalled by that of Leigh Kelway. The smith's sole comment on the situation was to unharness the filly, and drag her into the forge, where he tied her up. He then proceeded to whistle viciously on his fingers in the direction of a cottage, and to command, in tones of thunder, some unseen creature to bring over a couple of baskets of turf. The turf arrived in process of time, on a woman's back, and was arranged in a circle in a yard at the back of the forge. The tire was bedded on it, and the turf was with difficulty kindled at different points.

"Ye'll not get to the races this day," said the smith, yielding to a sardonic satisfaction; "the turf's wet, and I haven't one to do a hand's turn for me." He laid the wheel on the ground and lit his pipe.

Leigh Kelway looked pallidly about him over the spacious empty landscape of brown mountain slopes patched with golden furze and seamed with grey walls; I wondered if he were as hungry as I. We sat on stones opposite the smouldering ring of turf and smoked, and Flurry beguiled the smith into grim and calumnious confidences about every horse in the country. After about an hour, during which the turf went out three times, and the weather became more and more threatening, a girl with a red petticoat over her head appeared at the gate of the yard, and said to the smith:

"The horse is gone away from ye."

"Where?" exclaimed Flurry, springing to his feet.

"I met him walking wesht the road there below, and when I thought to turn him he commenced to gallop."

"Pulled her head out of the headstall," said Flurry, after a rapid survey of the forge. "She's near home by now."

It was at this moment that the rain began; the situation could scarcely have been better stage-managed. After reviewing the position, Flurry and I decided that the only thing to do was to walk to a public-house a couple of miles farther on, feed there if possible, hire a car, and go home.

It was an uphill walk, with mild, generous raindrops striking thicker and thicker on our faces; no one talked, and the grey clouds crowded up from behind the hills like billows of steam. Leigh Kelway bore it all with egregious resignation. I cannot pretend that I was at heart sympathetic, but by virtue of being his host I felt responsible for the breakdown, for his light suit, for everything, and divined his sentiment of horror at the first sight of the public-house.

It was a long, low cottage, with a line of dripping elm-trees overshadowing it; empty cars and carts round its door, and a babel from within made it evident that the racegoers were pursuing a gradual homeward route. The shop was crammed with steaming countrymen, whose loud brawling voices, all talking together, roused my English friend to his first remark since we had left the forge.

"Surely, Yeates, we are not going into that place?" he said severely; "those men are all drunk."

"Ah, nothing to signify!" said Flurry, plunging in and driving his way through the throng like a plough. "Here, Mary Kate!" he called to the girl behind the counter, "tell your mother we want some tea and bread and butter in the room inside."

The smell of bad tobacco and spilt porter was choking; we worked our way through it after him towards the end of the shop, intersecting at every hand discussions about the races.

"Tom was very nice. He spared his horse all along, and then he put into him—" "Well, at Goggin's corner the third horse was before the second, but he was goin' wake in himself." "I tell ye the mare had the hind leg fasht in the fore." "Clancy was dipping in the saddle." "'Twas a dam nice race what-ever—— "

We gained the inner room at last, a cheerless apartment, adorned with sacred pictures, a sewing-machine, and an array of supplementary tumblers and wineglasses; but, at all events, we had it so far to ourselves. At intervals during the next half-hour Mary Kate burst in with cups and plates, cast them on the table and disappeared, but of food there was no sign. After a further period of starvation and of listening to the noise in the shop, Flurry made a sortie, and, after lengthy and unknown adventures, reappeared carrying a huge brown tea-pot, and driving before him Mary Kate with the remainder of the repast. The bread tasted of mice, the butter of turf-smoke, the tea of brown paper, but we had got past the critical stage. I had entered upon my third round of bread and butter when the door was flung open, and my valued acquaintance, Slipper, slightly advanced in liquor, presented himself to our gaze. His bandy legs sprawled consequentially, his nose was redder than a coal of fire, his prominent eyes rolled crookedly upon us, and his left hand swept behind him the attempt of Mary Kate to frustrate his entrance.

"Good-evening to my vinerable friend, Mr. Flurry Knox!" he began, in the voice of a town crier, "and to the Honourable Major Yeates, and the English gintleman!"

This impressive opening immediately attracted an audience from the shop, and the doorway filled with grinning faces as Slipper advanced farther into the room.

"Why weren't ye at the races, Mr. Flurry?" he went on, his roving eye taking a grip of us all at the same time; "sure the Miss Bennetts and all the ladies was asking where were ye."

"It'd take some time to tell them that," said Flurry, with his mouth full; "but what about the races, Slipper? Had you good sport?"

"Sport it is? Divil so pleasant an afternoon ever you seen," replied Slipper. He leaned against a side table, and all the glasses on it jingled. Does your honour know O'Driscoll?" he went on irrelevantly. "Sure you do. He was in your honour's stable. It's what we were all sayin'; it was a great pity your honour was not there, for the likin' you had to Driscoll."

"That's thrue," said a voice at the door.

"There wasn't one in the Barony but was gethered in it, through and fro," continued Slipper, with a quelling glance at the interrupter; "and there was tints for sellin' porther, and whisky as pliable as new milk, and boys goin' round the tints outside, feeling for heads with the big ends of their black-thorns, and all kinds of recreations, and the Sons of Liberty's piffler and dhrum band from Skebawn; though faith! there was more of thim runnin' to look at the races than what was playin' in it; not to mintion different occasions that the bandmasther was atin' his lunch within in the whisky tint."

"But what about Driscoll?" said Flurry.

"Sure it's about him I'm tellin' ye," replied Slipper, with the practised orator's watchful eye on his growing audience. "'Twas within in the same whisky tint meself was, with the bandmasther and a few of the lads, an' we buyin' a ha'porth o' crackers, when I see me brave Driscoll landin' into the tint, and a pair o' thim long boots on him; him that hadn't a shoe nor a stocking to his foot when your honour had him picking grass out o' the stones behind in your yard. 'Well,', says I to meself, 'we'll knock some spoort out of Driscoll!'

"'Come here to me, acushla!' says I to him; 'I suppose it's some way wake in the legs y'are,' says I, 'an' the docthor put them on ye the way the people wouldn't thrample ye!'

"'May the divil choke ye!' says he, pleasant enough, but I knew by the blush he had he was vexed.

"'Then I suppose 'tis a left-tenant colonel y'are,' says I; 'yer mother must be proud out o' ye!' says I, 'an' maybe ye'll lend her a loan o' thim waders when she's rinsin' yer bauneen in the river!' says I.

"'There'll be work out o' this!' says he, lookin' at me both sour and bitther.

"'Well indeed, I was thinkin' you were blue moulded for want of a batin',' says I. He was for fightin' us then, but afther we had him pacificated with about a quarther of a naggin o' sperrits, he told us he was goin' ridin' in a race.

"'An' what'll ye ride?' says I.

"'Owld Bocock's mare,' says he.

"'Knipes!' says I, sayin' a great curse; 'is it that little staggeen from the mountains; sure she's somethin' about the one age with meself,' says I. 'Many's the time Jamesy Geoghegan and meself used to be dhrivin' her to Macroom with pigs an' all soorts,' says I; 'an' is it leppin' stone walls ye want her to go now?'

"'Faith, there's walls and every vari'ty of obstackle in it,' says he.

"'It'll be the best o' your play, so,' says I, 'to leg it away home out o' this.'

"'An' who'll ride her, so?' says he.

" 'Let the divil ride her,' says I."

Leigh Kelway, who had been leaning back seemingly half asleep, obeyed the hypnotism of Slipper's gaze, and opened his eyes.

" 'Let the divil ride her,' says I"

"That was now all the conversation that passed between himself and meself," resumed Slipper, "and there was no great delay afther that till they said there was a race startin' and the dickens a one at all was goin' to ride only two, Driscoll, and one Clancy. With that then I seen Mr. Kinahane, the Petty Sessions clerk, goin' round clearin' the coorse, an' I gethered

a few o' the neighbours, an' we walked the fields hither and
over till we seen the most of th' obstackles.

"'Stand aisy now by the plantation,' says I; 'if they get to
come as far as this, believe me ye'll see spoort,' says I, 'an' 'twill

Mr. Kinahane, the petty sessions clerk, goin' round clearin' the coorse

be a convanient spot to encourage the mare if she's anyway
wake in herself,' says I, cuttin' somethin' about five foot of an
ash sapling out o' the plantation.

"'That's yer sort!' says owld Bocock, that was thravellin' the
racecoorse, peggin' a bit o' paper down with a thorn in front
of every lep, the way Driscoll 'd know the handiest place to
face her at it.

"Well, I hadn't barely thrimmed the ash plant——"

"Have you any jam, Mary Kate?" interrupted Flurry, whose
meal had been in no way interfered with by either the story or
the highly-scented crowd who had come to listen to it.

"We have no jam, only thraycle, sir," replied the invisible Mary Kate.

"I hadn't the switch barely thrimmed," repeated Slipper firmly, "when I heard the people screechin', an' I seen Driscoll an' Clancy comin' on, leppin' all before them, an' owld Bocock's mare bellusin' an' powdherin' along, an' bedad! whatever obstackle wouldn't throw *her* down, faith, she'd throw *it* down, an' there's the thraffic they had in it.

" 'I declare to me sowl,' says I, 'if they continue on this way there's a great chance some one o' thim 'll win,' says I.

" 'Ye lie!' says the bandmasther, bein' a thrifle fulsome after his luncheon.

" 'I do not,' says I, 'in regard of seein' how soople them two boys is. Ye might observe,' says I, 'that if they have no convanient way to sit on the saddle, they'll ride the neck o' the horse till such time as they gets an occasion to lave it,' says I.

"Whatever obstackle wouldn't throw her down,
faith, she'd throw it down"

" 'Arrah, shut yer mouth!' says the bandmasther; 'they're puckin' out this way now, an' may the divil admire me!' says he, 'but Clancy has the other bet out, and the divil such leatherin' and beltin' of owld Bocock's mare ever you seen as what's in it!' says he.

"Well, when I seen them comin' to me, and Driscoll about the length of the plantation behind Clancy, I let a couple of bawls.

" 'Skelp her, ye big brute!' says I. 'What good's in ye that ye aren't able to skelp her?' "

" 'Skelp her, ye big brute!' says I"

The yell and the histrionic flourish of his stick with which Slipper delivered this incident brought down the house. Leigh Kelway was sufficiently moved to ask me in an undertone if "skelp" was a local term.

"Well, Mr. Flurry, and gintlemen," recommenced Slipper, "I declare to ye when owld Bocock's mare heard thim roars she sthretched out her neck like a gandher, and when she passed me out she give a couple of grunts, and looked at me as ugly as a Christian.

" 'Hah!' says I, givin' her a couple o' dhraws o' th' ash plant across the butt o' the tail, the way I wouldn't blind her; 'I'll make ye grunt!' says I, 'I'll nourish ye!'

"I knew well she was very frightful of th' ash plant since the winter Tommeen Sullivan had her under a sidecar. But now, in place of havin' any obligations to me, ye'd be surprised if ye heard the blaspheemious expressions of that young boy that was ridin' her; and whether it was over-anxious he was, turnin' around the way I'd hear him cursin', or whether it was some slither or slide came to owld Bocock's mare, I dunno, but she was bet up agin the last obstackle but two, and before ye could say 'Shnipes,' she was standin' on her two ears beyond in th' other field! I declare to ye, on the vartue of me oath, she stood that way till she reconnoithered what side would Driscoll fall, an' she turned about then and rolled on him as cosy as if he was meadow grass!"

Slipper stopped short; the people in the doorway groaned appreciatively; Mary Kate murmured "The Lord save us!"

"The blood was dhruv out through his nose and ears," continued Slipper, with a voice that indicated the cream of the narration, "and you'd hear his bones crackin' on the ground! You'd have pitied the poor boy."

"Good heavens!" said Leigh Kelway, sitting up very straight in his chair.

"Was he hurt, Slipper?" asked Flurry casually.

"Hurt is it?" echoed Slipper in high scorn; "killed on the spot!" He paused to relish the effect of the *dénouement* on Leigh Kelway. "Oh, divil so pleasant an afthernoon ever you seen; and indeed, Mr. Flurry, it's what we were all sayin', it was a great pity your honour was not there for the likin' you had for Driscoll."

As he spoke the last word there was an outburst of singing and cheering from a car-load of people who had just pulled up at the door. Flurry listened, leaned back in his chair, and began to laugh.

"It scarcely strikes one as a comic incident," said Leigh Kelway, very coldly to me; "in fact, it seems to me that the police ought——"

"Show me Slipper!" bawled a voice in the shop; "show me that dirty little undherlooper till I have his blood! Hadn't I the race won only for he souring the mare on me! What's that you say? I tell ye he did! He left seven slaps on her with the handle of a hay-rake——"

There was in the room in which we were sitting a second door, leading to the back yard, a door consecrated to the unobtrusive visits of so-called "Sunday travellers." Through it

Slipper faded away like a dream, and, simultaneously, a tall young man, with a face like a red-hot potato tied up in a bandage, squeezed his way from the shop into the room.

"Well, Driscoll," said Flurry, "since it wasn't the teeth of the rake he left on the mare, you needn't be talking!"

Leigh Kelway looked from one to the other with a wilder expression in his eye than I had thought it capable of. I read in it a resolve to abandon Ireland to her fate.

At eight o'clock we were still waiting for the car that we had been assured should be ours directly it returned from the races. At half-past eight we had adopted the only possible course that remained, and had accepted the offers of lifts on the laden cars that were returning to Skebawn, and I presently was gratified by the spectacle of my friend Leigh Kelway wedged between a roulette table and its proprietor on one side of a car, with Driscoll and Slipper, mysteriously reconciled and excessively drunk, seated, locked in each other's arms, on the other. Flurry and I, somewhat similarly placed, followed on two other cars. I was scarcely surprised when I was informed that the melancholy white animal in the shafts of the leading car was Owld Bocock's much-enduring steeplechaser.

The night was very dark and stormy, and it is almost superfluous to say that no one carried lamps; the rain poured upon us, and through wind and wet Owld Bocock's mare set the pace at a rate that showed she knew from bitter experience what was expected from her by gentlemen who had spent the evening in a public-house; behind her the other two tired horses followed closely, incited to emulation by shouting, singing, and a liberal allowance of whip. We were a good ten miles from Skebawn, and never had the road seemed so long. For mile after mile the half-seen low walls slid past us, with occasional plunges into caverns of darkness under trees. Sometimes from a wayside cabin a dog would dash out to bark at us as we rattled by; sometimes our cavalcade swung aside to pass, with yells and counter-yells, crawling carts filled with other belated race-goers.

I was nearly wet through, even though I received considerable shelter from a Skebawn publican, who slept heavily and irrepressibly on my shoulder. Driscoll, on the leading car, had struck up an approximation to the "Wearing of the Green," when a wavering star appeared on the road ahead of us. It grew momently larger; it came towards us apace. Flurry, on the car behind me, shouted suddenly—

"That's the mail car, with one of the lamps out! Tell those fellows ahead to look out!"

But the warning fell on deaf ears.

> "When laws can change the blades of grass
> From growing as they grow——"

howled five discordant voices, oblivious of the towering proximity of the star.

A Bianconi mail car is nearly three miles the size of an ordinary outside car, and when on a dark night it advances, Cyclops-like, with but one eye, it is difficult for even a sober driver to calculate its bulk. Above the sounds of melody there arose the thunder of heavy wheels, the splashing trample of three big horses, then a crash and a turmoil of shouts. Our cars pulled up just in time, and I tore myself from the embrace of my publican to go to Leigh Kelway's assistance.

The wing of the Bianconi had caught the wing of the smaller car, flinging Owld Bocock's mare on her side and throwing her freight headlong on top of her, the heap being surmounted by the roulette table. The driver of the mail car unshipped his solitary lamp and turned it on the disaster. I saw that Flurry had already got hold of Leigh Kelway by the heels, and was dragging him from under the others. He struggled up hatless, muddy, and gasping, with Driscoll hanging on by his neck, still singing the "Wearing of the Green."

A voice from the mail car said incredulously, *"Leigh Kelway!"* A spectacled face glared down upon him from under the dripping spikes of an umbrella.

It was the Right Honourable the Earl of Waterbury, Leigh Kelway's chief, returning from his fishing excursion.

Meanwhile Slipper, in the ditch, did not cease to announce that "Divil so pleasant an afthernoon ever ye seen as what was in it!"

Six

PHILIPPA'S FOX-HUNT

No one can accuse Philippa and me of having married in haste. As a matter of fact, it was but little under five years from that autumn evening on the river when I had said what is called in Ireland "the hard word," to the day in August when I was led to the altar by my best man, and was subsequently led away from it by Mrs. Sinclair Yeates. About two years out of the five had been spent by me at Shreelane in ceaseless warfare with drains, eaveshoots, chimneys, pumps; all those fundamentals, in short, that the ingenuous and improving tenant expects to find established as a basis from which to rise to higher things. As far as rising to higher things went, frequent ascents to the roof to search for leaks summed up my achievements; in fact, I suffered so general a shrinkage of my ideals that the triumph of making the hall-door bell ring blinded me to the fact that the rat-holes in the hall floor were nailed up with pieces of tin biscuit boxes, and that the casual visitor could, instead of leaving a card, have easily written his name in the damp on the walls.

Philippa, however, proved adorably callous to these and similar shortcomings. She regarded Shreelane and its floundering, foundering ménage of incapables in the light of a gigantic picnic in a foreign land; she held long conversations daily with Mrs. Cadogan, in order, as she informed me, to acquire the language; without any ulterior domestic intention she engaged kitchen-maids because of the beauty of their eyes, and housemaids because they had such delightfully pictur-esque old mothers, and she declined to correct the phraseol-ogy of the parlour-maid, whose painful habit it was to whisper "Do ye choose cherry or clarry?" when proffering the wine. Fast-days, perhaps, afforded my wife her first insight into the sterner realities of Irish housekeeping. Philippa had what are known as High Church proclivities, and took the matter seriously.

"I don't know how we are to manage for the servants' dinner to-morrow, Sinclair," she said, coming in to my office one Thursday morning; "Julia says she 'promised God this long time that she wouldn't eat an egg on a fast-day,' and the kitchen-maid says she won't eat herrings 'without they're fried with onions,' and Mrs. Cadogan says she will 'not go to them extremes for servants.'"

"I should let Mrs. Cadogan settle the menu herself," I suggested.

"I asked her to do that," replied Philippa, "and she only said she 'thanked God *she* had no appetite!'"

The lady of the house here fell away into unseasonable laughter.

I made the demoralising suggestion that, as we were going away for a couple of nights, we might safely leave them to fight it out, and the problem was abandoned.

Philippa had been much called on by the neighbourhood in all its shades and grades, and daily she and her trousseau frocks presented themselves at hall-doors of varying dimensions in due acknowledgment of civilities. In Ireland, it may be noted, the process known in England as "summering and wintering" a newcomer does not obtain; sociability and curiosity alike forbid delay. The visit to which we owed our escape from the intricacies of the fast-day was to the Knoxes of Castle Knox, relations in some remote and tribal way of my landlord, Mr. Flurry of that ilk. It involved a short journey by train, and my wife's longest basket-trunk; it also, which was more serious, involved my being lent a horse to go out cubbing the following morning.

At Castle Knox we sank into an almost forgotten environment of draught-proof windows and doors, of deep carpets, of silent servants instead of clattering belligerents. Philippa told me afterwards that it had only been by an effort that she had restrained herself from snatching up the train of her wedding-gown as she paced across the wide hall on little Sir Valentine's arm. After three weeks at Shreelane she found it difficult to remember that the floor was neither damp nor dusty.

I had the good fortune to be of the limited number of those who got on with Lady Knox, chiefly, I imagine, because I was as a worm before her, and thankfully permitted her to do all the talking.

"Your wife is extremely pretty," she pronounced autocratically, surveying Philippa between the candle-shades; "does she ride?"

Lady Knox was a short square lady, with a weather-beaten face, and an eye decisive from long habit of taking her own line across country and elsewhere. She would have made a very imposing little coachman, and would have caused her stable helpers to rue the day they had the presumption to be born; it struck me that Sir Valentine sometimes did so.

"I'm glad you like her looks," I replied, "as I fear you will find her thoroughly despicable otherwise; for one thing, she not only can't ride, but she believes that I can!"

"Oh come, you're not as bad as all that!" my hostess was good enough to say; "I'm going to put you up on Sorcerer to-morrow, and we'll see you at the top of the hunt—if there is one. That young Knox hasn't a notion how to draw these woods."

"Well, the best run we had last year out of this place was

with Flurry's hounds," struck in Miss Sally, sole daughter of Sir Valentine's house and home, from her place half-way down the table. It was not difficult to see that she and her mother held different views on the subject of Mr. Flurry Knox.

"I call it a criminal thing in any one's great-great-grandfather to rear up a preposterous troop of sons and plant them all out in his own country," Lady Knox said to me with apparent irrelevance. "I detest collaterals. Blood may be thicker than water, but it is also a great deal nastier. In this country I find that fifteenth cousins consider themselves near relations if they live within twenty miles of one!"

Lady Knox

Having before now taken in the position with regard to Flurry Knox, I took care to accept these remarks as generalities, and turned the conversation to other themes.

"I see Mrs. Yeates is doing wonders with Mr. Hamilton," said Lady Knox presently, following the direction of my eyes, which had strayed away to where Philippa was beaming upon her left-hand neighbour, a mildewed-looking old clergyman, who was delivering a long dissertation, the purport of which we were happily unable to catch.

"She has always had a gift for the Church," I said.

"Not curates?" said Lady Knox, in her deep voice.

I made haste to reply that it was the elders of the Church who were venerated by my wife.

"Well, she has her fancy in old Eustace Hamilton; he's elderly enough!" said Lady Knox. "I wonder if she'd venerate him as much if she knew that he had fought with his sister-in-law, and they haven't spoken for thirty years! though for the matter of that," she added, "I think it shows his good sense!"

"Mrs. Knox is rather a friend of mine," I ventured.

"Is she? H'm! Well, she's not one of mine!" replied my hostess, with her usual definiteness. "I'll say one thing for her, I believe she's always been a sportswoman. She's very rich, you know, and they say she only married old Badger Knox to save his hounds from being sold to pay his debts, and then she took the horn from him and hunted them herself. Has she been rude to your wife yet? No? Oh, well, she will. It's a mere question of time. She hates all English people. You know the story they tell of her? She was coming home from London, and when she was getting her ticket the man asked if she had said a ticket for York. 'No, thank God, Cork!' says Mrs. Knox."

"Well, I rather agree with her!" said I; "but why did she fight with Mr. Hamilton?"

"Oh, nobody knows. I don't believe they know themselves! Whatever it was, the old lady drives five miles to Fortwilliam every Sunday, rather than go to his church, just outside her own back gates," Lady Knox said with a laugh like a terrier's bark. "I wish I'd fought with him myself," she said; "he gives us forty minutes every Sunday."

As I struggled into my boots the following morning, I felt that Sir Valentine's acid confidences on cub-hunting, bestowed on me at midnight, did credit to his judgment. "A very moderate amusement, my dear Major," he had said, in his dry little voice; "you should stick to shooting. No one expects you to shoot before daybreak."

It was six o'clock as I crept downstairs, and found Lady Knox and Miss Sally at breakfast, with two lamps on the table, and a foggy daylight oozing in from under the half-raised blinds. Philippa was already in the hall, pumping up her bicycle, in a state of excitement at the prospect of her first experience of hunting that would have been more comprehensible to me had she been going to ride a strange horse, as I was. As I bolted my food I saw the horses being led past the windows, and a faint twang of a horn told that Flurry Knox and his hounds were not far off.

Miss Sally jumped up.

"If I'm not on the Cockatoo before the hounds come up, I shall never get there!" she said, hobbling out of the room in the toils of her safety habit. Her small, alert face looked very childish under her riding-hat; the lamp-light struck sparks out of her thick coil of golden-red hair: I wondered how I had ever thought her like her prim little father.

She was already on her white cob when I got to the hall-door, and Flurry Knox was riding over the glistening wet grass with his hounds, while his whip, Dr. Jerome Hickey, was having a stirring time with the young entry and the rabbit-holes. They moved on without stopping, up a back avenue, under tall and dripping trees, to a thick laurel covert, at some little distance from the house. Into this the hounds were thrown, and the usual period of fidgety inaction set in for the riders, of whom, all told, there were about half-a-dozen. Lady Knox, square and solid, on her big, confidential iron-grey, was near me, and her eyes were on me and my mount; with her rubicund face and white collar she was more than ever like a coachman.

"Sorcerer looks as if he suited you well," she said, after a few minutes of silence, during which the hounds rustled and crackled steadily through the laurels; "he's a little high on the leg, and so are you, you know, so you show each other off."

Sorcerer was standing like a rock, with his good-looking head in the air and his eyes fastened on the covert. His manners, so far, had been those of a perfect gentleman, and were in marked contrast to those of Miss Sally's cob, who was sidling, hopping, and snatching unappeasably at his bit. Philippa had disappeared from view down the avenue ahead. The fog was melting, and the sun threw long blades of light through the trees; everything was quiet, and in the distance the curtained windows of the house marked the warm repose of Sir Valentine, and those of the party who shared his opinion of cubbing.

"Hark! hark to cry there!"

It was Flurry's voice, away at the other side of the covert. The rustling and brushing through the laurels became more vehement, then passed out of hearing.

"He never will leave his hounds alone," said Lady Knox disapprovingly.

Miss Sally and the Cockatoo moved away in a series of heraldic capers towards the end of the laurel plantation, and at the same moment I saw Philippa on her bicycle shoot into view on the drive ahead of us.

"I've seen a fox!" she screamed, white with what I believe to have been personal terror, though she says it was excitement; "it passed quite close to me!"

"What way did he go?" bellowed a voice which I recognised as Dr. Hickey's, somewhere in the deep of the laurels.

"Down the drive!" returned Philippa, with a pea-hen quality in her tones with which I was quite unacquainted.

An electrifying screech of "Gone away!" was projected from the laurels by Dr. Hickey.

"Gone away!" chanted Flurry's horn at the top of the covert.

"This is what he calls cubbing!" said Lady Knox, "a mere farce!" but none the less she loosed her sedate monster into a canter.

Sorcerer got his hind-legs under him, and hardened his crest against the bit, as we all hustled along the drive after the flying figure of my wife. I knew very little about horses, but I realised that even with the hounds tumbling hysterically out of the covert, and the Cockatoo kicking the gravel into his face, Sorcerer comported himself with the manners of the best

society. Up a side road I saw Flurry Knox opening half of a
gate and cramming through it; in a moment we also had
crammed through, and the turf of a pasture field was under
our feet. Dr. Hickey leaned forward and took hold of his horse;
I did likewise, with the trifling difference that my horse took

Miss Sally and the cockatoo moved away

hold of me, and I steered for Flurry Knox with single-hearted
purpose, the hounds, already a field ahead, being merely an
exciting and noisy accompaniment of this endeavour. A heavy
stone wall was the first occurrence of note. Flurry chose a
place where the top was loose, and his clumsy-looking brown
mare changed feet on the rattling stones like a fairy. Sorcerer

came at it, tense and collected as a bow at full stretch, and sailed steeply into the air; I saw the wall far beneath me, with an unsuspected ditch on the far side, and I felt my hat following me at the full stretch of its guard as we swept over it, then, with a long slant, we descended to earth some sixteen feet from where we had left it, and I was possessor of the gratifying fact that I had achieved a good-sized "fly," and had not perceptibly moved in my saddle. Subsequent disillusioning experience has taught me that but few horses jump like Sorcerer, so gallantly, so sympathetically, and with such supreme mastery of the subject; but none the less the enthusiasm that he imparted to me has never been extinguished, and that October morning ride revealed to me the unsuspected intoxication of fox-hunting.

Behind me I heard the scrabbling of the Cockatoo's little hoofs among the loose stones, and Lady Knox, galloping on my left, jerked a maternal chin over her shoulder to mark her daughter's progress. For my part, had there been an entire circus behind me, I was far too much occupied with ramming on my hat and trying to hold Sorcerer, to have looked round, and all my spare faculties were devoted to steering for Flurry, who had taken a right-handed turn, and was at that moment surmounting a bank of uncertain and briary aspect. I surmounted it also, with the swiftness and simplicity for which the Quaker's methods of bank jumping had not prepared me, and two or three fields, traversed at the same steeplechase pace, brought us to a road and to an abrupt check. There, suddenly, were the hounds, scrambling in baffled silence down into the road from the opposite bank, to look for the line they had overrun, and there, amazingly, was Philippa, engaged in excited converse with several men with spades over their shoulders.

"Did ye see the fox, boys?" shouted Flurry, addressing the group.

"We did! we did!" cried my wife and her friends in chorus; "he ran up the road!"

"We'd be badly off without Mrs. Yeates!" said Flurry, as he whirled his mare round and clattered up the road with a hustle of hounds after him.

It occurred to me as forcibly as any mere earthly thing can occur to those who are wrapped in the sublimities of a run, that, for a young woman who had never before seen a fox out of a cage at the Zoo, Philippa was taking to hunting very kindly. Her cheeks were a most brilliant pink, her blue eyes shone.

"Oh, Sinclair!" she exclaimed, "they say he's going for Aussolas, and there's a road I can ride all the way!"

"Ye can, Miss! Sure we'll show you!" chorussed her *cortège*.

Her foot was on the pedal ready to mount. Decidedly my wife was in no need of assistance from me.

Up the road a hound gave a yelp of discovery, and flung himself over a stile into the fields; the rest of the pack went squealing and jostling after him, and I followed Flurry over one of those infinitely varied erections, pleasantly termed "gaps" in Ireland. On this occasion the gap was made of three razor-edged slabs of slate leaning against an iron bar, and Sorcerer conveyed to me his thorough knowledge of the matter by a lift of his hind-quarters that made me feel as if I were being skilfully kicked downstairs. To what extent I looked it, I cannot say, nor providentially can Philippa, as she had already started. I only know that undeserved good luck restored to me my stirrup before Sorcerer got away with me in the next field.

What followed was, I am told, a very fast fifteen minutes; for me time was not; the empty fields rushed past uncounted, fences came and went in a flash, while the wind sang in my ears, and the dazzle of the early sun was in my eyes. I saw the hounds occasionally, sometimes pouring over a green bank, as the charging breaker lifts and flings itself, sometimes driving across a field, as the white tongues of foam slide racing over the sand; and always ahead of me was Flurry Knox, going as a man goes who knows his country, who knows his horse, and whose heart is wholly and absolutely in the right place.

Do what I would, Sorcerer's implacable stride carried me closer and closer to the brown mare, till, as I thundered down the slope of a long field, I was not twenty yards behind Flurry. Sorcerer had stiffened his neck to iron, and to slow him down

I felt as if I were being skilfully kicked downstairs

was beyond me; but I fought his head away to the right, and found myself coming hard and steady at a stonefaced bank with broken ground in front of it. Flurry bore away to the left, shouting something that I did not understand. That Sorcerer shortened his stride at the right moment was entirely due to his own judgment; standing well away from the jump, he rose like a stag out of the tussocky ground, and as he swung my twelve stone six into the air the obstacle revealed itself to him and me as consisting not of one bank but of two, and between the two lay a deep grassy lane, half choked with furze. I have often been asked to state the width of the bohereen, and can only reply that in my opinion it was at least eighteen feet; Flurry Knox and Dr. Hickey, who did not jump it, say that it is not more than five. What Sorcerer did with it I cannot say; the sensation was of a towering flight with a kick back in it, a biggish drop, and a landing on cee-springs, still on the downhill grade. That was how one of the best horses in Ireland took one of Ireland's most ignorant riders over a very nasty place.

A sombre line of fir-wood lay ahead, rimmed with a grey wall, and in another couple of minutes we had pulled up on the Aussolas road, and were watching the hounds struggling over the wall into Aussolas demesne.

"No hurry now," said Flurry, turning in his saddle to watch the Cockatoo jump into the road, "he's to ground in the big earth inside. Well, Major, it's well for you that's a big-jumped horse. I thought you were a dead man a while ago when you faced him at the bohereen!"

I was disclaiming intention in the matter when Lady Knox and the others joined us.

"I thought you told me your wife was no sportswoman," she said to me, critically scanning Sorcerer's legs for cuts the while, "but when I saw her a minute ago she had abandoned her bicycle and was running across country like———"

"Look at her now!" interrupted Miss Sally. "Oh!—oh!" In the interval between these exclamations my incredulous eyes beheld my wife in mid-air, hand in hand with a couple of stalwart country boys, with whom she was leaping in unison from the top of a bank on to the road.

Every one, even the saturnine Dr. Hickey, began to laugh; I rode back to Philippa, who was exchanging compliments and congratulations with her escort.

"Oh, Sinclair!" she cried, "wasn't it splendid? I saw you jumping, and everything! Where are they going now?"

"My dear girl," I said, with marital disapproval, "you're killing yourself. Where's your bicycle?"

"Oh, it's punctured in a sort of lane, back there. It's all right; and then they"—she breathlessly waved her hand at her attendants—"they showed me the way."

"Begor! you proved very good, Miss!" said a grinning cavalier.

"Faith she did!' said another, polishing his shining brow with his white flannel coat-sleeve, "she lepped like a haarse!"

"And may I ask how you propose to go home?" said I.

"I don't know and I don't care! I'm not going home!" She cast an entirely disobedient eye at me. "And your eye-glass is hanging down your back and your tie is bulging out over your waist-coat!"

The little group of riders had begun to move away.

"We're going on into Aussolas," called out Flurry; "come on, and make my grandmother give you some breakfast, Mrs. Yeates; she always has it at eight o'clock."

The front gates were close at hand, and we turned in under the tall beech-trees, with the unswept leaves rustling round the horses' feet, and the lovely blue of the October morning sky filling the spaces between smooth grey branches and golden leaves. The woods rang with the voices of the hounds, enjoying an untrammelled rabbit hunt, while the Master and the Whip, both on foot, strolled along unconcernedly with their bridles over their arms, making themselves agreeable to my wife, an occasional touch of Flurry's horn, or a crack of Dr. Hickey's whip, just indicating to the pack that the authorities still took a friendly interest in their doings.

Down a grassy glade in the wood a party of old Mrs. Knox's young horses suddenly swept into view, headed by an old mare, who, with her tail over her back, stampeded ponderously past our cavalcade, shaking and swinging her handsome old head, while her youthful friends bucked and kicked and snapped at each other round her with the ferocious humour of their kind.

"Here, Jerome, take the horn," said Flurry to Dr. Hickey;

"I'm going to see Mrs. Yeates up to the house, the way these tomfools won't gallop on top of her."

From this point it seems to me that Philippa's adventures are more worthy of record than mine, and as she has favoured me with a full account of them, I venture to think my version may be relied on.

Mrs. Knox was already at breakfast when Philippa was led, quaking, into her formidable presence. My wife's acquaintance with Mrs. Knox was, so far, limited to a state visit on either side, and she found but little comfort in Flurry's assurances that his grandmother wouldn't mind if he brought all the hounds in to breakfast, coupled with the statement that she would put her eyes on sticks for the Major.

Whatever the truth of this may have been, Mrs. Knox received her guest with an equanimity quite unshaken by the fact that her boots were in the fender instead of on her feet, and that a couple of shawls of varying dimensions and degrees of age did not conceal the inner presence of a magenta flannel dressing-jacket. She installed Philippa at the table and plied her with food, oblivious as to whether the needful implements with which to eat it were forthcoming or no. She told Flurry where a vixen had reared her family, and she watched him ride away, with some biting comments on his mare's hocks screamed after him from the window.

The dining-room at Aussolas Castle is one of the many rooms in Ireland in which Cromwell is said to have stabled his horse (and probably no one would have objected less than Mrs. Knox had she been consulted in the matter). Philippa questions if the room had ever been tidied up since, and she endorses Flurry's observation that "there wasn't a day in the year you wouldn't get feeding for a hen and chickens on the floor." Opposite to Philippa, on a Louis Quinze chair, sat Mrs. Knox's woolly dog, its suspicious little eyes peering at her out of their setting of pink lids and dirty white wool. A couple of young horses outside the windows tore at the matted creepers on the walls, or thrust faces that were half-shy, half-impudent, into the room. Portly pigeons waddled to and fro on the broad window-sill, sometimes flying in to perch on the picture-frames, while they kept up incessantly a hoarse and pompous cooing.

Animals and children are, as a rule, alike destructive to conversation; but Mrs. Knox, when she chose, *bien entendu*, could have made herself agreeable in a Noah's ark, and Philippa has a gift of sympathetic attention that personal experience has taught me to regard with distrust as well as respect, while it has often made me realise the worldly wisdom of Kingsley's injunction:

"Be good, sweet maid, and let who will be clever."

Family prayers, declaimed by Mrs. Knox with alarming austerity, followed close on breakfast, Philippa and a vinegar-faced henchwoman forming the family. The prayers were long, and through the open window as they progressed came distantly a whoop or two; the declamatory tones staggered a little, and then continued at a distinctly higher rate of speed. "Ma'am! Ma'am!" whispered a small voice at the window.

Mrs. Knox made a repressive gesture and held on her way. A sudden outcry of hounds followed, and the owner of the whisper, a small boy with a face freckled like a turkey's egg, darted from the window and dragged a donkey and bath-chair into view. Philippa admits to having lost the thread of the discourse, but she thinks that the "Amen" that immediately ensued can hardly have come in its usual place. Mrs. Knox shut the book abruptly, scrambled up from her knees, and said, "They've found!"

In a surprisingly short space of time she had added to her attire her boots, a fur cape, and a garden hat, and was in the bath-chair, the small boy stimulating the donkey with the success peculiar to his class, while Philippa hung on behind.

The woods of Aussolas are hilly and extensive, and on that particular morning it seemed that they held as many foxes as hounds. In vain was the horn blown and the whips cracked, small rejoicing parties of hounds, each with a fox of its own, scoured to and fro: every labourer in the vicinity had left his work, and was sedulously heading every fox with yells that would have befitted a tiger hunt, and sticks and stones when occasion served.

"Will I pull out as far as the big rosydandhrum, ma'am?" inquired the small boy; "I seen three of the dogs go in it, and they yowling."

"You will," said Mrs. Knox, thumping the donkey on the back with her umbrella; "here! Jeremiah Regan! Come down out of that with that pitchfork! Do you want to kill the fox, you fool?"

"I do not, your honour, ma'am," responded Jeremiah Regan, a tall young countryman, emerging from a bramble brake.

"Did you see him?" said Mrs. Knox eagerly.

"I seen himself and his ten pups drinking below at the lake ere yestherday, your honour, ma'am, and he as big as a chestnut horse!" said Jeremiah.

"Faugh! Yesterday!" snorted Mrs. Knox; "go on to the rhododendrons, Johnny!"

The party, reinforced by Jeremiah and the pitchfork, progressed at a high rate of speed along the shrubbery path, encountering *en route* Lady Knox, stooping on to her horse's neck under the sweeping branches of the laurels.

"Your horse is too high for my coverts, Lady Knox," said the Lady of the Manor, with a malicious eye at Lady Knox's flushed face and dinged hat; "I'm afraid you will be left behind like Absalom when the hounds go away!"

"As they never do anything here but hunt rabbits," retorted her ladyship, "I don't think that's likely."

Mrs. Knox gave her donkey another whack, and passed on.

"Rabbits, my dear!" she said scornfully to Philippa. "That's all she knows about it. I declare it disgusts me to see a woman of that age making such a Judy of herself! Rabbits indeed!"

Down in the thicket of rhododendron everything was very

quiet for a time. Philippa strained her eyes in vain to see any of the riders; the horn blowing and the whip cracking passed on almost out of hearing. Once or twice a hound worked through the rhododendrons, glanced at the party, and hurried on, immersed in business. All at once Johnny, the donkey-boy, whispered excitedly:

"Look at he! Look at he!" and pointed to a boulder of grey rock that stood out among the dark evergreens. A big yellow cub was crouching on it; he instantly slid into the shelter of the bushes, and the irrepressible Jeremiah, uttering a rending shriek, plunged into the thicket after him. Two or three hounds came rushing at the sound, and after this Philippa says she finds some difficulty in recalling the proper order of events; chiefly, she confesses, because of the wholly ridiculous tears of excitement that blurred her eyes.

"We ran," she said, "we simply tore, and the donkey galloped, and as for that old Mrs. Knox, she was giving cracked screams to the hounds all the time, and they were screaming too; and then somehow we were all out on the road!"

What seems to have occurred was that three couple of hounds, Jeremiah Regan, and Mrs. Knox's equipage, amongst them somehow hustled the cub out of Aussolas demesne and up on to a hill on the farther side of the road. Jeremiah was sent back by his mistress to fetch Flurry, and the rest of the party pursued a thrilling course along the road, parallel with that of the hounds, who were hunting slowly through the gorse on the hillside.

"Upon my honour and word, Mrs. Yeates, my dear, we have the hunt to ourselves!" said Mrs. Knox to the panting Philippa, as they pounded along the road. "Johnny, d'ye see the fox?"

"I do, ma'am!" shrieked Johnny, who possessed the usual field-glass vision bestowed upon his kind. "Look at him over-right us on the hill above! Hi! The spotty dog have him! No, he's gone from him! *Gwan out o'that!*" This to the donkey, with blows that sounded like the beating of carpets, and produced rather more dust.

They had left Aussolas some half a mile behind, when, from a strip of wood on their right, the fox suddenly slipped over the bank on to the road just ahead of them, ran up it for a few yards and whisked in at a small entrance gate, with the three couple of hounds yelling on a red-hot scent, not thirty yards behind. The bath-chair party whirled in at their heels, Philippa and the donkey considerably blown, Johnny scarlet through his freckles, but as fresh as paint, the old lady blind and deaf to all things save the chase. The hounds went raging through the shrubs beside the drive, and away down a grassy slope towards a shallow glen, in the bottom of which ran a little stream, and after them over the grass bumped the bath-chair. At the stream they turned sharply and ran up the glen towards the avenue, which crossed it by means of a rough stone viaduct.

" 'Pon me conscience, he's into the old culvert!" exclaimed Mrs. Knox; "there was one of my hounds choked there once, long ago! Beat on the donkey, Johnny!"

At this juncture Philippa's narrative again becomes incoherent, not to say breathless. She is, however, positive that it was somewhere about here that the upset of the bath-chair occurred, but she cannot be clear as to whether she picked up the donkey or Mrs. Knox, or whether she herself was picked up by Johnny while Mrs. Knox picked up the donkey. From my knowledge of Mrs. Knox I should say she picked up herself and no one else. At all events, the next salient point is the palpitating moment when Mrs. Knox, Johnny, and Philippa successively applying an eye to the opening of the culvert by which the stream trickled under the viaduct, while five dripping hounds bayed and leaped around them, discovered by more senses than that of sight that the fox was in it, and furthermore that one of the hounds was in it too.

"There's a sthrong grating before him at the far end," said Johnny, his head in at the mouth of the hole, his voice sounding as if he were talking into a jug, "the two of them's fighting in it; they'll be choked surely!"

"Then don't stand gabbling there, you little fool, but get in and pull the hound out!" exclaimed Mrs. Knox, who was balancing herself on a stone in the stream.

"I'd be in dread, ma'am," whined Johnny.

"Balderdash!" said the implacable Mrs. Knox. "In with you!"

I understand that Philippa assisted Johnny into the culvert, and presume that it was in so doing that she acquired the two Robinson Crusoe bare footprints which decorated her jacket when I next met her.

"Have you got hold of him yet, Johnny?" cried Mrs. Knox up the culvert.

"I have, ma'am, by the tail," responded Johnny's voice, sepulchral in the depths.

"Can you stir him, Johnny?"

"I cannot, ma'am, and the wather is rising in it."

"Well, please God, they'll not open the mill dam!" remarked Mrs. Knox philosophically to Philippa, as she caught hold of Johnny's dirty ankles. "Hold on to the tail, Johnny!"

She hauled, with, as might be expected, no appreciable result. "Run, my dear, and look for somebody, and we'll have that fox yet!"

Philippa ran, whither she knew not, pursued by fearful visions of bursting mill-dams, and maddened foxes at bay. As she sped up the avenue she heard voices, robust male voices, in a shrubbery, and made for them. Advancing along an embowered walk towards her was what she took for one wild instant to be a funeral; a second glance showed her that it was a party of clergymen of all ages, walking by twos and threes in the dappled shade of the over-arching trees. Obviously she had intruded her sacrilegious presence into a Clerical Meeting. She acknowledges that at this awe-inspiring spectacle she faltered, but the thought of Johnny, the hound, and the fox, suffocating, possibly drowning together in the culvert, nerved her. She does not remember what she said or how she said it, but I fancy she must have conveyed to them the impression that old Mrs. Knox was being drowned, as she immediately found herself heading a charge of the Irish Church towards the scene of disaster.

Fate has not always used me well, but on this occasion it was mercifully decreed that I and the other members of the hunt should be privileged to arrive in time to see my wife and her rescue party precipitating themselves down the glen.

"Holy Biddy!" ejaculated Flurry, "is she running a paper-chase with all the parsons? But look! For pity's sake will you look at my grandmother and my Uncle Eustace?"

Mrs. Knox and her sworn enemy the old clergyman, whom I had met at dinner the night before, were standing, apparently in the stream, tugging at two bare legs that projected from a hole in the viaduct, and arguing at the top of their voices. The bath-chair lay on its side with the donkey grazing beside it, on the bank a stout Archdeacon was tendering advice, and the hounds danced and howled round the entire group.

"I tell you, Eliza, you had better let the Archdeacon try," thundered Mr. Hamilton.

"Then I tell you I will not!" vociferated Mrs. Knox, with a tug at the end of the sentence that elicited a subterranean lament from Johnny. "Now who was right about the second grating? I told you so twenty years ago!"

Exactly as Philippa and her rescue party arrived, the efforts of Mrs. Knox and her brother-in-law triumphed. The struggling, sopping form of Johnny was slowly drawn from the hole, drenched, speechless, but clinging to the stern of a hound, who, in its turn, had its jaws fast in the hind-quarters of a limp, yellow cub.

"Oh, it's dead!" wailed Philippa, "I *did* think I should have been in time to save it!"

"Well, if that doesn't beat all!" said Dr. Hickey.

Seven

A MISDEAL

THE wagonette slewed and slackened mysteriously on the top of the long hill above Drumcurran. So many remarkable things had happened since we had entrusted ourselves to the guidance of Mr. Bernard Shute that I rose in my place and possessed myself of the brake, and in so doing saw the horses with their heads hard in against their chests, and their quarters jammed crookedly against the splashboard, being apparently tied into knots by some inexplicable power.

"Some one's pulling the reins out of my hand!" exclaimed Mr. Shute.

The horses and pole were by this time making an acute angle with the wagonette, and the groom plunged from the box to their heads. Miss Sally Knox, who was sitting beside me, looked over the edge.

"Put on the brake! the reins are twisted round the axle!" she cried, and fell into a fit of laughter.

We all—that is to say, Philippa, Miss Shute, Miss Knox, and I—got out as speedily as might be; but, I think, without panic; Mr. Shute alone stuck to the ship, with the horses struggling and rearing below him. The groom and I contrived to back them, and by so doing caused the reins to unwind themselves from the axle.

"It was my fault," said Mr. Shute, hauling them in as fast as we could give them to him; "I broke the reins yesterday, and these are the phaeton ones, and about six fathoms long at that, and I forgot and let the slack go overboard. It's all right, I won't do it again."

With this reassurance we confided ourselves once more to the wagonette.

As we neared the town of Drumcurran the fact that we were on our way to a horse fair became alarmingly apparent. It is impossible to imagine how we pursued an uninjured course through the companies of horsemen, the crowded carts, the squealing colts, the irresponsible led horses, and, most immutable of all obstacles, the groups of countrywomen, with the hoods of their heavy blue cloaks over their heads. They looked like nuns of some obscure order; they were deaf and blind as ramparts of sandbags; nothing less callous to human life than a Parisian cabdriver could have burst a way through them. Many times during that drive I had cause to be thankful for the sterling qualities of Mr. Shute's brake; with its aid he dragged his over-fed bays into a crawl that finally, and not without injury to the varnish, took the wagonette to the Royal Hotel. Every available stall in the yard was by that time filled, and it was only by virtue of the fact that the kitchenmaid was nearly related to my cook that the indignant groom was permitted to stable the bays in a den known as the calf-house.

That I should have lent myself to such an expedition was wholly due to my wife. Since Philippa had taken up her residence in Ireland she had discovered a taste for horses that was not to be extinguished, even by an occasional afternoon on the Quaker, whose paces had become harder than rock in his many journeys to Petty Sessions; she had also discovered the Shutes, newcomers on the outer edge of our vast visiting district, and between them this party to Drumcurran Horse Fair had been devised. Philippa proposed to buy herself a hunter. Bernard Shute wished to do the same, possibly two hunters, money being no difficulty with this fortunate young man. Miss Sally Knox was of the company, and I also had been kindly invited, as to a missionary meeting, to come, and bring my cheque-book. The only saving clause in the affair was the fact that Mr. Flurry Knox was to meet us at the scene of action.

The fair was held in a couple of large fields outside the town, and on the farther bank of the Curranhilty River. Across a wide and glittering ford, horses of all sizes and sorts were splashing, and a long row of stepping-stones was hopped, and staggered, and scrambled over by a ceaseless variety of foot-passengers. A man with a cart plied as a ferry boat, doing a heavy trade among the applewomen and vendors of "crubeens," *alias* pigs' feet, a grisly delicacy peculiar to Irish open-air holiday-making, and the July sun blazed on a scene that even Miss Cecilia Shute found to be almost repayment enough for the alarms of the drive.

"As a rule, I am so bored by driving that I find it reviving to be frightened," she said to me, as we climbed to safety on a heathery ridge above the fields dedicated to galloping the horses; "but when my brother scraped all those people off one side of that car, and ran the pole into the cart of lemonade-bottles, I began to wish for courage to tell him I was going to get out and walk home."

"Well, if you only knew it," said Bernard, who was spreading rugs over the low furze bushes in the touching belief that the prickles would not come through, "the time you came nearest to walking home was when the lash of the whip got twisted round Nancy's tail. Miss Knox, you're an authority on these things—don't you think it would be a good scheme to have a light anchor in the trap, and when the horses began to play the fool, you'd heave the anchor over the fence and bring them up all standing?"

"They wouldn't stand very long," remarked Miss Sally.

"Oh, that's all right," returned the inventor; "I'd have a dodge to cast them loose, with the pole and the splinter-bar."

"You'd never see them again," responded Miss Knox demurely, "if you thought that mattered."

"It would be the brightest feature of the case," said Miss Shute.

She was surveying Miss Sally through her pince-nez as she spoke, and was, I have reason to believe, deciding that by the end of the day her brother would be well on in the first stages of his fifteenth love affair.

It has possibly been suspected that Mr. Bernard Shute was a sailor, had been a sailor rather, until within the last year, when he had tumbled into a fortune and a property, and out of the navy, in the shortest time on record. His enthusiasm for horses had been nourished by the hirelings of Malta, and other resorts of her Majesty's ships, and his knowledge of them was, so far, bounded by the fact that it was more usual to come off over their heads than their tails. For the rest, he was a clean-shaved and personable youth, with a laugh which I may, without offensive intention, define as possessing a what-cheeriness special to his profession, and a habit, engendered no doubt by long sojourns at the Antipodes, of getting his clothes in large hideous consignments from a naval outfitter.

It was eleven o'clock, and the fair was in full swing. Its vortex was in the centre of the field below us, where a low bank of sods and earth had been erected as a trial jump, with a yelling crowd of men and boys at either end, acting instead of the usual wings to prevent a swerve. Strings of reluctant horses were scourged over the bank by dozens of willing hands, while exhortation, cheers, and criticism were freely showered upon each performance.

"Give the knees to the saddle, boy, and leave the heels slack." "That's a nice horse. He'd keep a jock on his back where another'd throw him!" "Well jumped, begor! She fled that fairly!" as an ungainly three-year-old flounced over the bank without putting a hoof on it. Then her owner, unloosing his pride in simile after the manner of his race,

"Ah ha! when she give a lep, man, she's that free, she's like a hare for it!"

A giggling group of country girls elbowed their way past us out of the crowd of spectators, one of the number inciting her fellows to hurry on to the other field "until they'd see the lads galloping the horses," to which another responding that she'd "be skinned alive for the horses," the party sped on their way. We—*i.e.* my wife, Miss Knox, Bernard Shute, and myself—followed in their wake, a matter by no means as easy as it looked. Miss Shute had exhibited her wonted intelligence by remaining on the hilltop with the "Spectator"; she had not reached the happy point of possessing a mind ten years older than her age, and a face ten years younger, without also developing the gift of scenting boredom from afar. We squeezed past the noses and heels of fidgety horses, and circumnavigated their attendant groups of critics, while half-trained brutes in snaffles bolted to nowhere and back again, and whinnying foals ran to and fro in search of their mothers.

A moderate bank divided the upper from the lower fields, and as every feasible spot in it was commanded by a refusing horse, the choice of a place and moment for crossing it required judgment. I got Philippa across it in safety; Miss Knox, though as capable as any young woman in Ireland of getting over a bank, either on horseback or on her own legs, had to submit to the assistance of Mr. Shute, and the laws of dynamics decreed that a force sufficient to raise a bower anchor should hoist her seven stone odd to the top of the bank with such speed that she landed half on her knees and half in the arms of her pioneer. A group of portentously quiet men stood near, their eyes on the ground, their hands in their pockets; they were all dressed so much alike that I did not at first notice that Flurry Knox was among them; when I did, I perceived that his eyes, instead of being on the ground, were surveying Mr. Shute with that measure of disapproval that he habitually bestowed upon strange men.

"You're later than I thought you'd be," he said. "I have a

horse half-bought for Mrs. Yeates. It's that old mare of Bobby Bennett's; she makes a little noise, but she's a good mare, and you couldn't throw her down if you tried. Bobby wants thirty pounds for her, but I think you might get her for less. She's in the hotel stables, and you can see her when you go to lunch."

We moved on towards the rushy bank of the river, and Philippa and Sally Knox seated themselves on a low rock,

"Her grandsire was the Mountain Hare"

looking, in their white frocks, as incongruous in that dingy preoccupied assemblage as the dreamy meadow-sweet and purple spires of loosestrife that thronged the river banks. Bernard Shute had been lost in the shifting maze of men and horses, who were, for the most part, galloping with the blind fury of charging bulls; but presently, among a party who seemed to be riding the finish of a race, we descried our friend, and a second or two later he hauled a brown mare to a standstill in front of us.

"The fellow's asking forty-five pounds for her," he said to Miss Sally; "she's a nailer to gallop. I don't think it's too much?"

"Her grandsire was the Mountain Hare," said the owner of the mare, hurrying up to continue her family history, "and he was the grandest horse in the four baronies. He was forty-two years of age when he died, and they waked him the same as ye'd wake a Christian. They had whisky and porther—and bread—and a piper in it."

"Thim Mountain Hare colts is no great things," interrupted Mr. Shute's groom contemptuously. "I seen a colt once that was one of his stock, and if there was forty men and their wives, and they after him with sticks, he wouldn't lep a sod of turf."

"Lep, is it!" ejaculated the owner in a voice shrill with outrage. "You may lead that mare out through the counthry, and there isn't a fence in it that she wouldn't go up to it as indepindent as if she was going to her bed, and your honour's ladyship knows that dam well, Miss Knox."

"You want too much money for her, McCarthy," returned Miss Sally, with her little air of preternatural wisdom.

"God pardon you, Miss Knox! Sure a lady like you knows well that forty-five pounds is no money for that mare. Forty-five pounds!" He laughed. "It'd be as good for me to make her a present to the gentleman all out as take three farthings less for her! She's too grand entirely for a poor farmer like me, and if it wasn't for the long weak family I have, I wouldn't part with her under twice the money."

"Three fine lumps of daughters in America paying his rent for him," commented Flurry in the background. "That's the long weak family!"

Bernard dismounted and slapped the mare's ribs approvingly.

"I haven't had such a gallop since I was at Rio," he said. "What do you think of her, Miss Knox?" Then, without waiting for an answer, "I like her. I think I may as well give him the forty-five and have done with it!"

At these ingenuous words I saw a spasm of anguish cross the countenance of McCarthy, easily interpreted as the first pang of a life-long regret that he had not asked twice the money. Flurry Knox put up an eyebrow and winked at me; Mr. Shute's groom turned away for very shame. Sally Knox laughed with the deplorable levity of nineteen.

Thus, with a brevity absolutely scandalous in the eyes of all beholders, the bargain was concluded.

Flurry strolled up to Philippa, observing an elaborate remoteness from Miss Sally and Mr. Shute.

"I believe I'm selling a horse here myself to-day," he said; "would you like to have a look at him, Mrs. Yeates?"

"Oh, are you selling, Knox?" struck in Bernard, to whose brain the glory of buying a horse had obviously mounted like new wine; "I want another, and I know yours are the right sort."

"Well, as you seem fond of galloping," said Flurry sardonically, "this one might suit you."

"You don't mean the Moonlighter?" said Miss Knox, looking fixedly at him.

"Supposing I did, have you anything to say against him?" replied Flurry.

Decidedly he was in a very bad temper. Miss Sally shrugged her shoulders, and gave a little shred of a laugh, but said no more.

In a comparatively secluded corner of the field we came upon Moonlighter, sidling and fussing, with flickering ears, his tail tightly tucked in and his strong back humped in a manner that boded little good. Even to my untutored eye, he appeared to be an uncommonly good-looking animal, a well-bred grey, with shoulders that raked back as far as the eye could wish, the true Irish jumping hind-quarters, and a showy head and neck; it was obvious that nothing except Michael Hallahane's adroit chucks at his bridle kept him from displaying his jumping powers free of charge. Bernard stared at him in silence; not the pregnant and intimidating silence of the connoisseur, but the tongue-tied muteness of helpless ignorance. His eye for horses had most probably been formed on circus posters, and the advertisements of a well-known embrocation, and Moonlighter approximated in colour and conduct to these models.

"I can see he's a ripping fine horse," he said at length; "I think I should like to try him."

Miss Knox changed countenance perceptibly, and gave a

perturbed glance at Flurry. Flurry remained impenetrably unamiable.

"I don't pretend to be a judge of horses," went on Mr. Shute. "I dare say I needn't tell *you* that!" with a very engaging smile at Miss Sally; "but I like this one awfully."

As even Philippa said afterwards, she would not have given herself away like that over buying a reel of cotton.

"Are you quite sure that he's really the sort of horse you want?" said Miss Knox, with rather more colour in her face than usual; "he's only four years old, and he's hardly a finished hunter."

The object of her philanthropy looked rather puzzled. "What! can't he jump?" he said.

"Is it jump?" exclaimed Michael Hallahane, unable any longer to contain himself; "is it the horse that jumped five foot of a clothes line in Heffernan's yard, and not a one on his back but himself, and didn't leave so much as the thrack of his hoof on the quilt that was hanging on it!"

"That's about good enough," said Mr. Shute, with his large friendly laugh; "what's your price, Knox? I must have the horse that jumped the quilt! I'd like to try him, if you don't mind. There are some jolly-looking banks over there."

"My price is a hundred sovereigns," said Flurry; "you can try him if you like."

"Oh, don't!" cried Sally impulsively; but Bernard's foot was already in the stirrup. "I call it disgraceful!" I heard her say in a low voice to her kinsman—"you know he can't ride."

The kinsman permitted himself a malign smile. "That's his look-out," he said.

Perhaps the unexpected docility with which Moonlighter allowed himself to be manœuvred through the crowd was due to Bernard's thirteen stone; at all events, his progress through a gate into the next field was unexceptionable. Bernard, however, had no idea of encouraging this tranquillity. He had come out to gallop, and without further ceremony he drove his heels into Moonlighter's side, and took the consequences in the shape of a very fine and able buck. How he remained within even visiting distance of the saddle it is impossible to explain; perhaps his early experience in the rigging stood him in good stead in the matter of hanging on by his hands; but, however preserved, he did remain, and went away down the field at what he himself subsequently described as "the rate of knots."

Flurry flung away his cigarette and ran to a point of better observation. We all ran, including Michael Hallahane and various onlookers, and were in time to see Mr. Shute charging the least advantageous spot in a hollow-faced furzy bank. Nothing but the grey horse's extreme activity got the pair safely over; he jumped it on a slant, changed feet in the heart of a furze-bush, and was lost to view. In what relative positions Bernard and his steed alighted was to us a matter of conjecture; when we caught sight of them again, Moonlighter was running away, with his rider still on his back, while the slope of the ground lent wings to his flight.

"That young gentleman will be apt to be killed," said Michael Hallahane with composure, not to say enjoyment.

"He'll be into the long bog with him pretty soon," said Flurry, his keen eye tracking the fugitive.

"Oh!—I thought he was off that time!" exclaimed Miss Sally, with a gasp in which consternation and amusement were blended. "There! He *is* into the bog!"

It did not take us long to arrive at the scene of disaster, to which, as to a dog-fight, other foot-runners were already hurrying, and on our arrival we found things looking remarkably unpleasant for Mr. Shute and Moonlighter. The latter was sunk to his withers in the sheet of black slime into which he had stampeded; the former, submerged to the waist three yards further away in the bog, was trying to drag himself towards firm ground by the aid of tussocks of wiry grass.

"Hit him!" shouted Flurry. "Hit him! he'll sink if he stops there!"

Mr. Shute turned on his adviser a face streaming with black

mud, out of which his brown eyes and white teeth gleamed with undaunted cheerfulness.

"All jolly fine," he called back; "if I let go this grass I'll sink too!"

A shout of laughter from the male portion of the spectators sympathetically greeted this announcement, and a dozen equally futile methods of escape were suggested. Among those who had joined us was, fortunately, one of the many boys who pervaded the fair selling halters, and, by means of several of these knotted together, a line of communication was established. Moonlighter, who had fallen in the state of inane stupor in which horses in his plight so often indulge, was roused to activity by showers of stones and imprecations but faintly chastened by the presence of ladies. Bernard, hanging on to his tail, belaboured him with a cane, and, finally, the reins proving good, the task of towing the victims ashore was achieved.

"He's mine, Knox, you know," were Mr. Shute's first words as he scrambled to his feet; "he's the best horse I ever got across—worth twice the money!"

"Faith, he's aisy plased!" remarked a bystander.

"Oh, do go and borrow some dry clothes," interposed Philippa practically; "surely there must be some one————"

"There's a shop in the town where he can strip a peg for 13s. 9d.," said Flurry grimly; "I wouldn't care myself about the clothes you'd borrow here!"

The morning sun shone jovially upon Moonlighter and his rider, caking momently the black bog stuff with which both were coated, and as the group disintegrated, and we turned to go back, every man present was pleasurably aware that the buttons of Mr. Shute's riding breeches had burst at the knee, causing a large triangular hiatus above his gaiter.

"Well," said Flurry conclusively to me as we retraced our steps, "I always thought the fellow was a fool, but I never thought he was such a damned fool."

It seemed an interminable time since breakfast when our

party, somewhat shattered by the stirring events of the morning, found itself gathered in an upstairs room at the Royal Hotel, waiting for a meal that had been ordained some two hours before. The air was charged with the mingled odours of boiling cabbage and frying mutton; we affected to speak of them with disgust, but our souls yearned to them. Female ministrants, with rustling skirts and pounding feet, raced along the passages with trays that were never for us, and opening doors released roaring gusts of conversation, blended with the clatter of knives and forks, and still we starved. Even the ginger-coloured check suit, lately labelled "The Sandringham. Wonderful value, 16s. 9d." in the window of Drumcurran's leading mart, and now displayed upon Mr. Shute's all too lengthy limbs, had lost its power to charm.

"Oh, don't tear that bell quite out by the roots, Bernard," said his sister, from the heart of a lamentable yawn. "I dare say it only amuses them when we ring, but it may remind them that we are still alive. Major Yeates, do you or do you not regret the pigs' feet?"

"More than I can express," I said, turning from the window, where I had been looking down at the endless succession of horses' backs and men's hats, moving in two opposing currents in the street below. "I dare say if we talk about them for a little we shall feel ill, and that will be better than nothing."

At this juncture, however, a heavy-laden tray thumped against the door, and our repast was borne into the room by a hot young woman in creaking boots, who hoarsely explained that what kept her was waiting on the potatoes, and that the ould pan that was in it was playing Puck with the beefsteaks.

"Well," said Miss Shute, as she began to try conclusions between a blunt knife and a bullet-proof mutton chop. "I have never lived in the country before, but I have always been given to understand that the village inn was one of its chief attractions." She delicately moved the potato dish so as to cover the traces of a bygone egg, and her glance lingered on the flies that dragged their way across a melting mound of salt butter. "I like local colour, but I don't care about it on the tablecloth."

"Well, I'm feeling quite anxious about Irish country hotels now," said Bernard; "they're getting so civilised and respectable. After all, when you go back to England no one cares a pin to hear that you've been done up to the knocker. That don't amuse them a bit. But all my friends are as pleased as anything when I tell them of the pothouse where I slept in my clothes rather than face the sheets, or how, when I complained to the landlady next day, she said, 'Cock ye up! Wasn't it his Reverence the Dean of Kilcoe had them last!'"

We smiled wanly; what I chiefly felt was respect for any hungry man who could jest in presence of such a meal.

"All this time my hunter hasn't been bought," said Philippa presently, leaning back in her chair, and abandoning the unequal contest with her beef-steak. "Who is Bobby Bennett? Will his horse carry a lady?"

Sally Knox looked at me and began to laugh.

"You should ask Major Keates about Bobby Bennett," she said.

Confound Miss Sally! It had never seemed worth while to tell Philippa all that story about my doing up Miss Bobby Bennett's hair, and I sank my face in my tumbler of stagnant whiskey-and-soda to conceal the colour that suddenly adorned it. Any intelligent man will understand that it was a situation calculated to amuse the ungodly, but without any real fun in it. I explained Miss Bennett as briefly as possible, and at all the more critical points Miss Sally's hazel-green eyes roamed slowly and mercilessly towards me.

"You haven't told Mrs. Yeates that she's one of the greatest horse-copers in the country," she said, when I had got through somehow; "she can sell you a very good horse sometimes, and a very bad one too, if she gets the chance."

"No one will ever explain to me," said Miss Shute, scanning us all with her dark, half-amused, and wholly sophisticated eyes, "why horse-coping is more respectable than cheating at cards. I rather respect people who are able to cheat at cards; if every one did, it would make whist so much more cheerful; but there is no forgiveness for dealing yourself the right card, and there is no condemnation for dealing your neighbour a very wrong horse!"

"Your neighbour is supposed to be able to take care of himself," said Bernard.

"Well, why doesn't that apply to card-players?" returned his sister; "are they all in a state of helpless innocence?"

"I'm helplessly innocent," announced Philippa, "so I hope Miss Bennett won't deal me a wrong horse."

"Oh, her mare is one of the right ones," said Miss Sally; "she's a lovely jumper, and her manners are the very best."

The door opened, and Flurry Knox put in his head. "Bobby Bennett's downstairs," he said to me mysteriously.

I got up, not without consciousness of Miss Sally's eye, and prepared to follow him. "You'd better come too, Mrs. Yeates, to keep an eye on him. Don't let him give her more than thirty, and if he gives that she should return him two sovereigns." This last injunction was bestowed in a whisper as we descended the stairs.

Miss Bennett was in the crowded yard of the hotel, looking handsome and overdressed, and she greeted me with just that touch of Auld Lang Syne in her manner that I could best have dispensed with. I turned to the business in hand without delay. The brown mare was led forth from the stable and paraded for our benefit; she was one of those inconspicuous, meritorious animals about whom there seems nothing particular to say, and I felt her legs and looked hard at her hocks, and was not much the wiser.

"It's no use my saying she doesn't make a noise," said Miss Bobby, "because every one in the country will tell you she does. You can have a vet, if you like, and that's the only fault he can find with her. But if Mrs. Yeates hasn't hunted before now, I'll guarantee Cruiskeen as just the thing for her. She's really safe and confidential. My little brother Georgie has hunted her—*you* remember Georgie, Major Yeates?—the night of the ball, you know—and he's only eleven. Mr. Knox can tell you what sort she is."

"Oh, she's a grand mare," said Mr. Knox, thus appealed to; "you'd hear her coming three fields off like a German band!"

"And well for you if you could keep within three fields of her!" retorted Miss Bennett. "At all events, she's not like the hunter you sold Uncle, that used to kick the stars as soon as I put my foot in the stirrup!"

"'Twas the size of the foot frightened him," said Flurry.

"Do you know how Uncle cured him?" said Miss Bennett, turning her back on her adversary; "he had him tied head and tail across the yard gate, and every man that came in had to get over his back!"

"That's no bad one!" said Flurry.

Philippa looked from one to the other in bewilderment, while the badinage continued, swift and unsmiling, as became two hierarchs of horse-dealing; it went on at intervals for the next ten minutes, and at the end of that time I had bought the mare for thirty pounds. As Miss Bennett said nothing about giving me back two of them, I had not the nerve to suggest it.

After this Flurry and Miss Bennett went away, and were swallowed up in the fair; we returned to our friends upstairs, and began to arrange about getting home. This, among other difficulties, involved the tracking and capture of the Shutes' groom, and took so long that it necessitated tea. Bernard and I had settled to ride our new purchases home, and the groom was to drive the wagonette—an alteration ardently furthered by Miss Shute. The afternoon was well advanced when Bernard and I struggled through the turmoil of the hotel yard in search of our horses, and, the hotel hostler being nowhere to be found, the Shutes' man saddled our animals for us, and then withdrew, to grapple single-handed with the bays in the calf-house.

"Good business for me, that Knox is sending the grey horse

home for me," remarked Barnard as his new mare followed him tractably out of the stall. "He'd have been rather a handful in this hole of a place."

He shoved his way out of the yard in front of me, seemingly quite comfortable and at home upon the descendant of the Mountain Hare, and I followed as closely as drunken carmen and shafts of erratic carts would permit. Cruiskeen evinced a decided tendency to turn to the right on leaving the yard, but she took my leftward tug in good part, and we moved on through the streets of Drumcurran with a dignity that was only impaired by the irrepressible determination of Mr. Shute's new trousers to run up his leg. It was a trifle disappointing that Cruiskeen should carry her nose in the air like a camel, but I set it down to my own bad hands, and to that cause I also imputed her frequent desire to stop, a desire that appeared to coincide with every fourth or fifth public-house on the line of march. Indeed, at the last corner before we left the town, Miss Bennett's mare and I had a serious difference of opinion, in the course of which she mounted the pavement and remained planted in front of a very disreputable public-house, whose owner had been before me several times for various infringements of the Licensing Acts. Bernard and the corner-boys were of course much pleased; I inwardly resolved to let Miss Bennett know how her groom occupied his time in Drumcurran.

We got out into the calm of the country roads without further incident, and I there discovered that Cruiskeen was possessed of a dromedary swiftness in trotting, that the action was about as comfortable as the dromedary's, and that it was extremely difficult to moderate the pace.

"I say! This is something like going!" said Bernard, cantering hard beside me with slack rein and every appearance of happiness. "Do you mean to keep it up all the way?"

"You'd better ask this devil," I replied, hauling on the futile ring snaffle. "Miss Bennett must have an arm like a prize-

*She mounted the pavement in front of a very disreputable
public-house*

fighter. If this is what she calls confidential, I don't want her confidences."

After another half-mile, during which I cursed Flurry Knox, and registered a vow that Philippa should ride Cruiskeen in a cavalry bit, we reached the cross-roads at which Bernard's way parted from mine. Another difference of opinion between my wife's hunter and me here took place, this time on the subject of parting from our companion, and I experienced that peculiar inward sinking that accompanies the birth of the conviction one has been stuck. There were still some eight miles between me and home, but I had at least the consolation of knowing that the brown mare would easily cover it in forty minutes. But in this also disappointment awaited me. Dropping her head to about the level of her knees, the mare subsided into a walk as slow as that of the slowest cow, and very similar in general style. In this manner I progressed for a further mile, breathing forth, like St. Paul, threatenings and slaughters against Bobby Bennett and all her confederates; and then the idea occurred to me that many really first-class hunters were very poor hacks. I consoled myself with this for a further period, and presently an opportunity for testing it presented itself. The road made a long loop round the flank of a hill, and it was possible to save half a mile or so by getting into the fields. It was a short cut I had often taken on the Quaker, and it involved nothing more serious than a couple of low stone "gaps" and an infantine bank. I turned Cruiskeen at the first of these. She was evidently surprised. Being in an excessively bad temper, I beat her in a way that surprised her even more, and she jumped the stones precipitately and with an ease that showed she knew quite well what she was about. I vented some further emotion upon her by the convenient medium of my cane, and galloped her across the field and over the bank, which, as they say in these parts, she "fled" without putting an iron on it. It was not the right way to jump it, but it was inspiriting, and when she had disposed of the next gap without hesitation my waning confidence in Miss Bennett began to revive. I cantered over the ridge of the hill, and down it towards the cottage near which I was accustomed to get out on to the road again. As I neared my wonted opening in the fence, I saw that it had been filled by a stout pole, well fixed into the bank at each end, but not more than three feet high. Cruiskeen pricked her ears at it with intelligence; I trotted her at it, and gave her a whack.

Ages afterwards there was some one speaking on the blurred edge of a dream that I was dreaming about nothing in particular. I went on dreaming, and was impressed by the shape of a fat jug, mottled white and blue, that intruded itself painfully, and I again heard voices, very urgent and full of effort, but quite outside any concern of mine.

I also made an effort of some kind; I was doing my very best to be good and polite, but I was dreaming in a place that whirred, and was engrossing, and daylight was cold and let in some unknown unpleasantness. For that time the dream got the better of the daylight , and then, *apropos* of nothing, I was standing up in a house with some one's arm round me; the mottled jug was there, so was the unpleasantness, and I was talking with most careful, old-world politeness.

"Sit down now, you're all right," said Miss Bobby Bennett, who was mopping my face with a handkerchief dipped in the jug.

I perceived that I was asking what had happened.

"She fell over the stick with you," said Miss Bennett; "the dirty brute!"

With another great effort I hooked myself on to the march of events, as a truck is dragged out of a siding and hooked to a train.

"Oh, the Lord save us!" said a grey-haired woman who held the jug, "ye're desthroyed entirely, asthore! Oh, glory be to the merciful will of God, me heart lepped across me shesht when I seen him undher the horse!"

"Go out and see if the trap's coming," said Miss Bennett; "he should have found the doctor by this." She stared very closely at my face, and seemed to find it easier to talk in short sentences.

"We must get those cuts looking better before Mrs. Yeates comes."

After an interval, during which unexpected places in my head ached from the cold water, the desire to be polite and coherent again came upon me.

"I am sure it was not your mare's fault," I said.

Miss Bennett laughed a very little. I was glad to see her laugh; it had struck me her face was strangely haggard and frightened.

"Well, of course it wasn't poor Cruiskeen's fault," she said. "She's nearly home with Mr. Shute by now. That's why I came after you!"

"Mr. Shute!" I said; "wasn't he at the fair that day?"

"He was," answered Miss Bobby, looking at me with very

compassionate eyes; "you and he got on each other's horses by mistake at the hotel, and you got the worst of the exchange!"

"Oh!" I said, without even trying to understand.

"He's here within, your honour's ladyship, Mrs. Yeates, ma'am," shouted the grey-haired woman at the door; "don't be unaisy, achudth; he's doing grand. Sure, I'm telling Miss Binnitt if she was his wife itself, she couldn't give him betther care!"

The grey-haired woman laughed.

Eight

THE HOLY ISLAND

For three days of November a white fog stood motionless over the country. All day and all night smothered booms and bangs away to the south-west told that the Fastnet gun was hard at work, and the sirens of the American liners uplifted their monstrous female voices as they felt their way along the coast of Cork. On the third afternoon the wind began to whine about the windows of Shreelane, and the barometer fell like a stone. At 11 P.M. the storm rushed upon us with the roar and the suddenness of a train; the chimneys bellowed, the tall old house quivered, and the yelling wind drove against it, as a man puts his shoulder against a door to burst it in.

We none of us got much sleep, and if Mrs. Cadogan is to be believed—which experience assures me she is not—she spent the night in devotional exercises, and in ministering to the panic-stricken kitchen-maid by the light of a Blessed candle. All that day the storm screamed on, dry-eyed; at nightfall the rain began, and next morning, which happened to be Sunday, every servant in the house was a messenger of Job, laden with tales of leakages, floods, and fallen trees, and inflated with the ill-concealed glory of their kind in evil tidings. To Peter

Cadogan, who had been to early Mass, was reserved the crowning satisfaction of reporting that a big vessel had gone on the rocks at Yokahn Point the evening before, and was breaking up fast; it was rumoured that the crew had got ashore, but this feature, being favourable and uninteresting, was kept as much as possible in the background. Mrs. Cadogan, who had been to America in an ocean liner, became at once the latest authority on shipwrecks, and was of opinion that "whoever would be dhrownded, it wouldn't be thim lads o' sailors. Sure wasn't there the greatest storm ever was in it the time meself was on the say, and what'd thim fellows do but to put us below entirely in the ship, and close down the doors on us, the way theirselves'd leg it when we'd be dhrownding!"

This view of the position was so startlingly novel that Philippa withdrew suddenly from the task of ordering dinner, and fell up the kitchen stairs in unsuitable laughter. Philippa has not the most rudimentary capacity for keeping her countenance.

That afternoon I was wrapped in the slumber, balmiest and most profound, that follows on a wet Sunday luncheon, when Murray, our D.I. of police, drove up in uniform, and came into the house on the top of a gust that set every door banging and every picture dancing on the walls. He looked as if his eyes had been blown out of his head, and he wanted something to eat very badly.

"I've been down at the wreck since ten o'clock this morning," he said, "waiting for her to break up, and once she does there'll be trouble. She's an American ship, and she's full up with rum, and bacon, and butter, and all sorts. Bosanquet is there with all his coastguards, and there are five hundred country people on the strand at this moment, waiting for the fun to begin. I've got ten of my fellows there, and I wish I had as many more. You'd better come back with me, Yeates, we may want the Riot Act before all's done!"

The heavy rain had ceased, but it seemed as if it had fed the wind instead of calming it, and when Murray and I drove out of Shreelane, the whole dirty sky was moving, full sailed, in from the south-west, and the telegraph wires were hanging in a loop from the post outside the gate. Nothing except a Skebawn car-horse would have faced the whooping charges of the wind that came at us across Corran Lake; stimulated mysteriously by whistles from the driver, Murray's yellow hireling pounded woodenly along against the blast, till the smell of the torn sea-weed was borne upon it, and we saw the Atlantic waves come towering into the bay of Tralagough.

The ship was, or had been, a three-masted barque; two of her masts were gone, and her bows stood high out of water on the reef that forms one of the shark-like jaws of the bay. The long strand was crowded with black groups of people, from the bank of heavy shingle that had been hurled over on to the road, down to the slope where the waves pitched themselves and climbed and fought and tore the gravel back with them, as though they had dug their fingers in. The people were nearly all men, dressed solemnly and hideously in their Sunday clothes; most of them had come straight from Mass without any dinner, true to that Irish instinct that places its fun before its food. That the wreck was regarded as a spree of the largest kind was sufficiently obvious. Our car pulled up at a public-house that stood askew between the road and the shingle; it was humming with those whom Irish publicans are pleased to call "Bonâ feeds," and sundry of the same class were clustered round the door. Under the wall on the leeside was seated a bagpiper, droning out "The Irish Washerwoman" with nodding head and tapping heel, and a young man was cutting a few steps of a jig for the delectation of a group of girls.

So far Murray's constabulary had done nothing but exhibit their imposing chest measurement and spotless uniforms to the Atlantic, and Bosanquet's coastguards had only salvaged some spars, the débris of a boat, and a dead sheep, but their time was coming. As we stumbled down over the shingle, battered by the wind and pelted by clots of foam, some one beside me shouted, "She's gone!" A hill of water had smoth-

ered the wreck, and when it fell from her again nothing was
left but the bows, with the bowsprit hanging from them in a
tangle of rigging. The clouds, bronzed by an unseen sunset,
hung low over her; in that greedy pack of waves, with the
remorseless rocks above and below her, she seemed the most
lonely and tormented of creatures.

About half-an-hour afterwards the cargo began to come
ashore on the top of the rising tide. Barrels were plunging and
diving in the trough of the waves, like a school of porpoises;
they were pitched up the beach in waist-deep rushes of foam;
they rolled down again, and were swung up and shouldered
by the next wave, playing a kind of Tom Tiddler's ground with
the coastguards. Some of the barrels were big and dangerous,
some were small and nimble like young pigs, and the blue-
jackets were up to their middles as their prey dodged and
ducked, and the police lined out along the beach to keep back
the people. Ten men of the R.I.C. can do a great deal, but they
cannot be in more than twenty or thirty places at the same
instant; therefore they could hardly cope with a scattered and
extremely active mob of four or five hundred, many of whom
had taken advantage of their privileges as "bona-fide travellers," and all of whom were determined on getting at the rum.

As the dusk fell the thing got more and more out of hand;
the people had found out that the big puncheons held the rum,
and had succeeded in capturing one. In the twinkling of an eye
it was broached, and fifty backs were shoving round it like a
football scrummage. I have heard many rows in my time: I
have seen two Irish regiments—one of them Militia—at each
other's throats in Fermoy barracks; I have heard Philippa's
water spaniel and two fox-terriers hunting a strange cat round
the dairy; but never have I known such untrammelled bedlam
as that which yelled round the rum-casks on Tralagough
strand. For it was soon not a question of one broached cask, or
even of two. The barrels were coming in fast, so fast that it was
impossible for the representatives of law and order to keep on
any sort of terms with them. The people, shouting with

laughter, stove in the casks, and drank rum at 34° above proof, out of their hands, out of their hats, out of their boots. Women came fluttering over the hillsides through the twilight, carrying jugs, milk-pails, anything that would hold the liquor; I saw one of them, roaring with laughter, tilt a filthy zinc bucket to an old man's lips.

With the darkness came anarchy. The rising tide brought more and yet more booty: great spars came lunging in on the

Out of their books

lap of the waves, mixed up with cabin furniture, seamen's chests, and the black and slippery barrels, and the country people continued to flock in, and the drinking became more and more unbridled. Murray sent for more men and a doctor, and we slaved on hopelessly in the dark; collaring half-drunken men, shoving pig-headed casks up hills of shingle, hustling in among groups of roaring drinkers—we rescued perhaps one barrel in half-a-dozen. I began to know that there were men there who were not drunk and were not idle; I was also aware, as the strenuous hours of darkness passed, of an occasional rumble of cart wheels on the road. It was evident that the casks which were broached were the least part of the looting, but even they were beyond our control. The most that Bosanquet, Murray, and I could do was to concentrate our forces on the casks that had been secured, and to organise charges upon the swilling crowds in order to upset the casks that they had broached. Already men and boys were lying about, lump as leeches, motionless as the dead.

"They'll kill themselves before morning, at this rate!" shouted Murray to me. "They're drinking it by the quart! Here's another barrel; come on!"

We rallied our small forces, and after a brief but furious struggle succeeded in capsizing it. It poured away in a flood over the stones, over the prostrate figures that sprawled on them, and a howl of reproach followed.

"If ye pour away any more o' that, Major," said an unctuous voice in my ear, "ye'll intoxicate the stones and they'll be getting up and knocking us down!"

I had been aware of a fat shoulder next to mine in the throng as we heaved the puncheon over, and I now recognised the ponderous wit and Falstaffian figure of Mr. James Canty, a noted member of the Skebawn Board of Guardians, and the owner of a large farm near at hand.

"I never saw worse work on this strand," he went on. "I considher these debaucheries a disgrace to the counthry."

Mr. Canty was famous as an orator, and I presume that it was from long practice among his fellow P.L.G.'s that he was able, without apparent exertion, to out-shout the storm.

At this juncture the long-awaited reinforcements arrived, and along with them came Dr. Jerome Hickey, armed with a black bag. Having mentioned that the bag contained a pump—not one of the common or garden variety—and that no pump on board a foundering ship had more arduous labours to perform, I prefer to pass to other themes. The wreck, which had at first appeared to be as inexhaustible and as variously stocked as that in the "Swiss Family Robinson," was beginning to fail in its supply. The crowd were by this time for the most part incapable from drink, and the fresh contingent of police tackled their work with some prospect of success by the light of a tar barrel, contributed by the owner of the public-house. At about the same time I began to be aware that I was aching with fatigue, that my clothes hung heavy and soaked upon me, that my face was stiff with the salt spray and the bitter wind, and that it was two hours past dinnertime. The possibility of fried salt herrings and hot whiskey and water at the public-house rose dazzlingly before my mind, when Mr. Canty again crossed my path.

Mr. James Canty

"In my opinion ye have the whole cargo under conthrol now, Major," he said, "and the police and the sailors should be able to account for it all now by the help of the light. Wasn't I the finished fool that I didn't think to send up to my house for a tar barrel before now! Well—we're all foolish sometimes! But indeed it's time for us to give over, and that's what I'm after saying to the Captain and Mr. Murray. You're exhausted now the three of ye, and if I might make so bold, I'd suggest that ye'd come up to my little place and have what'd warm ye before ye'd go home. It's only a few perches up the road."

The tide had turned, the rain had begun again, and the tar barrel illumined the fact that Dr. Hickey's dreadful duties alone were pressing. We held a council and finally followed Mr. Canty, picking our way through wreckage of all kinds, including the human variety. Near the public-house I stumbled over something that was soft and had a squeak in it; it was the piper, with his head and shoulders in an overturned rum-barrel, and the bagpipes still under his arm.

I knew the outward appearance of Mr. Canty's house very well. It was a typical southern farmhouse, with dirty whitewashed walls, a slated roof, and small, hermetically-sealed windows staring at the morass of manure which constituted the yard. We followed Mr. Canty up the filthy lane that led to it, picked our way round vague and squelching spurs of the manure heap, and were finally led through the kitchen into a stifling best parlour. Mrs. Canty, a vast and slatternly matron, had evidently made preparations for us; there was a newly-lighted fire pouring flame up the chimney from layers of bogwood, there were whisky and brandy on the table, and a plateful of biscuits sugared in white and pink. Upon our hostess was a black silk dress which indifferently concealed the fact that she was short of boot-laces, and that the boots themselves had made many excursions to the yard and none to the blacking-bottle. Her manners, however, were admirable, and while I live I shall not forget her potato cakes. They came in hot and hot from a pot-oven, they were speckled with caraway seeds, they swam in salt butter, and we ate them shamelessly and greasily, and washed them down with hot whisky and water; I knew to a nicety how ill I should be next day, and heeded not.

"Well, gentlemen," remarked Mr. Canty later on, in his best Board of Guardians' manner, "I've seen many wrecks between this and the Mizen Head, but I never witnessed a scene of more disgraceful ex-cess than what was in it to-night."

"Hear, hear!" murmured Bosanquet with unseemly levity.

"I should say," went on Mr. Canty, "there was at one time to-night upwards of one hundred men dead dhrunk on the strand, or anyway so dhrunk that if they'd attempt to spake they'd foam at the mouth."

"The craytures!" interjected Mrs. Canty sympathetically.

"But if they're dhrunk to-day," continued out host, "it's nothing at all to what they'll be to-morrow and afther to-morrow, and it won't be on the strand they'll be dhrinkin' it."

"Why, where will it be?" said Bosanquet, with his disconcerting English way of asking a point-blank question.

Mr. Canty passed his hand over his red cheeks.

"There'll be plenty asking that before all's said and done, Captain," he said, with a compassionate smile, "and there'll be plenty that could give the answer if they'll like, but by dam I don't think ye'll be apt to get much out of the Yokahn boys!"

"The Lord save us, 'twould be better to keep out from the likes o' thim!" put in Mrs. Canty, sliding a fresh avalanche of potato cakes on to the dish; "didn't they pull the clothes off the gauger and pour potheen down his throath till he ran screeching through the streets o' Skebawn!"

James Canty chuckled.

"I remember there was a wreck here one time, and the undherwriters put me in charge of the cargo. Brandy it was—cases of the best Frinch brandy. The people had a song about it, what's this the first verse was—

> "One night to the rocks of Yokahn
> Came the barque *Isabella* so dandy,
> To pieces she went before dawn,
> Herself and her cargo of brandy.
> And all met a wathery grave
> Excepting the vessel's car*pen*ther,
> Poor fellow, so far from his home."

Mr. Canty chanted these touching lines in a tuneful if wheezy tenor. "Well, gentlemen, we're all friends here," he continued, "and it's no harm to mention that this man below at the public-house came askin' me would I let him have some of it for a consideration. 'Sullivan,' says I to him, 'if ye ran down gold in a cup in place of the brandy, I wouldn't give it to you. Of coorse,' says I, 'I'm not sayin' but that if a bottle was to get a crack of a stick, and it to be broken, and a man to drink a glass out of it, that would be no more than an accident.' 'That's no good to me,' says he, 'but if I had twelve gallons of that brandy in Cork,' says he, 'by the Holy German!' says he, saying an awful curse, 'I'd sell twenty-five out of it!' Well, indeed, it was true for him; it was grand stuff. As the saying is, it would make a horse out of a cow!"

"It appears to be a handy sort of place for keeping a pub," said Bosanquet.

"Shut to the door, Margaret," said Mr. Canty with elaborate caution. "It'd be a queer place that wouldn't be handy for Sullivan!"

A further tale of great length was in progress when Dr. Hickey's Mephistophelian nose was poked into the best parlour.

"Hullo, Hickey! Pumped out? eh?" said Murray.

"If I am, there's plenty more like me," replied the Doctor enigmatically, "and some of them three times over! James, did these gentlemen leave you a drop of anything that you'd offer me?"

"Maybe ye'd like a glass of rum, Doctor?" said Mr. Canty with a wink at his other guests.

Dr. Hickey shuddered.

I had next morning precisely the kind of mouth that I had anticipated, and it being my duty to spend the better part of the day administering justice in Skebawn, I received from Mr. Flurry Knox and other of my brother magistrates precisely the class of condolences on my "Monday head" that I found least amusing. It was unavailing to point out the resemblance between hot potato cakes and molten lead, or to dilate on their equal power of solidifying; the collective wisdom of the Bench decided that I was suffering from contraband rum, and rejoiced over me accordingly.

During the next three weeks Murray and Bosanquet put in a time only to be equalled by that of the heroes in detective romances. They began by acting on the hint offered by Mr. Canty, and were rewarded by finding eight barrels of bacon and three casks of rum in the heart of Mr. Sullivan's turf rick, placed there, so Mr. Sullivan explained with much detail, by enemies, with the object of getting his licence taken away. They stabbed potato gardens with crowbars to find the buried barrels, they explored the chimneys, they raided the cow-houses; and in every possible and impossible place they found some of the cargo of the late barque *John D. Williams*, and, as the sympathetic Mr. Canty said, "For as much as they found, they left five times as much afther them!"

It was a wet, lingering autumn, but towards the end of November the rain dried up, the weather stiffened, and a week of light frosts and blue skies was offered as a tardy apology. Philippa possesses, in common with many of her sex, an inappeasable passion for picnics, and her ingenuity for devising occasions for them is only equalled by her gift for enduring their rigours. I have seen her tackle a moist chicken pie with a splinter of slate and my stylograph pen. I have known her to take the tea-basket to an auction, and make tea in a four-wheeled inside car, regardless of the fact that it was coming under the hammer in ten minutes, and that the kettle took twenty minutes to boil. It will therefore be readily understood that the rare occasions when I was free to go out with a gun were not allowed to pass uncelebrated by the tea-basket.

"You'd much better shoot Corran Lake to-morrow," my wife said to me one brilliant afternoon. "We could send the punt over, and I could meet you on Holy Island with——"

The rest of the sentence was concerned with ways, means, and the tea-basket, and need not be recorded.

I had taken the shooting of a long snipe bog that trailed from Corran Lake almost to the sea at Tralagough, and it was my custom to begin to shoot from the seaward end of it, and finally to work round the lake after duck.

To-morrow proved a heavenly morning, touched with frost, gilt with sun. I started early, and the mists were still smoking up from the calm, all-reflecting lake, as the Quaker stepped out along the level road, smashing the thin ice on the puddles with his big feet. Behind the calves of my legs sat Maria, Philippa's brown Irish water-spaniel, assiduously licking the barrels of my gun, as was her custom when the ecstasy of going out shooting was hers. Maria had been given to Philippa as a wedding-present, and since then it had been my wife's ambition that she should conform to the Beth Gelert standard of being "a lamb at home, a lion in the chase." Maria did pretty well as a lion: she hunted all dogs unmistakably smaller than herself, and whenever it was reasonably possible to do so she devoured the spoils of the chase, notably jack snipe. It was as a lamb that she failed; objectionable as I have no doubt a lamb would be as a domestic pet, it at least would not snatch the cold beef from the luncheon-table, nor yet, if banished for its crimes, would it spend the night in scratching the paint off the hall door. Maria bit beggars (who valued their disgusting limbs at five shillings the square inch), she bullied the servants, she concealed ducks' claws and fishes' backbones behind the sofa cushions, and yet, when she laid her brown snout upon my knee, and rolled her blackguard amber eyes upon me, and smote me with her feathered paw, it was impossible to remember her iniquities against her. On shooting mornings Maria ceased to be a buccaneer, a glutton, and a hypocrite. From the moment when I put my gun together her breakfast stood untouched until it suffered the final degradation of being eaten by the cats, and now in the trap she was shivering with excitement, and agonising in her soul lest she should even yet be left behind.

Slipper met me at the cross roads from which I had sent back the trap; Slipper, redder in the nose than anything I had ever seen off the stage, very husky as to the voice, and going rather tender on both feet. He informed me that I should have a grand day's shooting, the head-poacher of the locality having, in a most gentlemanlike manner, refrained from exercising his sporting rights the day before, on hearing that I was coming. I understood that this was to be considered as a mark of high personal esteem, and I set to work at the bog with suitable gratitude.

In spite of Mr. O'Driscoll's magnanimity, I had not a very good morning. The snipe were there, but in the perfect stillness of the weather it was impossible to get near them, and five times out of six they were up, flickering and dodging, before I was within shot. Maria became possessed of seven devils and broke away from heel the first time I let off my gun, ranging far and wide in search of the bird I had missed, and putting up every live thing for half a mile round, as she went splashing and steeple-chasing through the bog. Slipper expressed his opinion of her behaviour in language more appallingly picturesque and resourceful than any I have heard, even in the Skebawn Court-house; I admit that at the time I thought he spoke very suitably. Before she was recaptured every remaining snipe within earshot was lifted out of it by Slipper's steam-engine whistles and my own infuriated bellows; it was fortunate that the bog was spacious and that there was still a long tract of it ahead, where beyond these voices there was peace.

I worked my way on, jumping treacle-dark drains, floundering through the rustling yellow rushes, circumnavigating the bog-holes, and taking every possible and impossible chance of a shot; by the time I had reached Corran Lake I had got two and a half brace, retrieved by Maria with a perfection that showed what her powers were when the sinuous adroitness of Slipper's woodbine stick was fresh in her mind. But with Maria it was always the unexpected that happened. My last snipe, a jack, fell in the lake, and Maria, bursting through the reeds with kangaroo bounds, and cleaving the water like a torpedo-boat, was a model of all the virtues of her kind. She picked up the bird with a snake-like dart of her head, clambered with it on to a tussock, and there, well out of reach of the arm of the law, before our indignant eyes crunched in twice and bolted it.

"Well," said Slipper complacently, some ten minutes afterwards, "divil such a bating ever I gave a dog since the day Prince killed owld Mrs. Knox's paycock! Prince was a lump of a brown tarrier I had one time, and faith I kicked the toes out o' me owld boots on him before I had the owld lady composed!"

However composing Slipper's methods may have been to Mrs. Knox, they had quite the contrary effect upon a family party of duck that had been lying in the reeds. With horrified outcries they broke into flight, and now were far away on the ethereal mirror of the lake, among strings of their fellows that were floating and quacking in preoccupied indifference to my presence.

A promenade along the lake-shore demonstrated the fact that without a boat there was no more shooting for me; I looked across to the island where, some time ago, I had seen Philippa and her punt arrive. The boat was tied to an overhanging tree, but my wife was nowhere to be seen. I was opening my mouth to give a hail, when I saw her emerge precipitately from among the trees and jump into the boat; Philippa had not in vain spent many summers on the Thames, she was under way in a twinkling, sculled a score of strokes at the rate of a finish, then stopped and stared at the peaceful island. I called to her, and in a minute or two the punt had crackled through the reeds, and shoved its blunt nose ashore at the spot where I was standing.

"Sinclair," said Philippa in awe-struck tones, "there's something on the island!"

"I hope there's something to eat there," said I.

"I tell you there *is* something there, alive," said my wife with her eyes as large as saucers; "it's making an awful sound like snoring."

"That's the fairies, ma'am," said Slipper with complete certainty; "sure I known them that seen fairies in that island as thick as the grass, and every one o' them with little caps on them."

Philippa's wide gaze wandered to Slipper's hideous pug face and back to me.

"It was not a human being, Sinclair!" she said combatively, though I had not uttered a word.

Maria had already, after the manner of dogs, leaped, dripping, into the boat: I prepared to follow her example.

"Major," said Slipper, in a tragic whisper, "there was a man was a night on that island one time, watching duck, and Thim People cot him, and dhragged him through Hell and through Death, and threw him in the tide——"

"Shove off the boat," I said, too hungry for argument.

Slipper obeyed, throwing his knee over the gunwale as he did so, and tumbling into the bow; we could have done without him very comfortably, but his devotion was touching.

Holy Island was perhaps a hundred yards long, and about half as many broad; it was covered with trees and a dense growth of rhododendrons; somewhere in the jungle was a ruined fragment of a chapel, smothered in ivy and briars, and in a little glade in the heart of the island there was a holy well. We landed, and it was obviously a sore humiliation to Philippa that not a sound was to be heard in the spell-bound silence of the island, save the cough of a heron on a tree-top.

"It *was* there," she said, with an unconvinced glance at the surrounding thickets.

"Sure, I'll give a thrawl through the island, ma'am," volunteered Slipper with unexpected gallantry, "an' if it's the divil himself is in it, I'll rattle him into the lake!"

He went swaggering on his search, shouting, "Hi, cock!" and whacking the rhododendrons with his stick, and after an interval returned and assured us that the island was uninhabited. Being provided with refreshments he again withdrew, and Philippa and Maria and I fed variously and at great length, and washed the plates with water from the holy well. I was smoking a cigarette when we heard Slipper addressing the solitudes at the farther end of the island, and ending with one of his whisky-throated crows of laughter.

He presently came lurching towards us through the bushes, and a glance sufficed to show even Philippa—who was as incompetent a judge of such matters as many of her sex—that he was undeniably screwed.

"Major Yeates!" he began, "and Mrs. Major Yeates, with respex to ye, I'm bastely dhrunk! Me head is light since the 'fluenzy, and the docthor told me I should carry a little bottle-een o' sperrits——"

"Look here," I said to Philippa, "I'll take him across, and bring the boat back for you."

"Sinclair," responded my wife with concentrated emotion, "I would rather die than stay on this island alone!"

Slipper was getting drunker every moment, but I managed to stow him on his back in the bows of the punt, in which position he at once began to uplift husky and wandering strains of melody. To this accompaniment we, as Tennyson says,

> "moved from the brink like some full-breasted swan,
> That, fluting a wild carol ere her death,
> Ruffles her pure cold plume, and takes the flood
> With swarthy web."

Slipper would certainly have been none the worse for taking the flood, and, as the burden of "Lannigan's Ball" strengthened and spread along the tranquil along the tranquil lake, and the duck once more fled in justifiable consternation, I felt much inclined to make him do so.

We made for the end of the lake that was nearest Shreelane, and, as we rounded the point of the island, another boat presented itself to our view. It contained my late entertainer, Mrs. Canty, seated bulkily in the stern, while a small boy bowed himself between the two heavy oars.

"It's a lovely evening, Major Yeates," she called out. "I'm just going to the island to get some water from the holy well for me daughter that has an impression on her chest. Indeed,

I thought 'twas yourself was singing a song for Mrs. Yeates when I heard you coming, but sure Slipper is a great warrant himself for singing."

"May the divil crack the two legs undher ye!" bawled Slipper in acknowledgment of the compliment.

Mrs. Canty laughed genially, and her boat lumbered away.

I shoved Slipper ashore at the nearest point; Philippa and I paddled to the end of the lake, and abandoning the duck as a bad business, walked home.

A few days afterwards it happened that it was incumbent upon me to attend the funeral of the Roman Catholic Bishop of the diocese. It was what is called in France *"un bel enterrement,"* with inky flocks of tall-hatted priests, and countless yards of white scarves, and a repast of monumental solidity at the Bishop's residence. The actual interment was to take place in Cork, and we moved in long and imposing procession to the railway station, where a special train awaited the cortège. My friend Mr. James Canty was among the mourners: an important and active personage, exchanging condolences with the priests, giving directions to porters, and blowing his nose with a trumpeting mournfulness that penetrated all the other noises of the platform. He was condescending enough to notice my presence, and found time to tell me that he had given Mr. Murray "a sure word" with regard to some of *"the wreckage"*—this with deep significance, and a wink of an inflamed and tearful eye. I saw him depart in a first-class carriage, and the odour of sanctity; seeing that he was accompanied by seven priests, and that both windows were shut, the latter must have been considerable.

Afterwards, in the town, I met Murray, looking more pleased with himself than I had seen him since he had taken up the unprofitable task of smuggler-hunting.

"Come along and have some lunch," he said, "I've got a real good thing on this time! That chap Canty came to me late last night, and told me that he knew for a fact that the island on Corran Lake was just stiff with barrels of bacon and rum, and that I'd better send every man I could spare to-day to get them into the town. I sent the men out at eight o'clock this morning; I think I've gone one better than Bosanquet this time!"

I began to realise that Philippa was going to score heavily on the subject of the fairies that she had heard snoring on the island, and I imparted to Murray the leading features of our picnic there.

"Oh, Slipper's been up to his chin in that rum from the first," said Murray. "I'd like to know who his sleeping partner was!"

It was beginning to get dark before the loaded carts of the salvage party came lumbering past Murray's windows and into the yard of the police-barrack. We followed them, and in so doing picked up Flurry Knox, who was sauntering in the same direction. It was a good haul, five big casks of rum, and at least a dozen smaller barrels of bacon and butter, and Murray and his Chief Constable smiled seraphically on one another as the spoil was unloaded and stowed in a shed.

"Wouldn't it be as well to see how the butter is keeping?" remarked Flurry, who had been looking on silently, with, as I had noticed, a still and amused eye. "The rim of that small keg there looks as if it had been shifted lately."

The sergeant looked hard at Flurry; he knew as well as most people that a hint from Mr. Knox was usually worth taking. He turned to Murray.

"Will I open it, sir?"

"Oh! open it if Mr. Knox wishes," said Murray, who was not famous for appreciating other people's suggestions.

The keg was opened.

"Funny butter," said Flurry.

The sergeant said nothing. The keg was full of black bog-mould. Another was opened, and another, all with the same result.

"Damnation!" said Murray, suddenly losing his temper.

"What's the use of going on with those? Try one of the rum casks."

A few moments passed in total silence while a tap and a spigot were sent for and applied to the barrel. The sergeant drew off a mugful and put his nose to it with the deliberation of a connoisseur.

"Water, sir," he pronounced, "dirty water, with a small indication of sperrits."

A junior constable tittered explosively, met the light blue glare of Murray's eye, and withered away.

"Perhaps it's holy water!" said I, with a wavering voice.

Murray's glance pinned me like an assegai, and I also faded into the background.

"Well," said Flurry in dulcet tones, "if you want to know where the stuff is that was in those barrels, I can tell you, for I was told it myself half-an-hour ago. It's gone to Cork with the Bishop by special train!"

Mr. Canty was undoubtedly a man of resource. Mrs. Canty had mistakenly credited me with an intelligence equal to her own, and on receiving from Slipper a highly coloured account of how audibly Mr. Canty had slept off his potations, had regarded the secret of Holy Island as having been given away. That night and the two succeeding ones were spent in the transfer of the rum to bottles, and the bottles and the butter to fish boxes; these were, by means of a slight lubrication of the railway underlings loaded into a truck as "Fresh Fish, Urgent," and attached to the Bishop's funeral train, while the police, decoyed far from the scene of action, were breaking their backs over barrels of bog-water. "I suppose," continued Flurry pleasantly, "you don't know the pub that Canty's brother has in Cork. Well, I do. I'm going to buy some rum there next week, cheap."

"I shall proceed against Canty!" said Murray, with fateful calm.

"You won't proceed far," said Flurry; "you'll not get as much evidence out of the whole country as'd hang a cat."

"Who was your informant?" demanded Murray.

Flurry laughed. "Well, by the time the train was in Cork, yourself and the Major were the only two men in the town that weren't talking about it."

Nine

THE POLICY OF THE CLOSED DOOR

THE disasters and humiliations that befell me at Drum-curran Fair may yet be remembered. They certainly have not been forgotten in the regions about Skebawn, where the tale of how Bernard Shute and I stole each other's horses has passed into history. The grand-daughter of the Mountain Hare, bought by Mr. Shute with such light-hearted enthusiasm, was restored to that position between the shafts of a cart that she was so well fitted to grace; Moonlighter, his other purchase, spent the two months following on the fair in "favouring" a leg with a strained sinew, and in receiving visits from the local vet., who, however uncertain in his diagnosis of Moonlighter's leg, had accurately estimated the length of Bernard's foot.

Miss Bennett's mare Cruiskeen, alone of the trio, was immediately and thoroughly successful. She went in harness like a hero, she carried Philippa like an elder sister, she was never sick or sorry; as Peter Cadogan summed her up, "That one 'd live where another 'd die." In her safe keeping Philippa made her *début* with hounds at an uneventful morning's cubbing, with no particular result, except that Philippa returned home so stiff that she had to go to bed for a day, and arose more determined than ever to be a fox-hunter.

The opening meet of Mr. Knox's foxhounds was on November 1, and on that morning Philippa on Cruiskeen, accompanied by me on the Quaker, set out for Ardmeen Cross, the time-honoured fixture for All Saints' Day. The weather was grey and quiet, and full of all the moist sweetness of an Irish autumn. There had been a great deal of rain during the past month; it had turned the bracken to a purple brown, and had filled the hollows with shining splashes of water. The dead leaves were slippery under foot, and the branches above were thinly decked with yellow, where the pallid survivors of summer still clung to their posts. As Philippa and I sedately approached the meet the red coats of Flurry Knox and his whip, Dr. Jerome Hickey, were to be seen on the road at the top of the hill; Cruiskeen put her head in the air, and stared at them with eyes that understood all they portended.

"Sinclair," said my wife hurriedly, as a straggling hound, flogged in by Dr. Hickey, uttered a grievous and melodious howl, "remember, if they find, it's no use to talk to me, for I shan't be able to speak."

I was sufficiently acquainted with Philippa in moments of enthusiasm to exhibit silently the corner of a clean pocket-handkerchief; I have seen her cry when a police constable won a bicycle race in Skebawn; she has wept at hearing Sir Valentine Knox's health drunk with musical honours at a tenants' dinner. It is an amiable custom, but, as she herself admits, it is unbecoming.

An imposing throng, in point of numbers, was gathered at the cross-roads, the riders being almost swamped in the crowd of traps, outside cars, bicyclists, and people on foot. The field was an eminently representative one. The Clan Knox was, as usual, there in force, its more aristocratic members dingily respectable in black coats and tall hats that went impartially to weddings, funerals, and hunts, and, like a horse that is past mark of mouth, were no longer to be identified with any special epoch; there was a humbler squireen element in tweeds and flat-brimmed pot-hats, and a good muster of farmers, men of the spare, black-muzzled, West of Ireland type, on horses that ranged from the cart mare, clipped trace high, to shaggy and leggy three-year-olds, none of them hunters, but all of them able to hunt. Philippa and I worked our way to the heart of things, where was Flurry, seated on his brown mare, in what appeared to be a somewhat moody silence. As we exchanged greetings I was aware that his eye was resting with extreme disfavour upon two approaching figures. I put up my eye-glass, and perceived that one of them was Miss Sally Knox, on a tall grey horse; the other was Mr. Bernard Shute, in all the flawless beauty of his first pink coat, mounted on Stockbroker, a well-known, hard-mouthed, big-jumping bay, recently purchased from Dr. Hickey.

During the languors of a damp autumn the neighbourhood had been much nourished and sustained by the privilege of observing and diagnosing the progress of Mr. Shute's flirtation with Miss Sally Knox. What made it all the more enjoyable for the lookers-on—or most of them—was, that although Bernard's courtship was of the nature of a proclamation from the housetops, Miss Knox's attitude left everything to the imagination. To Flurry Knox the romantic but despicable position of slighted rival was comfortably allotted; his sole sympathisers were Philippa and old Mrs. Knox of Aussolas, but no one knew if he needed sympathisers. Flurry was a man of mystery.

Mr. Shute and Miss Knox approached us rapidly, the latter's mount pulling hard.

"Flurry," I said, "isn't that grey the horse Shute bought from you last July at the fair?"

Flurry did not answer me. His face was as black as thunder. He turned his horse round, cursing two country boys who got in his way, with low and concentrated venom, and began to move forward, followed by the hounds. If his wish was to avoid speaking to Miss Sally it was not to be gratified.

"Good-morning, Flurry," she began, sitting close down to

Moonlighter's ramping jog as she rode up beside her cousin. "What a hurry you're in! We passed no end of people on the road who won't be here for another ten minutes."

"No more will I," was Mr. Knox's cryptic reply, as he spurred the brown mare into a trot.

Moonlighter made a vigorous but frustrated effort to buck, and indemnified himself by a successful kick at a hound.

"Bother you, Flurry! Can't you walk for a minute?" exclaimed Miss Sally, who looked about as large, in relation to her horse, as the conventional tomtit on a round of beef. "You might have more sense than to crack your whip under this horse's nose! I don't believe you know what horse it is even!"

I was not near enough to catch Flurry's reply.

"Well, if you did'nt want him to be lent to me you should'nt have sold him to Mr. Shute!" retorted Miss Knox, in her clear, provoking little voice.

"I suppose he's afraid to ride him himself," said Flurry, turning his horse in at a gate. "Get ahead there, Jerome, can't you? It's better to put them in at this end than to have every one riding on top of them!"

Miss Sally's cheeks were still very pink when I came up and began to talk to her, and her grey-green eyes had a look in them like those of an angry kitten.

The riders moved slowly down a rough pasture-field, and took up their position along the brow of Ardmeen covert, into which the hounds had already hurled themselves with their customary contempt for the convenances. Flurry's hounds, true to their nationality, were in the habit of doing the right thing in the wrong way.

Untouched by autumn, the furze bushes of Ardmeen covert were darkly green, save for a golden fleck of blossom here and there, and the glistening grey cobwebs that stretched from spike to spike. The look of the ordinary gorse covert is familiar to most people as a tidy enclosure of an acre or so, filled with low plants of well-educated gorse; not so many will be found who have experience of it as a rocky, sedgy wilderness, half a mile square, garrisoned with brigades of furze bushes, some of them higher than a horse's head, lean, strong, and cunning, like the foxes that breed in them, impenetrable, with their bristling spikes, as a hedge of bayonets. By dint of infinite leisure and obstinate greed, the cattle had made paths for themselves through the bushes to the patches of grass that they hemmed in; their hoofprints were guides to the explorer, down muddy staircases of rock, and across black intervals of unplumbed bog. The whole covert slanted gradually down to a small river that raced round three sides of it, and beyond the stream, in agreeable contrast, lay a clean and wholesome country of grass fields and banks.

The hounds drew slowly along and down the hill towards the river, and the riders hung about outside the covert, and tried—I can answer for at least one of them—to decide which was the least odious of the ways through it, in the event of the fox breaking at the far side. Miss Sally took up a position not very far from me, and it was easy to see that she had her hands full with her borrowed mount, on whose temper the delay and suspense were visibly telling. His iron-grey neck was white from the chafing of the reins; had the ground under his feet been red-hot he could hardly have sidled and hopped more uncontrollably; nothing but the most impassioned conjugation of the verb to condemn could have supplied any human equivalent for the manner in which he tore holes in the sedgy grass with a furious forefoot. Those who were even superficial judges of character gave his heels a liberal allowance of sea-room, and Mr. Shute, who could not be numbered among such, and had, as usual, taken up a position as near Miss Sally as possible, was rewarded by a double knock on his horse's ribs that was a cause of heartless mirth to the lady of his affections.

Not a hound had as yet spoken, but they were forcing their way through the gorse forest and shoving each other jealously aside with growing excitement, and Flurry could be seen at intervals, moving forward in the direction they were indicating. It was at this juncture that the ubiquitous Slipper presented himself at my horse's shoulder.

"'Tis for the river he's making, Major," he said, with an upward roll of his squinting eyes, that nearly made me sea-sick. "He's a Castle Knox fox that came in this morning, and ye should get ahead down to the ford!"

A tip from Slipper was not to be neglected, and Philippa and I began a cautious progress through the gorse, followed by Miss Knox as quietly as Moonlighter's nerves would permit.

"Wishful has it!" she exclaimed, as a hound came out into view, uttered a sharp yelp, and drove forward.

"Hark! hark!" roared Flurry with at least three *r*'s reverberating in each "hark;" at the same instant came a holloa from the farther side of the river, and Dr. Hickey's renowned and blood-curdling screech was uplifted at the bottom of the covert. Then babel broke forth, as the hounds, converging from every quarter, flung themselves shrieking on the line. Moonlighter went straight up on his hind-legs, and dropped again with a bound that sent him crushing past Philippa and Cruiskeen; he did it a second time, and was almost on to the tail of the Quaker, whose bulky person was not to be hurried in any emergency.

"Get on if you can, Major Yeates!" called out Sally, steadying the grey as well as she could in the narrow pathway between the great gorse bushes.

Other horses were thundering behind us, men were shouting to each other in similar passages right and left of us, the cry of the hounds, filled the air with a kind of delirium. A low wall with a stick laid along it barred the passage in front of me, and the Quaker firmly and immediately decided not to have it until some one else had dislodged the pole.

"Go ahead!" I shouted, squeezing to one side with heroic disregard of the furze bushes and my new tops.

The words were hardly out of my mouth when Moonlighter, mad with thwarted excitement, shot by me, hurtling over the obstacle with extravagant fury, landed twelve feet beyond it on clattering slippery rock, saved himself from falling with an eel-like forward buck on to sedgy ground, and bolted at full speed down the muddy cattle track. There are corners—rocky, most of them—in that cattle track, that Sally has told me she will remember to her dying day; boggy holes of any depth, ranging between two feet and half-way to Australia, that she says she does not fail to mention in the General Thanksgiving; but at the time they occupied mere fractions of the strenuous seconds in which it was hopeless for her to do anything but try to steer, trust to luck, sit hard down into the saddle and try to stay there. (For my part, I would as soon try to adhere to the horns of a charging bull as to the crutches of a side-saddle, but happily the necessity is not likely to arise.) I saw Flurry Knox a little ahead of her on the same track, jamming his mare into the furze bushes to get out of her way; he shouted something after her about the ford, and started to gallop for it himself by a breakneck short cut.

The hounds were already across the river, and it was obvious that, ford or no ford, Moonlighter's intentions might be simply expressed in the formula "Be with them I will." It was all down-hill to the river, and among the furze bushes and rocks there was neither time nor place to turn him. He rushed at it with a shattering slip upon a streak of rock, with a heavy plunge in the deep ground by the brink; it was as bad a take-off for twenty feet of water as could well be found. The grey horse rose out of the boggy stuff with all the impetus that pace and temper could give, but it was not enough. For one instant the twisting, sliding current was under Sally, the next a veil of water sprang up all round her, and Moonlighter was rolling and lurching in the desperate effort to find foothold in the rocky bed of the stream.

I was following at the best pace I could kick out of the Quaker, and saw the water swirl into her lap as her horse rolled to the near-side. She caught the mane to save herself, but he struggled on to his legs again, and came floundering broadside on to the further bank. In three seconds she had got out of the saddle and flung herself at the bank, grasping the rushes, and trying, in spite of the sodden weight of her habit, to drag herself out of the water.

At the same instant I saw Flurry and the brown mare dashing through the ford, twenty yards higher up. He was off his horse and beside her with that uncanny quickness that Flurry reserved for moments of emergency, and, catching her by the arms, swung her on to the bank as easily as if she had been the kennel terrier.

"Catch the horse!" she called out, scrambling to her feet.

"Damn the horse!" returned Flurry, in the rage that is so often the reaction from a bad scare.

I turned along the bank and made for the ford; by this time it was full of hustling, splashing riders, through whom Bernard Shute, furiously picking up a bad start, drove a devastating way. He tried to turn his horse down the bank towards Miss Knox, but the hounds were running hard, and, to my intense amusement, Stockbroker refused to abandon the chase, and swept his rider away in the wake of his stable companion, Dr. Hickey's young chestnut. By this time two country boys had, as is usual in such cases, risen from the earth, and fished Moonlighter out of the stream. Miss Sally wound up an acrimonious argument with her cousin by observing that she didn't care what he said, and placing her water-logged boot in his obviously unwilling hand, in a second was again in the saddle, gathering up the wet reins with the trembling, clumsy fingers of a person who is thoroughly chilled and in a violent hurry. She set Moonlighter going, and was away in a moment, galloping him at the first fence at a pace that suited his steeplechasing ideas.

"Mr. Knox!" panted Philippa, who had by this time joined us, "make her go home!"

"She can go where she likes as far as I'm concerned," responded Mr. Knox, pitching himself on his mare's back and digging in the spurs.

Moonlighter had already glided over the bank in front of us,

with a perfunctory flick at it with his heels; Flurry's mare and
Cruiskeen jumped it side by side with equal precision. It was
a bank of some five feet high; the Quaker charged it enthusiastically, refused it abruptly, and, according to his infuriating
custom at such moments, proceeded to tear hurried mouthfuls
of grass.

"Will I give him a couple o' belts, your Honour?" shouted
one of the running accompaniment of country boys.

"You will!" said I, with some further remarks to the Quaker
that I need not commit to paper.

Swish! Whack! The sound was music in my ears, as the
good, remorseless ash sapling bent round the Quaker's
dappled hind-quarters. At the third stripe he launched both his
heels in the operator's face; at the fourth he reared undecid-
edly; at the fifth he bundled over the bank in a manner purged
of hesitation.

"Ha!" yelled my assistants, "that'll put the fear o' God in
him!" as the Quaker fled head-long after the hunt. "He'll be
the betther o' that while he lives!"

Without going quite as far as this, I must admit that for the
next half-hour he was astonishingly the better of it.

The Castle Knox fox was making a very pretty line of it over
the seven miles that separated him from his home. He headed
through a grassy country of Ireland's mild and brilliant green,
fenced with sound and buxom banks, enlivened by stone walls,
uncompromised by the presence of gates, and yet comfortably
laced with lanes for the furtherance of those who had laid to
heart Wolsey's valuable advice: "Fling away ambition: by that
sin fell the angels." The flotsam and jetsam of the hunt
pervaded the landscape: standing on one long bank, three
dismounted farmers flogged away at the refusing steeds below
them, like anglers trying to rise a sulky fish; half-a-dozen hats,
bobbing in a string, showed where the road riders followed the
delusive windings of a bohireen. It was obvious that in the
matter of ambition they would not have caused Cardinal

"He'll be the betther o' that while he lives!"

Wolsey a moment's uneasiness; whether angels or otherwise, they were not going to run any risk of falling.

Flurry's red coat was like a beacon two fields ahead of me, with Philippa following in his tracks; it was the first run worthy of the name that Philippa had ridden, and I blessed Miss Bobby Bennett as I saw Cruiskeen's undefeated fencing. An encouraging twang of the Doctor's horn notified that the hounds were giving us a chance; even the Quaker pricked his blunt ears and swerved in his stride to the sound. A stone wall, a rough patch of heather, a boggy field, dinted deep and black with hoof marks, and the stern chase was at an end. The hounds had checked on the outskirts of a small wood, and the field, thinned down to a panting dozen or so, viewed us with the disfavour shown by the first flight towards those who unexpectedly add to their select number. In the depths of the wood Dr. Hickey might be heard uttering those singular little yelps of encouragement that to the irreverent suggest a milkman in his dotage. Bernard Shute, who neither knew nor cared what the hounds were doing, was expatiating at great length to an uninterested squireen upon the virtues and perfections of his new mount.

"I did all I knew to come and help you at the river," he said, riding up to the splashed and still dripping Sally, "but Stockbroker wouldn't hear of it. I pulled his ugly head round till his nose was on my boot, but he galloped away just the same!"

"He was quite right," said Miss Sally; "I didn't want you in the least."

As Miss Sally's red gold coil of hair was turned towards me during this speech, I could only infer the glance with which it was delivered, from the fact that Mr. Shute responded to it with one of those firm gazes of adoration in which the neighbourhood took such an interest, and crumbled away into incoherency.

A shout from the top of a hill interrupted the amenities of the check; Flurry was out of the wood in half-a-dozen seconds, blowing shattering blasts upon his horn, and the hounds rushed to him, knowing the "gone away" note that was never blown in vain. The brown mare came out through the trees and the undergrowth like a woodcock down the wind, and jumped across a stream on to a more than questionable bank; the hounds splashed and struggled after him, and, as they landed, the first ecstatic whimpers broke forth. In a moment it was full cry, discordant, beautiful, and soul-stirring, as the pack spread and sped, and settled to the line. I saw the absurd dazzle of tears in Philippa's eyes, and found time for the insulting proffer of the clean pocket-handkerchief, as we all galloped hard to get away on good terms with the hounds.

It was one of those elect moments in fox-hunting when the fittest alone have survived; even the Quaker's sluggish blood was stirred by good company, and possibly by the remembrance of the singing ash-plant, and he lumbered up tall stone-faced banks and down heavy drops, and across wide ditches, in astounding adherence to the line cut out by Flurry. Cruiskeen went like a book—a story for girls, very pleasant and safe, but rather slow. Moonlighter was pulling Miss Sally on to the sterns of the hounds, flying his banks, rocketing like a pheasant over three-foot walls—committing, in fact, all the crimes induced by youth and over-feeding; he would have done very comfortably with another six or seven stone on his back.

Why Bernard Shute did not come off at every fence and generally die a thousand deaths I cannot explain. Occasionally I rather wished he would, as, from my secure position in the rear, I saw him charging his fences at whatever pace and place seemed good to the thoroughly demoralised Stockbroker, and in so doing cannon heavily against Dr. Hickey on landing over a rotten ditch, jump a wall with his spur rowelling Charlie Knox's boot, and cut in at top speed in front of Flurry, who was scientifically cramming his mare up a very awkward scramble. In so far as I could think of anything beyond Philippa and myself and the next fence, I thought there would be trouble for Mr. Shute in consequence of this last feat. It was a half-hour long to be remembered, in spite of the Quaker's ponderous and unalterable gallop, in spite of the thump with which he came down off his banks, in spite of the confiding manner in which he hung upon my hand.

We were nearing Castle Knox, and the riders began to edge away from the hounds towards a gate that broke the long barrier of the demesne wall. Steaming horses and purple-faced riders clattered and crushed in at the gate; there was a moment of pulling up and listening, in which quivering tails and pumping sides told their own story. Cruiskeen's breathing suggested a cross between a grampus and a gramaphone; Philippa's hair had come down, and she had a stitch in her side. Moonlighter, fresher than ever, stamped and dragged at his bit; I thought little Miss Sally looked very white. The bewildering clamour of the hounds was all through the wide laurel plantations. At a word from Flurry, Dr. Hickey shoved his horse ahead and turned down a ride, followed by most of the field.

"Philippa," I said severely, "you've had enough, and you know it."

"Do go up to the house and make them give you something to eat," struck in Miss Sally, twisting Moonlighter round to keep his mind occupied.

"And as for you, Miss Sally," I went on, in the manner of Mr. Fairchild, "the sooner you get off that horse and out of those wet things the better."

Flurry, who was just in front of us, said nothing, but gave a short and most disagreeable laugh. Philippa accepted my suggestion with the meekness of exhaustion, but under the circumstances it did not surprise me that Miss Sally did not follow her example.

Then ensued an hour of woodland hunting at its worst and most bewildering. I galloped after Flurry and Miss Sally up and down long glittering lanes of laurel, at every other moment burying my face in the Quaker's coarse white mane to avoid the slash of the branches, and receiving down the back of my neck showers of drops stored up from the rain of the day before; playing an endless game of hide-and-seek with the hounds, and never getting any nearer to them, as they turned and doubled through the thickets of evergreens. Even to my limited understanding of the situation it became clear at length that two foxes were on foot; most of the hounds were hard at work a quarter of a mile away, but Flurry, with a grim face and a faithful three couple, stuck to the failing line of the hunted fox.

There came a moment when Miss Sally and I—who through many vicissitudes had clung to each other—found ourselves at a spot where two rides crossed. Flurry was waiting there, and a little way up one of the rides a couple of hounds were hustling to and fro, with the thwarted whimpers half breaking from them; he held up his hand to stop us, and at that identical moment Bernard Shute, like a bolt from the blue, burst upon our vision. It need scarcely be mentioned that he was going at full gallop—I have rarely seen him ride at any other pace—and as he bore down upon Flurry and the hounds, ducking and dodging to avoid the branches, he shouted something about a fox having gone away at the other side of the covert.

"Hold hard!" roared Flurry; "don't you see the hounds, you fool?"

Mr. Shute, to do him justice, held hard with all the strength in his body, but it was of no avail. The bay horse had got his head down and his tail up, there was a piercing yell from a hound as it was ridden over, and Flurry's brown mare will not soon forget the moment when Stockbroker's shoulder took her on the point of the hip and sent her staggering into the laurel branches. As she swung round, Flurry's whip went up, and with a swift backhander the cane and the looped thong caught Bernard across his broad shoulders.

"O Mr. Shute!" shrieked Miss Sally, as I stared dumfoundered; "did that branch hurt you?"

"All right! Nothing to signify!" he called out as he bucketed past, tugging at his horse's head. "Thought some one had hit me at first! Come on, we'll catch 'em up this way!"

He swung perilously into the main ride and was gone, totally unaware of the position that Miss Sally's quickness had saved.

Flurry rode straight up to his cousin, with a pale, dangerous face.

"I suppose you think I'm to stand being ridden over and having my hounds killed to please you," he said; "but you're mistaken, You were very smart, and you may think you've saved him his licking, but you needn't think he won't get it. He'll have it in spite of you, before he goes to his bed this night!"

A man who loses his temper badly because he is badly in love is inevitably ridiculous, far though he may be from thinking himself so. He is also a highly unpleasant person to argue with, and Miss Sally and I held our peace respectfully. He turned his horse and rode away.

Almost instantly the three couple of hounds opened in the underwood near us with a deafening crash, and not twenty yards ahead the hunted fox, dark with wet and mud, slunk across the ride. The hounds were almost on his brush; Moonlighter reared and chafed; the din was redoubled, passed away to a little distance, and suddenly seemed stationary in the middle of the laurels.

"Could he have got into the old ice-house?" exclaimed Miss Sally, with reviving excitement. She pushed ahead, and turned down the narrowest of all the rides that had that day been my portion. At the end of the green tunnel there was a comparatively open space; Flurry's mare was standing in it, riderless, and Flurry himself was hammering with a stone at the padlock of a door that seemed to lead into the heart of a laurel clump. The hounds were baying furiously somewhere back of the entrance, among the laurel stems.

"He's got in by the old ice drain," said Flurry, addressing himself sulkily to me, and ignoring Miss Sally. He had not the least idea of how absurd was his scowling face, draped by the luxuriant hart's-tongues that overhung the doorway.

The padlock yielded, and the opening door revealed a low, dark passage, into which Flurry disappeared, lugging a couple of hounds with him by the scruff of the neck; the remaining two couple bayed implacably at the mouth of the drain. The croak of a rusty bolt told of a second door at the inner end of the passage.

"Look out for the steps, Flurry, they're all broken," called out Miss Sally in tones of honey.

There was no answer. Miss Sally looked at me; her face was serious, but her mischievous eyes made a confederate of me.

"He's in an *awful* rage!" she said. "I'm afraid there will certainly be a row."

A row there certainly was, but it was in the cavern of the ice-house, where the fox had evidently been discovered. Miss Sally suddenly flung Moonlighter's reins to me and slipped off his back.

"Hold him!" she said, and dived into the doorway under the overhanging branches.

Things happened after that with astonishing simultaneousness. There was a shrill exclamation from Miss Sally, the inner door was slammed and bolted, and at one and the same moment the fox darted from the entry, and was away into the wood before one could wink.

"What's happened?" I called out, playing the refractory Moonlighter like a salmon.

Miss Sally appeared at the doorway, looking half scared and half delighted.

"I've bolted him in, and I won't let him out till he promises to be good! I was only just in time to slam the door after the box bolted out!"

"Great Scott!" I said helplessly.

Miss Sally vanished again into the passage, and the imprisoned hounds continued to express their emotions in the echoing vault of the ice-house. Their master remained mute as the dead, and I trembled.

"Flurry!" I heard Miss Sally say. "Flurry, I—I've locked you in!"

This self-evident piece of information met with no response.

"Shall I tell you why?"

A keener note seemed to indicate that a hound had been kicked.

"I don't care whether you answer me or not, I'm going to tell you!"

There was a pause; apparently telling him was not as simple as had been expected.

"I won't let you out till you promise me something. Ah, Flurry, don't be so cross! What do you say?——Oh, that's a ridiculous thing to say. You know quite well it's not on his account!"

There was another considerable pause.

"Flurry!" said Miss Sally again, in tones that would have wiled a badger from his earth. "Dear Flurry——"

At this point I hurriedly flung Moonlighter's bridle over a branch and withdrew.

My own subsequent adventures are quite immaterial, until the moment when I encountered Miss Sally on the steps of the hall door at Castle Knox.

"I'm just going in to take off these wet things," she said airily.

This was no way to treat a confederate.

"Well?" I said, barring her progress.

"Oh—he—he promised. It's all right," she replied, rather breathlessly.

There was no one about; I waited resolutely for further information. It did not come.

"Did he try to make his own terms?" said I, looking hard at her.

"Yes, he did." She tried to pass me.

"And what did you do?"

"I refused them!" she said, with the sudden stagger of a sob in her voice, as she escaped into the house.

Now what on earth was Sally Knox crying about?

Ten

THE HOUSE OF FAHY

NOTHING could shake the conviction of Maria that she was by nature and by practice a house dog. Every one of Shreelane's many doors had, at one time or another, slammed upon her expulsion, and each one of them had seen her stealthy, irrepressible return to the sphere that she felt herself so eminently qualified to grace. For her the bone, thriftily interred by Tim Connor's terrier, was a mere diversion; even the fruitage of the ashpit had little charm for an accomplished *habitué* of the kitchen. She knew to a nicety which of the doors could be burst open by assault, at which it was necessary to whine sycophantically; and the clinical thermometer alone could furnish a parallel for her perception of mood in those in authority. In the case of Mrs. Cadogan she knew that there were seasons when instant and complete self-effacement was the only course to pursue; therefore when, on a certain morning in July, on my way through the downstairs regions to my office, I saw her approach the kitchen door with her usual circumspection, and, on hearing her name enunciated indignantly by my cook, withdraw swiftly to a city of refuge at the back of the hayrick, I drew my own conclusions.

Had she remained, as I did, she would have heard the disclosure of a crime that lay more heavily on her digestion than her conscience.

"I can't put a thing out o' me hand but he's watching me to whip it away!" declaimed Mrs. Cadogan, with all the disregard of her kind for the accident of sex in the brute creation. "'Twas only last night I was back in the scullery when I heard Bridget let a screech, and there was me brave dog up on the table eating the roast beef that was after coming out from the dinner!"

"Brute!" interjected Philippa, with what I well knew to be a simulated wrath.

"And I had planned that bit of beef for the luncheon," continued Mrs. Cadogan in impassioned lamentation, "the way we wouldn't have to inthrude on the cold turkey! Sure he has it that dhragged, that all we can do with it now is run it through the mincing machine for the Major's sandwiches."

At this appetising suggestion I thought fit to intervene in the deliberations.

"One thing," I said to Philippa afterwards, as I wrapped up a bottle of Yanatas in a Cardigan jacket and rammed it into an already apoplectic Gladstone bag, "that I do draw the line at, is taking that dog with us. The whole business is black enough as it is."

"Dear," said my wife, looking at me with almost clairvoyant abstraction, "I could manage a second evening dress if you didn't mind putting my tea-jacket in your portmanteau."

Little, thank Heaven! as I know about yachting, I knew enough to make pertinent remarks on the incongruity of an ancient 60-ton hireling and a fleet of smart evening dresses; but none the less I left a pair of indispensable boots behind, and the tea-jacket went into my portmanteau.

It is doing no more than the barest justice to the officers of the Royal Navy to say that, so far as I know them, they cherish no mistaken enthusiasm for a home on the rolling deep when a home anywhere else presents itself. Bernard Shute had unfortunately proved an exception to this rule. During the winter, the invitation to go for a cruise in the yacht that was in process of building for him hung over me like a cloud; a timely strike in the builder's yard brought a respite, and, in fact, placed the completion of the yacht at so safe a distance that I was betrayed into specious regrets, echoed with an atrocious sincerity by Philippa. Into a life pastorally compounded of Petty Sessions and lawn-tennis parties, retribution fell when it was least expected. Bernard Shute hired a yacht in Queenstown, and one short week afterwards the worst had happened, and we were packing our things for a cruise in her, the only alleviation being the knowledge that, whether by sea or land, I was bound to return to my work in four days.

We left Shreelane at twelve o'clock, a specially depressing hour for a start, when breakfast has died in you, and lunch is still remote. My last act before mounting the dogcart was to put her collar and chain on Maria and immure her in the potato-house, whence, as we drove down the avenue, her wails rent the heart of Philippa and rejoiced mine. It was a very hot day, with a cloudless sky; the dust lay thick on the white road, and on us also, as, during two baking hours, we drove up and down the long hills and remembered things that had been left behind, and grew hungry enough to eat sandwiches that tasted suspiciously of roast beef.

The yacht was moored in Clountiss Harbour; we drove through the village street, a narrow and unlovely thoroughfare, studded with public-houses, swarming with children and poultry, down through an ever-growing smell of fish, to the quay.

Thence we first viewed our fate, a dingy-looking schooner, and the hope I had secretly been nourishing that there was not wind enough for her to start, was dispelled by the sight of her topsail going up. More than ever at that radiant moment—as the reflection of the white sail quivered on the tranquil blue, and the still water flattered all it reproduced, like a fashionable photographer—did I agree with George Herbert's advice, "Praise the sea, but stay on shore."

"We must hail her, I suppose," I said drearily. I assailed the *Eileen Oge*, such being her inappropriate name, with desolate cries, but achieved no immediate result beyond the assembling of some village children round us and our luggage.

"Mr. Shute and the two ladies was after screeching here for the boat awhile ago," volunteered a horrid little girl, whom I had already twice frustrated in the attempt to seat an infant relative on our bundle of rugs. "Timsy Hallahane says 'twould be as good for them to stay ashore, for there isn't as much wind outside as'd out a candle."

With this encouraging statement the little girl devoted herself to the alternate consumption of gooseberries and cockles.

All things come to those who wait, and to us arrived at length the gig of the *Eileen Oge*, and such, by this time, were the temperature and the smells of the quay that I actually welcomed the moment that found us leaving it for the yacht.

"Now, Sinclair, aren't you glad we came?" remarked Philippa, as the clear green water deepened under us, and a light briny air came coolly round us with the motion of the boat.

As she spoke, there was an outburst of screams from the children on the quay, followed by a heavy splash.

"Oh stop!" cried Philippa in an agony; "one of them has fallen in! I can see its poor little brown head!"

"'Tis a dog, ma'am," said briefly the man who was rowing stroke.

"One might have wished it had been that little girl," said I, as I steered to the best of my ability for the yacht.

We had traversed another twenty yards or so, when Philippa, in a voice in which horror and triumph were strangely blended, exclaimed, "She's following us!"

"Who? The little girl?" I asked callously.

"No," returned Philippa; "worse."

I looked round, not without a prevision of what I was to see, and beheld the faithful Maria swimming steadily after us, with her brown muzzle thrust out in front of her, ripping through the reflections like a plough.

"Go home!" I roared, standing up and gesticulating in fury that I well knew to be impotent. "Go home, you brute!"

Maria redoubled her efforts, and Philippa murmured uncontrollably—

"She's following us!"

"Well, she *is* a dear!"

Had I had a sword in my hand I should undoubtedly have slain Philippa; but before I could express my sentiments in any way, a violent shock flung me endways on top of the man who was pulling stroke. Thanks to Maria, we had reached our destination all unawares; the two men, respectfully awaiting my instructions, had rowed on with disciplined steadiness, and, as a result, we had rammed the *Eileen Oge* amidships, with a vigour that brought Mr. Shute tumbling up the companion to see what had happened.

"Oh, it's you, is it?" he said, with his mouth full. "Come in; don't knock! Delighted to see you, Mrs. Yeates; don't apologise. There's nothing like a hired ship after all—it's quite jolly to see the splinters fly—shows you're getting your money's worth. Hullo! who's this?"

This was Maria, feigning exhaustion, and noisily treading water at the boat's side.

"What, poor old Maria? Wanted to send her ashore, did he? Heartless ruffian!"

Thus was Maria installed on board the *Eileen Oge*, and the element of fatality had already begun to work.

There was just enough wind to take us out of Clountiss Harbour, and with the last of the out-running tide we crept away to the west. The party on board consisted of our host's sister, Miss Cecilia Shute, Miss Sally Knox, and ourselves; we sat about in conventional attitudes in deck chairs and on adamantine deck bosses, and I talked to Miss Shute with feverish brilliancy, and wished the patience-cards were not in the cabin; I knew the supreme importance of keeping one's mind occupied, but I dared not face the cabin. There was a long, almost imperceptible swell, with little queer seabirds that I have never seen before—and trust I never shall again— dotted about on its glassy slopes. The coast-line looked low and grey and dull, as, I think, coast-lines always do when viewed from the deep. The breeze that Bernard had promised us we should find outside was barely enough to keep us moving. The burning sun of four o'clock focussed its heat on the deck; Bernard stood up among us, engaged in what he was pleased to call "handling the stick," and beamed almost as offensively as the sun.

"Oh, we're slipping along," he said, his odiously healthy face glowing like copper against the blazing blue sky. "You're going a great deal faster than you think, and the men say we'll pick up a breeze once we're round the Mizen."

I made no reply; I was not feeling ill, merely thoroughly disinclined for conversation. Miss Sally smiled wanly, and closing her eyes, laid her head on Philippa's knee. Instructed by a dread free-masonry, I knew that for her the moment had come when she could no longer bear to see the rail rise slowly above the horizon, and with an equal rhythmic slowness sink below it. Maria moved restlessly to and fro, panting and yawning, and occasionally rearing herself on her hind-legs against the side, and staring forth with wild eyes at the headachy sliding of the swell. Perhaps she was meditating suicide; if so I sympathised with her, and since she was obviously going to be sick I trusted that she would bring off the suicide with as little delay as possible. Philippa and Miss Shute sat in unaffected serenity in deck chairs, and stitched at white things—teacloths for the *Eileen Oge*, I believe, things in themselves a mockery—and talked untiringly, with that singular indifference to their marine surroundings that I have often observed in ladies who are not sea-sick. It always stirs me afresh to wonder why they had not remained ashore; nevertheless, I prefer their tranquil and total lack of interest in seafaring matters to the blatant Vikingism of the average male who is similarly placed.

Somehow, I know not how, we crawled onwards, and by about five o'clock we had rounded the Mizen, a gaunt spike of a headland that starts up like a boar's tusk above the ragged lip of the Irish coast, and the *Eileen Oge* was beginning to swing and wallop in the long sluggish rollers that the American liners know and despise. I was very far from despising them. Down in the west, resting on the sea's rim, a purple bank of clouds lay awaiting the descent of the sun, as seductively and as malevolently as a damp bed at a hotel awaits a traveller.

The end, so far as I was concerned, came at tea-time. The meal had been prepared in the saloon, and thither it became incumbent on me to accompany my hostess and my wife. Miss Sally, long past speech, opened, at the suggestion of tea, one eye, and disclosed a look of horror. As I tottered down the companion I respected her good sense. The *Eileen Oge* had been built early in the sixties, and head-room was not her strong point; neither, apparently, was ventilation. I began by dashing my forehead against the frame of the cabin door, and then, shattered morally and physically, entered into the atmosphere of the pit. After which things, and the sight of a plate of rich cake, I retired in good order to my cabin, and began upon the Yanatas.

I pass over some painful intermediate details and resume at the moment when Bernard Shute woke me from a drugged slumber to announce that dinner was over.

"It's been raining pretty hard," he said, swaying easily with the swing of the yacht; "but we've got a clinking breeze, and we ought to make Lurriga Harbour to-night. There's good anchorage there, the men say. They're rather a lot of swabs, but they know this coast, and I don't. I took 'em over with the ship all standing."

"Where are we now?" I asked, something heartened by the blessed word "anchorage."

"You're running up Sheepskin Bay—it's a thundering big bay; Lurriga's up at the far end of it, and the night's as black as the inside of a cow. Dig out and get something to eat, and come on deck—What! no dinner?"—I had spoken morosely, with closed eyes—"Oh, rot! you're on an even keel now. I promised Mrs. Yeates I'd make you dig out. You're as bad as a soldier officer that we were ferrying to Malta one time in the old *Tamar*. He got one leg out of his berth when we were going down the Channel, and he was too sick to pull it in again till we got to Gib!"

I compromised on a drink and some biscuits. The ship was certainly steadier, and I felt sufficiently restored to climb weakly on deck. It was by this time past ten o'clock, and heavy clouds blotted out the last of the afterglow, and smothered the stars at their birth. A wet warm wind was lashing the *Eileen Oge* up a wide estuary; the waves were hunting her, hissing under her stern, racing up to her, crested with the white glow of phosphorus, as she fled before them. I dimly discerned in the greyness the more solid greyness of the shore. The mainsail loomed out into the darkness, nearly at right angles to the yacht, with the boom creaking as the following wind gave us an additional shove. I know nothing of yacht sailing, but I can appreciate the grand fact that in running before a wind the boom is removed from its usual sphere of devastation.

I sat down beside a bundle of rugs that I had discovered to be my wife, and thought of my whitewashed office at Shreelane and its bare but stationary floor, with a yearning that was little short of passion. Miss Sally had long since succumbed; Miss Shute was tired, and had turned in soon after dinner.

"I suppose she's overdone by the delirious gaiety of the afternoon," said I acridly, in reply to this information.

Philippa cautiously poked forth her head from the rugs, like a tortoise from under its shell, to see that Bernard, who was standing near the steersman, was out of hearing.

"In all your life, Sinclair," she said impressively, "you never knew such a time as Cecilia and I have had down there! We've had to wash *everything* in the cabins, and remake the beds, and *hurl* the sheets away—they were covered with black finger-marks—and while we were doing that, in came the creature that calls himself the steward, to ask if he might get something of his that he had left in Miss Shute's 'birthplace'! and he rooted out from under Cecilia's mattress a pair of socks and half a loaf of bread!"

"Consolation to Miss Shute to know her berth has been well aired," I said, with the nearest approach to enjoyment I had known since I came on board; "and has Sally made any equally interesting discoveries?"

"She said she didn't care what her bed was like; she just

dropped into it. I must say I am sorry for her," went on Philippa; "she hated coming. Her mother made her accept."

"I wonder if Lady Knox will make her accept *him!*" I said. "How often has Sally refused him, does any one know?"

"Oh, about once a week," replied Philippa; "just the way I kept on refusing you, you know!"

Something cold and wet was thrust into my hand, and the aroma of damp dog arose upon the night air; Maria had issued from some lair at the sound of our voices, and was now, with palsied tremblings, slowly trying to drag herself on to my lap.

"Poor thing, she's been so dreadfully ill," said Philippa. "Don't send her away, Sinclair. Mr. Shute found her lying on his berth not able to move; didn't you, Mr. Shute?"

"She found out that she was able to move," said Bernard, who had crossed to our side of the deck; "it was somehow borne in upon her when I got at her with a boot-tree. I wouldn't advise you to keep her in your lap, Yeates. She stole half a ham after dinner, and she might take a notion to make the only reparation in her power."

I stood up and stretched myself stiffly. The wind was freshening, and though the growing smoothness of the water told that we were making shelter of some kind, for all that I could see of land we might as well have been in mid-ocean. The heaving lift of the deck under my feet, and the lurching swing when a stronger gust filled the ghostly sails, were more disquieting to me in suggestion than in reality, and, to my surprise, I found something almost enjoyable in rushing through darkness at the pace at which we were going.

"We're a small bit short of the mouth of Lurriga Harbour yet, sir," said the man who was steering, in reply to a question from Bernard. "I can see the shore well enough; sure I know every yard of wather in the bay——"

As he spoke he sat down abruptly and violently; so did Bernard, so did I. The bundle that contained Philippa collapsed upon Maria.

"Main sheet!" bellowed Bernard, on his feet in an instant, as the boom swung in and out again with a terrific jerk. "We're ashore!"

In response to this order three men in succession fell over me while I was still struggling on the deck, and something that was either Philippa's elbow, or the acutest angle of Maria's skull, hit me in the face. As I found my feet the cabin skylight was suddenly illuminated by a wavering glare. I got across the slanting deck somehow, through the confusion of shouting men and the flapping thunder of the sails, and saw through the skylight a gush of flame rising from a pool of fire around an overturned lamp on the swing-table. I avalanched down the companion and was squandered like an avalanche on the floor at the foot of it. Even as I fell, McCarthy the steward dragged the strip of carpet from the cabin floor and threw it on the blaze; I found myself, in some unexplained way, snatching a railway rug from Miss Shute and applying it to the same purpose, and in half-a-dozen seconds we had smothered the flame and were left in total darkness. The most striking feature of the situation was the immovability of the yacht.

"Great Ned!" said McCarthy, invoking I know not what heathen deity, "is it on the bottom of the say we are? Well, whether or no, thank God we have the fire quinched!"

We were not, so far, at the bottom of the sea, but during the next ten minutes the chances seemed in favour of our getting there. The yacht had run her bows upon a sunken ridge of rock, and after a period of feminine indecision as to whether she were going to slide off again, or roll over into deep water, she elected to stay where she was, and the gig was lowered with all speed, in order to tow her off before the tide left her.

My recollection of this interval is but hazy, but I can certify that in ten minutes I had swept together an assortment of necessaries and knotted them into my counterpane, had broken the string of my eye-glass, and lost my silver matchbox; had found Philippa's curling-tongs and put them in my pocket; had carted all the luggage on deck; had then applied myself to the manly duty of reassuring the ladies, and had found Miss Shute merely bored, Philippa enthusiastically anxious to be allowed to help to pull the gig, and Miss Sally radiantly restored to health and spirits by the cessation of movement and the probability of an early escape from the yacht.

The rain had, with its usual opportuneness, begun again; we stood in it under umbrellas, and watched the gig jumping on its tow-rope like a dog on a string, as its crew plied the labouring oar in futile endeavour to move the *Eileen Oge*. We had run on the rock at half-tide, and the increasing slant of the deck as the tide fell brought home to us the pleasing probability that at low water—viz, about 2 A.M.—we should roll off the rock and go to the bottom. Had Bernard Shute wished to show himself in the most advantageous light to Miss Sally he could scarcely have bettered the situation. I looked on in helpless respect while he whom I had known as the scourge of the hunting field, the terror of the shooting party, rose to the top of a difficult position and kept there, and my respect was, if possible, increased by the presence of mind with which he availed himself of all critical moments to place a protecting arm round Miss Knox.

By about 1 A.M. the two gaffs with which Bernard had contrived to shore up the slowly heeling yacht began to show signs of yielding, and, in approved shipwreck fashion, we took to the boats, the yacht's crew in the gig remaining in attendance on what seemed likely to be the last moments of the *Eileen Oge*, while we, in the dinghy, sought for the harbour. Owing to the tilt of the yacht's deck, and the roughness of the broken water round her, getting into the boat was no mean feat of gymnastics. Miss Sally did it like a bird, alighting in the inevitable arms of Bernard; Miss Shute followed very badly, but, by innate force of character, successfully; Philippa, who was enjoying every moment of her shipwreck, came last, launching herself into the dinghy with my silver shoe-horn clutched in one hand, and in the other the tea-basket. I heard the hollow clank of its tin cups as she sprang, and appreciated the heroism with which Bernard received one of its corners in his waist. How or when Maria left the yacht I know not, but when I applied myself to the bow oar I led off with three crabs, owing to the devotion with which she thrust her head into my lap.

I am no judge of these matters, but in my opinion we ought to have been swamped several times during that row. There was nothing but the phosphorus of breaking waves to tell us where the rocks were, and nothing to show where the harbour was except a solitary light, a masthead light, as we supposed. The skipper had assured us that we could not go wrong if we kept "a westerly course with a little northing in it;" but it seemed simpler to steer for the light, and we did so. The dinghy climbed along over the waves with an agility that was safer than it felt; the rain fell without haste and without rest, the oars were as inflexible as crowbars, and somewhat resembled them in shape and weight; nevertheless, it was Elysium when compared with the afternoon leisure of the deck of the *Eileen Oge*.

At last we came, unexplainably, into smooth water, and it was at about this time that we were first aware that the darkness was less dense than it had been, and that the rain had ceased. By imperceptible degrees a greyness touched the back of the waves, more a dreariness than a dawn, but more welcome than thousands of gold and silver. I looked over my shoulder and discerned vague bulky things ahead; as I did so, my oar was suddenly wrapped in seaweed. We crept on; Maria stood up with her paws on the gunwale, and whined in high agitation. The dark objects ahead resolved themselves into rocks, and without more ado Maria pitched herself into the water. In half a minute we heard her shaking herself on shore. We slid on; the water swelled under the dinghy, and lifted her keel on to grating gravel.

"We couldn't have done it better if we'd been the Hydrographer Royal," said Bernard, wading knee-deep in a light wash of foam, with the painter in his hand; "but all the same, that masthead light is some one's bedroom candle!"

We landed, hauled up the boat, and then feebly sat down on our belongings to review the situation, and Maria came and shook herself over each of us in turn. We had run into a little cove, guided by the philanthropic beam of a candle in the upper window of a house about a hundred yards away. The candle still burned on, and the anæmic day-light exhibited to us our surroundings, and we debated as to whether we could at 2.45 A.M. present ourselves as objects of compassion to the owner of the candle. I need hardly say that it was the ladies who decided on making the attempt, having, like most of their sex, a courage incomparably superior to ours in such matters; Bernard and I had not a grain of genuine compunction in our souls, but we failed in nerve.

We trailed up from the cove, laden with emigrants' bundles, stumbling on wet rocks in the half-light, and succeeded in making our way to the house.

It was a small two-storeyed building, of that hideous breed of architecture usually dedicated to the rectories of the Irish Church; we felt that there was something friendly in the presence of a pair of carpet slippers in the porch, but there was a hint of exclusiveness in the fact that there was no knocker and that the bell was broken. The light still burned in the upper window, and with a faltering hand I flung gravel at the glass. This summons was appallingly responded to by a shriek; there was a flutter of white at the panes, and the candle was extinguished.

"Come away!" exclaimed Miss Shute, "it's a lunatic asylum!"

We stood our ground, however, and presently heard a footstep within, a blind was poked aside in another window, and we were inspected by an unseen inmate; then some one came downstairs, and the hall door was opened by a small man with a bald head and a long sandy beard. He was attired in a brief dressing-gown, and on his should sat, like an angry ghost, a large white cockatoo. Its crest was up on end, its beak was a good two inches long and curved like a Malay kris; its claws gripped the little man's shoulder. Maria uttered in the background a low and thunderous growl.

"Don't take any notice of the bird, please," said the little man nervously, seeing our united gaze fixed upon this apparition; "he's extremely fierce if annoyed."

Our entertainer

The majority of our party here melted away to either side of the hall door, and I was left to do the explaining. The tale of our misfortunes had its due effect, and we were ushered into a small drawing-room, our host holding open the door for us, like a nightmare footman with bare shins, a gnome-like bald head, and an unclean spirit swaying on his shoulder. He opened the shutters, and we sat decorously round the room, as at an afternoon party, while the situation was further expounded on both sides. Our entertainer, indeed, favoured us with the leading items of his family history, amongst them the facts that he was a Dr. Fahy from Cork, who had taken somebody's rectory for the summer, and had been prevailed on by some of his patients to permit them to join him as paying guests.

"I said it was a lunatic asylum," murmured Miss Shute to me.

"In point of fact," went on our host, "there isn't an empty room in the house, which is why I can only offer your party the use of this room and the kitchen fire, which I make a point of keeping burning all night."

He leaned back complacently in his chair, and crossed his legs; then, obviously remembering his costume, sat bolt upright again. We owed the guiding beams of the candle to the owner of the cockatoo, an old Mrs. Buck, who was, we gathered, the most paying of all the patients, and also, obviously, the one most feared and cherished by Dr. Fahy. "She has a candle burning all night for the bird, and her door open to let him walk about the house when he likes," said Dr. Fahy; "indeed, I may say her passion for him amounts to dementia. He's very fond of me, and Mrs. Fahy's always telling me I should be thankful, as whatever he did we'd be bound to put up with it!"

Dr. Fahy had evidently a turn for conversation that was unaffected by circumstance; the first beams of the early sun were lighting up the rep chair covers before the door closed upon his brown dressing-gown, and upon the stately white back of the cockatoo, and the demoniac possession of laughter that had wrought in us during the interview burst forth unchecked. It was most painful and exhausting, as such laughter always is; but by far the most serious part of it was that Miss Sally, who was sitting in the window, somehow drove her elbow through a pane of glass, and Bernard, in pulling down the blind to conceal the damage, tore it off the roller.

There followed on this catastrophe a period during which reason tottered and Maria barked furiously. Philippa was the first to pull herself together, and to suggest an adjournment to the kitchen fire that, in honour of the paying guests, was never quenched, and, respecting the repose of the household, we proceeded thither with a stealth that convinced Maria we were engaged in a rat hunt. The boots of paying guests littered the floor, the débris of their last repast covered the table; a cat in some unseen fastness crooned a war song to Maria, who feigned unconsciousness and fell to scientific research in the scullery.

We roasted our boots at the range, and Bernard, with all a sailor's gift for exploration and theft, prowled in noisome purlieus and emerged with a jug of milk and a lump of salt butter. No one who has not been a burglar can at all realise what it was to roam through Dr. Fahy's basement storey, with the rookery of paying guests asleep above, and to feel that, so far, we had repaid his confidence by breaking a pane of glass and a blind, and putting the scullery tap out of order. I have always maintained that there was something wrong with it before I touched it, but the fact remains that when I had filled Philippa's kettle, no human power could prevail upon it to stop flowing. For all I know to the contrary it is running still.

It was in the course of our furtive return to the drawing-room that we were again confronted by Mrs. Buck's cockatoo. It was standing in malign meditation on the stairs, and on seeing us it rose, without a word of warning, upon the wing, and with a long screech flung itself at Miss Sally's golden-red head, which a ran of sunlight had chanced to illumine. There was a moment of stampede, as the selected victim, pursued by the cockatoo, fled into the drawing-room; two chairs were upset (one, I think, broken), Miss Sally enveloped herself in a window curtain, Philippa and Miss Shute effaced themselves beneath a table; the cockatoo, foiled of its prey, skimmed, still screeching, round the ceiling. It was Bernard who, with a well-directed sofa-cushion, drove the enemy from the room. There was only a chink of the door open, but the cockatoo turned on his side as he flew, and swung through it like a woodcock.

We slammed the door behind him, and at the same instant there came a thumping on the floor overhead, muffled, yet peremptory.

"That's Mrs. Buck!" said Miss Shute, crawling from under the table; "the room over this is the one that had the candle in it."

We sat for a time in awful stillness, but nothing further happened, save a distant shriek overhead, that told the cockatoo had sought and found sanctuary in his owner's room. We had tea *sotto voce*, and then, one by one, despite the amazing discomfort of the drawing-room chairs, we dozed off to sleep.

It was at about five o'clock that I woke with a stiff neck and an uneasy remembrance that I had last seen Maria in the kitchen. The others, looking, each of them, about twenty years older than their age, slept in various attitudes of exhaustion. Bernard opened his eyes as I stole forth to look for Maria, but none of the ladies awoke. I went down the evil-smelling passage that led to the kitchen stairs, and, there on a mat, regarding me with intelligent affection, was Maria; but what—oh what was the white thing that lay between her forepaws?

The situation was too serious to be coped with alone. I fled noiselessly back to the drawing-room and put my head in; Bernard's eyes—blessed be the light sleep of sailors!—opened again, and there was that in mine that summoned him forth. (Blessed also be the light step of sailors!)

We took the corpse from Maria, withholding perforce the language and the slaughtering that our hearts ached to bestow. For a minute or two our eyes communed.

"I'll get the kitchen shovel," breathed Bernard; "you open the hall door!"

A moment later we passed like spirits into the open air, and on into a little garden at the end of the house. Maria followed us, licking her lips. There were beds of nasturtiums, and of purple stocks, and of marigolds. We chose a bed of stocks, a plump bed, that looked like easy digging. The windows were all tightly shut and shuttered, and I took the cockatoo from under my coat and hid it, temporarily, behind a box border. Bernard had brought a shovel and a coal scoop. We dug like badgers. At eighteen inches we got down into shale and stones, and the coal scoop struck work.

"Never mind," said Bernard; "we'll plant the stocks on top of him."

It was a lovely morning, with a new-born blue sky and a light northerly breeze. As we returned to the house, we looked across the wavelets of the little cove and saw, above the rocky point round which we had groped last night, a triangular white patch moving slowly along.

"The tide's lifted her!" said Bernard, standing stock-still. He looked at Mrs. Buck's window and at me. "Yeates!" he whispered, "let's quit!"

It was now barely six o'clock, and not a soul was stirring. We woke the ladies and convinced them of the high importance of catching the tide. Bernard left a note on the hall table for Dr. Fahy, a beautiful note of leave-taking and gratitude, and apology for the broken window (for which he begged to enclose half-a-crown). No allusion was made to the other casualties. As we neared the strand he found an occasion to say to me:

"I put in a postscript that I thought it best to mention that I had seen the cockatoo in the garden, and hoped it would get back all right. That's quite true, you know! But look here, whatever you do, you must keep it all dark from the ladies——"

At this juncture Maria overtook us with the cockatoo in her mouth.

Eleven

OCCASIONAL LICENSES

"IT's out of the question," I said, looking forbiddingly at Mrs. Moloney through the spokes of the bicycle that I was pumping up outside the grocer's in Skebawn.

"Well, indeed, Major Yeates," said Mrs. Moloney, advancing excitedly, and placing on the nickel plating a hand that I had good and recent cause to know was warm, "sure I know well that if th' angel Gabriel came down from heaven looking for a license for the races, your honour wouldn't give it to him without a charackther, but as for Michael! Sure, the world knows what Michael is!"

I had been waiting for Philippa for already nearly half-an-hour, and my temper was not at its best.

"Character or no character, Mrs. Moloney," said I with asperity, "the magistrates have settled to give no occasional licenses, and if Michael were as sober as——"

"Is it sober! God help us!" exclaimed Mrs. Moloney with an upward rolling of her eye to the Recording Angel; "I'll tell your honour the truth. I'm his wife, now, fifteen years, and I never seen the sign of dhrink on Michael only once, and that was when he went out o' good nature helping Timsy Ryan to whitewash his house, and Timsy and himself had a couple o' pots o' porther, and look, he was as little used to it that his head got light, and he walked away out to dhrive in the cows and it no more than eleven o'clock in the day! And the cows, the craytures, as much surprised, goin' hither and over the four corners of the road from him! Faith, ye'd have to laugh. 'Michael,' says I to him, 'ye're dhrunk!' 'I am,' says he, and the tears rained from his eyes. I turned the cows from him. 'Go home,' I says, 'and lie down on Willy Tom's bed——'"

At this affecting point my wife came out of the grocer's with a large parcel to be strapped to my handlebar, and the history of Mr. Moloney's solitary lapse from sobriety got no further than Willy Tom's bed.

"You see," I said to Philippa, as we bicycled quietly home through the hot June afternoon, "we've settled we'll give no licenses for the sports. Why even young Sheehy, who owns three pubs in Skebawn, came to me and said he hoped the magistrates would be firm about it, as these one-day licenses were quite unnecessary, and only led to drunkenness and fighting, and every man on the Bench has joined in promising not to grant any."

"How nice, dear!" Philippa absently. "Do you know Mrs. McDonnell can only let me have three dozen cups and saucers; I wonder if that will be enough?"

"Do you mean to say you expect three dozen people?" said I.

"Oh, it's always well to be prepared," replied my wife evasively.

During the next few days I realised the true inwardness of what it was to be prepared for an entertainment of this kind. Games were not at a high level in my district. Football, of a wild, guerilla species, was waged intermittently, blended in some inextricable way with Home Rule and a brass band, and on Sundays gatherings of young men rolled a heavy round stone along the roads, a rudimentary form of sport, whose fascination lay primarily in the fact that it was illegal, and, in lesser degree, in betting on the length of each roll. I had had a period of enthusiasm, during which I thought I was going to be the apostle of cricket in the neighbourhood, but my mission dwindled to single wicket with Peter Cadogan, who was indulgent but bored, and I swiped the ball through the dining-room window, and some one took one of the stumps to poke the laundry fire. Once a year, however, on that festival of the Roman Catholic Church which is familiarly known as "Pether and Paul's day," the district was wont to make a spasmodic effort at athletic sports, which were duly patronised by the gentry and promoted by the publicans, and this year the honour of a steward's green rosette was conferred upon me. Philippa's genius for hospitality here saw its chance, and broke forth into unbridled tea-party in connection with the sports, even involving me in the hire of a tent, the conveyance of chairs and tables, and other large operations.

It chanced that Flurry Knox had on this occasion lent the fields for the sports, with the proviso that horse-races and a tug-of-war were to be added to the usual programme; Flurry's participation in events of this kind seldom failed to be of an inflaming character. As he and I planted larch spars for the high jump, and stuck furze-bushes into hurdles (locally known as "hurrls"), and skirmished hourly with people who wanted to sell drink on the course, I thought that my next summer leave would singularly coincide with the festival consecrated to St. Peter and St. Paul. We made a grand stand of quite four feet high, out of old fish-boxes, which smelt worse and worse as the day wore on, but was, none the less, as sought after by those for whom it was not intended, as is the Royal enclosure at Ascot; we broke gaps in all the fences to allow carriages on to the ground, we armed a gang of the worst blackguards in Skebawn with cart-whips, to keep the course, and felt that organisation could go no further.

The momentous day of Pether and Paul opened badly, with heavy clouds and every indication of rain, but after a few thunder showers things brightened, and it seemed within the bounds of possibility that the weather might hold up. When I got down to the course on the day of the sports the first thing I saw was a tent of that peculiar filthy grey that usually enshrines the sale of porter, with an array of barrels in a crate beside it; I bore down upon it in all the indignant majesty of the law, and in so doing came upon Flurry Knox, who was engaged in flogging boys off the Grand Stand.

"Sheehy's gone one better than you!" he said, without taking any trouble to conceal the fact that he was amused.

"Sheehy!" I said; "why, Sheehy was the man who went to every magistrate in the country to ask them to refuse a license for the sports."

"Yes, he took some trouble to prevent any one else having a look in," replied Flurry; "he asked every magistrate but one, and that was the one that gave him the license."

"You don't mean to say that it was you?" I demanded in high wrath and suspicion, remembering that Sheehy bred horses, and that my friend Mr. Knox was a person of infinite resource in the matter of a deal.

"Well, well," said Flurry, rearranging a disordered fish-box, "and me that's a churchwarden, and sprained my ankle a month ago with running downstairs at my grandmother's to be in time for prayers! Where's the use of a good character in this country?"

"Not much when you keep it eating its head off for want of exercise," I retorted; "but if it wasn't you, who was it?"

"Do you remember old Moriarty out at Castle Ire?"

I remembered him extremely well as one of those representatives of the people with whom a paternal Government had leavened the effete ranks of the Irish magistracy.

"Well," resumed Flurry, "that license was as good as a five-pound note in his pocket."

I permitted myself a comment on Mr. Moriarty suitable to the occasion.

"Oh, that's nothing," said Flurry easily; "he told me one day when he was half screwed that his Commission of the Peace was worth a hundred and fifty a year to him in turkeys and whisky, and he was telling the truth for once."

At this point Flurry's eye wandered, and following its direction I saw Lady Knox's smart 'bus cleaving its way through the throngs of country people, lurching over the ups and downs of the field like a ship in a sea. I was too blind to make out the component parts of the white froth that crowned it on top, and seethed forth from it when it had taken up a position near the tent in which Philippa was even now propping the legs of the tea-table, but from the fact that Flurry addressed himself to the door, I argued that Miss Sally had gone inside.

Lady Knox's manner had something more than its usual bleakness. She had brought, as she promised, a large contingent, but from the way that the strangers within her gates melted impalpably and left me to deal with her single-handed, I drew the further deduction that all was not well.

"Did you ever in your life see such a gang of women as I have brought with me?" she began with her wonted directness, as I piloted her to the Grand Stand, and placed her on the stoutest looking of the fish-boxes. "I have no patience with men who yacht! Bernard Shute has gone off to the Clyde, and I had counted on his being a man at my dance next week. I suppose you'll tell me you're going away too."

I assured Lady Knox that I would be a man to the best of my ability.

"This is the last dance I shall give," went on her ladyship, unappeased; "the men in this country consist of children and cads."

I admitted that we were but a poor lot, "but," I said, "Miss Sally told me——"

"Sally's a fool!" said Lady Knox, with a falcon eye at her daughter, who happened to be talking to her distant kinsman, Mr. Flurry of that ilk.

The races had by this time begun with a competition known as the "Hop, Step, and Lep"; this, judging by the yells, was a highly interesting display, but as it was conducted between two impervious rows of onlookers, the aristocracy on the fish-boxes saw nothing save the occasional purple face of a competitor, starting into view above the wall of backs like a jack-in-the-box. For me, however, the odorous sanctuary of the fish-boxes was not to be. I left it guarded by Slipper with

a cart-whip of flail-like dimensions, as disreputable an object as could be seen out of low comedy, with some one's old white cords on his bandy legs, butcher-boots three sizes too big for him, and a black eye. The small boys fled before him; in the glory of his office he would have flailed his own mother off the fish-boxes had occasion served.

I had an afternoon of decidedly mixed enjoyment. My stewardship blossomed forth like Aaron's rod, and added to itself the duties of starter, handicapper, general referee, and chucker-out, besides which I from time to time strove with emissaries who came from Philippa with messages about water

He would have flailed his own mother had occasion served

and kettles. Flurry and I had to deal single-handed with the foot-races (our brothers in office being otherwise engaged at Mr. Sheehy's), a task of many difficulties, chiefest being that the spectators all swept forward at the word "Go!" and ran the race with the competitors, yelling curses, blessings, and advice upon them, taking short cuts over anything and everybody,

and mingling inextricably with the finish. By fervent applica-
tions of the whips, the course was to some extent purged for
the quarter-mile, and it would, I believe, have been a triumph
of handicapping had not an unforeseen disaster overtaken the
favourite—old Mrs. Knox's bath-chair boy. Whether, as was
alleged, his braces had or had not been tampered with by a
rival was a matter that the referee had subsequently to deal
with in the thick of a free fight; but the painful fact remained
that in the course of the first lap what were described as "his
galluses" abruptly severed their connection with the garments
for whose safety they were responsible, and the favourite
was obliged to seek seclusion in the crowd.

The tug-of-war followed close on this *contretemps*, and had
the excellent effect of drawing away, like a blister, the inflam-
mation set up by the grievances of the bath-chair boy. I cannot
at this moment remember of how many men each team
consisted; my sole aim was to keep the numbers even, and to
baffle the volunteers who, in an ecstasy of sympathy, attached
themselves to the tail of the rope at moments when their
champions weakened. The rival forces dug their heels in and
tugged, in an uproar that drew forth the innermost line of
customers from Mr. Sheehy's porter tent, and even attracted
"the quality" from the haven of the fish-boxes, Slipper, in the
capacity of Squire of Dames, pioneering Lady Knox through
the crowd with the cart-whip, and with language whose nature
was providentially veiled, for the most part, by the din. The tug-
of-war continued unabated. One team was getting the worst of
it, but hung doggedly on, sinking lower and lower till they
gradually sat down; nothing short of the trump of judgment
could have conveyed to them that they were breaking rules,
and both teams settled down by slow degrees on to their sides,
with the rope under them, and their heels still planted in the
ground, bringing about complete deadlock. I do not know
the record duration for a tug-of-war, but I can certify that the
Cullinagh and Knockranny teams lay on the ground at full
tension for half-an-hour, like men in apoplectic fits, each man

with his respective adherents howling over him, blessing him, and adjuring him to continue.

With my own nauseated eyes I saw a bearded countryman, obviously one of Mr. Sheehy's best customers, fling himself on his knees beside one of the combatants, and kiss his crimson and streaming face in a rapture of encouragement. As he shoved unsteadily past me on his return journey to Mr. Sheehy's, I heard him informing a friend that "he cried a handful over Danny Mulloy, when he seen the poor brave boy so shtubborn, and, indeed, he couldn't say why he cried."

"For good nature ye'd cry," suggested the friend.

"Well, just that, I suppose," returned Danny Mulloy's admirer resignedly; "indeed, if it was only two cocks ye seen fightin' on the road, yer heart'd take part with one o' them!"

I had begun to realise that I might as well abandon the tug-of-war and occupy myself elsewhere, when my wife's much harassed messenger brought me the portentous tidings that Mrs. Yeates wanted me at the tent at once. When I arrived I found the tent literally bulging with Philippa's guests; Lady Knox, seated on a hamper, was taking off her gloves, and loudly announcing her desire for tea, and Philippa, with a flushed face and a crooked hat, breathed into my ear the awful news that both the cream and the milk had been forgotten.

"But Flurry Knox says he can get me some," she went on; "he's gone to send people to milk a cow that lives near here. Go out and see if he's coming."

I went out and found, in the first instance, Mrs. Cadogan, who greeted me with the prayer that the divil might roast Julia McCarthy, that legged it away to the races like a wild goose, and left the cream afther her on the servants' hall table. "Sure, Misther Flurry's gone looking for a cow, and what cow would there be in a backwards place like this? And look at me shtriving to keep the kettle simpering on the fire, and not as much coals undher it as'd redden a pipe!"

"Where's Mr. Knox?" I asked.

"Himself and Slipper's galloping the counthry like the deer. I believe it's to the house above they went, sir."

I followed up a rocky hill to the house above, and there found Flurry and Slipper engaged in the patriarchal task of driving two brace of coupled and spancelled goats into a shed.

"It's the best we can do," said Flurry briefly; "there isn't a cow to be found, and the people are all down at the sports. Be d——d to you, Slipper, don't let them go from you!" as the goats charged and doubled like football players.

"But goats' milk!" I said, paralysed by horrible memories of what tea used to taste like at Gib.

"They'll never know it!" said Flurry, cornering a venerable nanny; "here, hold this divil, and hold her tight!"

I have no time to dwell upon the pastoral scene that followed. Suffice it to say, that at the end of ten minutes of scorching profanity from Slipper, and incessant warfare with the goats, the latter had reluctantly yielded two small jugfuls, and the dairymaids had exhibited a nerve and skill in their trade that won my lasting respect.

"I knew I could trust *you*, Mr. Knox!" said Philippa, with shining eyes, as we presented her with the two foaming beakers. I suppose a man is never a hero to his wife, but if she could have realised the bruises on my legs, I think she would have reserved a blessing for me also.

What was thought of the goats' milk I gathered symptomatically from a certain fixity of expression that accompanied the first sip of the tea, and from observing that comparatively few ventured on second cups. I also noted that after a brief conversation with Flurry, Miss Sally poured hers secretly on to the grass. Lady Knox had throughout the day preserved an aspect so threatening that no change was perceptible in her demeanour. In the throng of hungry guests I did not for some time notice that Mr. Knox had withdrawn until something in Miss Sally's eye summoned me to her, and she told me she had a message from him for me.

"Couldn't we come outside?" she said.

Outside the tent, within less than six yards of her mother, Miss Sally confided to me a scheme that made my hair stand on end. Summarised, it amounted to this: That, first, she was in the primary stage of a deal with Sheehy for a four-year-old chestnut colt, for which Sheehy was asking double its value on the assumption that it had no rival in the country; that, secondly, they had just heard it was going to run in the first race; and, thirdly and lastly, that as there was no other horse available, Flurry was going to take old Sultan out of the 'bus and ride him in the race; and that Mrs. Yeates had promised to keep mamma safe in the tent, while the race was going on, and "you know, Major Yeates, it would be delightful to beat Sheehy after his getting the better of you all about the license!"

With this base appeal to my professional feelings, Miss Knox paused, and looked at me insinuatingly. Her eyes were greeny-grey, and very beguiling.

"Come on," she said; "they want you to start them!"

Pursued by visions of the just wrath of Lady Knox, I weakly followed Miss Sally to the farther end of the second field, from which point the race was to start. The course was not a serious one: two or three natural banks, a stone wall, and a couple of "hurrls." There were but four riders, including Flurry, who was seated composedly on Sultan, smoking a cigarette and talking confidentially to Slipper. Sultan, although something stricken in years and touched in the wind, was a brown horse who in his day had been a hunter of no mean repute; even now he occasionally carried Lady Knox in a sedate and gentlemanly manner, but it struck me that it was trying him rather high to take him from the pole of the 'bus after twelve miles on a hilly road, and hustle him over a country against a four-year-old. My acutest anxiety, however, was to start the race as quickly as possible, and to get back to the tent in time to establish an *alibi*; therefore I repressed my private sentiments, and, tying my handkerchief to a stick, determined that no time should be fashionably frittered away in false starts.

They got away somehow; I believe Sheehy's colt was facing the wrong way at the moment when I dropped the flag, but a friend turned him with a stick, and, with a cordial and timely whack, speeded him on his way on sufficiently level terms, and then somehow, instead of returning to the tent, I found myself with Miss Sally on the top of a tall narrow bank, in a precarious line of other spectators, with whom we toppled and swayed, and, in moments of acuter emotion, held on to each other in unaffected comradeship.

Flurry started well, and from our commanding position we could see him methodically riding at the first fence at a smart hunting canter, closely attended by James Canty's brother on a young black mare, and by an unknown youth on a big white horse. The hope of Sheehy's stable, a leggy chestnut, ridden by a cadet of the house of Sheehy, went away from the friend's stick like a rocket, and had already refused the first bank twice before old Sultan decorously changed feet on it and dropped down into the next field with tranquil precision. The white horse scrambled over it on his stomach, but landed safely, despite the fact that his rider clasped him round the neck during the process; the black mare and the chestnut shouldered one another over at the hole the white horse had left, and the whole party went away in a bunch and jumped the ensuing hurdle without disaster. Flurry continued to ride at the same steady hunting pace, accompanied respectfully by the white horse and by Jerry Canty on the black mare. Sheehy's colt had clearly the legs of the party, and did some showy galloping between the jumps, but as he refused to face the banks without a lead, the end of the first round found the field still a sociable party personally conducted by Mr. Knox.

"That's a dam nice horse," said one of my hangers-on, looking approvingly at Sultan as he passed us at the beginning of the second round, making a good deal of noise but apparently going at his ease; "you might depind your life on him, and he have the crabbedest jock in the globe of Ireland on him this minute."

"Canty's mare's very sour," said another; "look at her now, baulking the bank! she's as cross as a bag of weasels."

"Begob, I wouldn't say but she's a little sign lame," resumed the first; "she was going light on one leg on the road a while ago."

"I tell you what it is," said Miss Sally, very seriously, in my ear, "that chestnut of Sheehy's is settling down. I'm afraid he'll gallop away from Sultan at the finish, and the wall won't stop him. Flurry can't get another inch out of Sultan. He's riding him well," she ended in a critical voice, which yet was not quite like her own. Perhaps I should not have noticed it but for the fact that the hand that held my arm was trembling. As for me, I thought of Lady Knox, and trembled too.

There now remained but one bank, the trampled remnant of the furze hurdle, and the stone wall. The pace was beginning to improve, and the other horses drew away from Sultan; they charged the bank at full gallop, the black mare and the chestnut flying it perilously, with a windmill flourish of legs and arms from their riders, the white horse racing up to it with a gallantry that deserted him at the critical moment, with the result that his rider turned a somersault over his head and landed, amidst the roars of the onlookers, sitting on the fence facing his horse's nose. With creditable presence of mind he remained on the bank, towed the horse over, scrambled on to his back again and started afresh. Sultan, thirty yards to the bad, pounded doggedly on, and Flurry's cane and heels remained idle; the old horse, obviously blown, slowed cautiously coming in at the jump. Sally's grip tightened on my arm, and the crowd yelled as Sultan, answering to a hint from the spurs and a touch at his mouth, heaved himself on to the bank. Nothing but sheer riding on Flurry's part got him safe off it, and saved him from the consequences of a bad peck on landing; none the less, he pulled himself together and went away down the hill for the stone wall as stoutly as ever. The high-road skirted the last two fields, and there was a gate in the roadside fence beside the place where the stone wall met it at right angles. I had noticed this gate, because during the first round Slipper had been sitting on it, demonstrating with his usual fevour. Sheehy's colt was leading, with his nose in the air, his rider's hands going like a circular saw, and his temper, as a bystander remarked, "up on end"; the black mare, half mad from spurring, was going hard at his heels, completely out of hand; the white horse was steering steadily for the wrong side of the flag, and Flurry, by dint of cutting corners and of saving every yard of ground, was close enough to keep his antagonists' heads over their shoulders, while their right arms rose and fell in unceasing flagellation.

"There'll be a smash when they come to the wall! If one falls they'll all go!" panted Sally. "Oh!—— Now! Flurry! Flurry!——"

What had happened was that the chestnut colt had suddenly perceived that the gate at right angles to the wall was standing wide open, and, swinging away from the jump, he had bolted headlong out on to the road, and along it at top speed for his home. After him fled Canty's black mare, and with her, carried away by the spirit of stampede, went the white horse.

Flurry stood up in his stirrups and gave a view-halloa as he cantered down to the wall. Sultan came at it with the send of the hill behind him, and jumped it with a skill that intensified, if that were possible, the volume of laughter and yells around us. By the time the black mare and the white horse had returned and ignominiously bundled over the wall to finish as best they might, Flurry was leading Sultan towards us.

"That blackguard, Slipper!" he said, grinning; "every one'll say I told him to open the gate! But look here, I'm afraid we're in for trouble. Sultan's given himself a bad over-reach; you could never drive him home to-night. And I've just seen Norris lying blind drunk under a wall!"

Now Norris was Lady Knox's coachman. We stood aghast at this "horror on horror's head," the blood trickled down Sultan's heel, and the lather lay in flecks on his dripping, heaving sides, in irrefutable witness to the iniquity of Lady Knox's only daughter. Then Flurry said:

"Thank the Lord, here's the rain!"

At the moment I admit that I failed to see any cause for gratitude in this occurrence, but later on I appreciated Flurry's grasp of circumstances.

That appreciation was, I think, at its highest development about half-an-hour afterwards, when I, an unwilling conspirator (a part with which my acquaintance with Mr. Knox had rendered me but too familiar) unfurled Mrs. Cadogan's umbrella over Lady Knox's head, and hurried her through the rain from the tent to the 'bus, keeping it and my own person well between her and the horses. I got her in, with the rest of her bedraggled and exhausted party, and slammed the door.

"Remember, Major Yeates," she said through the window, "you are the *only* person here in whom I have any confidence. I don't wish *any* one else to touch the reins!" this with a glance towards Flurry, who was standing near.

"I'm afraid I'm only a moderate whip," I said.

"My dear man," replied Lady Knox testily, "those horses could drive themselves!"

I slunk round to the front of the 'bus. Two horses, carefully rugged, were in it, with the inevitable Slipper at their heads.

"Slipper's going with you," whispered Flurry, stepping up to me; "she won't have me at any price. He'll throw the rugs over them when you get to the house, and if you hold the umbrella well over her she'll never see. I'll manage to get Sultan over somehow, when Norris is sober. That will be all right."

I climbed to the box without answering, my soul being bitter within me, as is the soul of a man who has been persuaded by womankind against his judgment.

"Never again!" I said to myself, picking up the reins; "let her marry him or Bernard Shute, or both of them if she likes, but I won't be roped into this kind of business again!"

Slipper drew the rugs from the horses, revealing on the near side Lady Knox's majestic carriage horse, and on the off, a thick-set brown mare of about fifteen hands.

"What brute is this?" said I to Slipper, as he swarmed up beside me.

"I don't rightly know where Misther Flurry got her," said Slipper, with one of his hiccoughing crows of laughter; "give her the whip, Major, and"—here he broke into song:

> "Howld to the shteel,
> Honamaundhiaoul; she'll run off like an eel!'

"If you don't shut your mouth," said I, with pent-up ferocity, "I'll chuck you off the 'bus."

Slipper was but slightly drunk, and, taking this delicate rebuke in good part, he relapsed into silence.

Wherever the brown mare came from, I can certify that it was not out of double harness. Though humble and anxious to oblige, she pulled away from the pole as if it were red hot, and at critical moments had a tendency to sit down. However, we squeezed without misadventure among the donkey carts and between the groups of people, and bumped at length in safety out on to the high-road.

Here I thought it no harm to take Slipper's advice, and I applied the whip to the brown mare, who seemed inclined to turn round. She immediately fell into an uncertain canter that no effort of mine could frustrate; I could only hope that Miss Sally would foster conversation inside the 'bus and create a distraction; but judging from my last view of the party, and of Lady Knox in particular, I thought she was not likely to be successful. Fortunately the rain was heavy and thick, and a rising west wind gave every promise of its continuance. I had little doubt but that I should catch cold, but I took it to my bosom with gratitude as I reflected how it was drumming on the roof of the 'bus and blurring the windows.

We had reached the foot of a hill, about a quarter of a mile from the racecourse; the Castle Knox horse addressed himself to it with dignified determination, but the mare showed a sudden and alarming tendency to jib.

"Belt her, Major!" vociferated Slipper, as she hung back from the pole chain, with the collar half-way up her ewe neck, "and give it to the horse, too! He'll dhrag her!"

I was in the act of "belting," when a squealing whinny struck upon my ear, accompanied by a light pattering gallop on the road behind us; there was an answering roar from the brown mare, a roar, as I realised with a sudden drop of the heart, of outraged maternal feeling, and in another instant a pale, yellow foal sprinted up beside us, with shrill whickerings of joy. Had there at this moment been a boghole handy, I should have turned the 'bus into it without hesitation; as there was no accommodation of the kind, I laid the whip severely into everything I could reach, including the foal. The result was that we topped the hill at a gallop, three abreast, like a Russian troitska; it was like my usual luck that at this identical moment we should meet the police patrol, who saluted respectfully.

"That the divil may blisther Michael Moloney!" ejaculated Slipper, holding on to the rail; "didn't I give him the foaleen and a halther on him to keep him! I'll howld you a pint 'twas the wife let him go, for she being vexed about the license! Sure that one's a March foal, an' he'd run from here to Cork!"

There was no sign from my inside passengers, and I held on at a round pace, the mother and child galloping absurdly, the carriage horse pulling hard, but behaving like a gentleman. I wildly revolved plans of how I would make Slipper turn the foal in at the first gate we came to, of what I should say to Lady Knox supposing the worst happened and the foal accompanied us to her hall door, and of how I would have Flurry's blood at the earliest possible opportunity, and here the fateful sound of galloping behind us was again heard.

"It's impossible!" I said to myself; "she can't have twins!"

The galloping came nearer, and Slipper looked back.

"Murdher alive!" he said in a stage whisper; "Tom Sheehy's afther us on the butcher's pony!"

"What's that to me?" I said, dragging my team aside to let him pass; "I suppose he's drunk, like every one else!"

Then the voice of Tom Sheehy made itself heard.

"Shtop! Shtop thief!" he was bawling; "give up my mare! How will I get me porther home!"

That was the closest shave I have ever had, and nothing could have saved the position but the torrential nature of the rain and the fact that Lady Knox had on a new bonnet. I explained to her at the door of the bus that Sheehy was drunk (which was the one unassailable feature of the case), and had come after

"Shtop! Shtop thief!"

his foal, which, with the fatuity of its kind, had escaped from a field and followed us. I did not mention to Lady Knox that when Mr. Sheehy retreated, apologetically, dragging the foal after him in a halter belonging to one of her own carriage horses, he had a sovereign of mine in his pocket, and during the narration I avoided Miss Sally's eye as carefully as she avoided mine.

The only comments on the day's events that are worthy of record were that Philippa said to me that she had not been able to understand what the curious taste in the tea had been till Sally told her it was turf-smoke, and that Mrs. Cadogan said to Philippa that night that "the Major was that dhrinched that if he had a shirt between his skin and himself he could have wrung it," and that Lady Knox said to a mutual friend that though Major Yeates had been extremely kind and obliging he was an uncommonly bad whip.

Twelve

<hr/>

"OH LOVE! OH FIRE!"

IT was on one of the hottest days of a hot August that I walked over to Tory Lodge to inform Mr. Flurry Knox, M.F.H., that the limits of human endurance had been reached, and that either Venus and her family, or I and mine, must quit Shreelane. In a moment of impulse I had accepted her and her numerous progeny as guests in my stable-yard, since when Mrs. Cadogan had given warning once or twice a week, and Maria, lawful autocrat of the ashpit, had had—I quote the kitchenmaid—"tin battles for every male she'd ate."

The walk over the hills was not of a nature to lower the temperature, moral or otherwise. The grassy path was as slippery as glass, the rocks radiated heat, the bracken radiated horseflies. There was no need to nurse my wrath to keep it warm.

I found Flurry seated in the kennel-yard in a long and unclean white linen coat, engaged in clipping hieroglyphics on the ears of a young outgoing draft, an occupation in itself unfavourable to argument. The young draft had already monopolised all possible forms of remonstrance, from snarling in the obscurity behind the meal sack in the boiler-house, to hysterical yelling as they were dragged forth by the tail; but through these alarms and excursions I denounced Venus and all her works, from slaughtered Wyandottes to broken dishes. Even as I did so I was conscious of something chastened in Mr. Knox's demeanour, some touch of remoteness and melancholy with which I was quite unfamiliar; my indictment weakened and my grievances became trivial when laid before this grave and almost religiously gentle young man.

"I'm sorry you and Mrs. Yeates should be vexed by her. Send her back when you like. I'll keep her. Maybe it'll not be for so long after all."

When pressed to expound this dark saying Flurry smiled wanly and snipped a second line in the hair of the puppy that was pinned between his legs. I was almost relieved when a hard try to bite on the part of the puppy imparted to Flurry's language a transient warmth; but the reaction was only temporary.

"It'd be as good for me to make a present of this lot to old Welby as to take the price he's offering me," he went on, as he got up and took off his highly-scented kennel-coat, "but I couldn't be bothered fighting him. Come on in and have something. I drink tea myself at this hour."

If he had said toast and water it would have seemed no more than was suitable to such a frame of mind. As I followed him to the house I thought that when the day came that Flurry Knox could not be bothered with fighting old Welby things were becoming serious, but I kept this opinion to myself and merely offered an admiring comment on the roses that were blooming on the front of the house.

"I put up every stick of that trellis myself with my own hands," said Flurry, still gloomily; "the roses were trailing all over the place for the want of it. Would you like to have a look at the garden while they're getting tea? I settled it up a bit since you saw it last."

I acceded to this almost alarmingly ladylike suggestion, marvelling greatly.

Flurry certainly was a changed man, and his garden was a changed garden. It was a very old garden, with unexpected arbours madly overgrown with flowering climbers, and a flight of grey steps leading to a terrace, where a moss-grown sundial and ancient herbaceous plants strove with nettles and briars; but I chiefly remembered it as a place where washing was wont to hang on black-currant bushes, and the kennel terrier matured his bones and hunted chickens. There was now rabbit wire on the gate, the walks were cleaned, the beds weeded. There was even a bed of mignonette, a row of sweet pea, and a blazing party of sunflowers, and Michael, once second in command in many a filibustering expedition, was now on his knees, ingloriously tying carnations to little pieces of cane.

We walked up the steps to the terrace. Down below us the rich and southern blue of the sea filled the gaps between scattered fir-trees; the hillside above was purple with heather; a bay mare and her foal were moving lazily through the bracken, with the sun glistening on it and them. I looked back at the house, nestling in the hollow of the hill, I smelled the smell of the mignonette in the air, I regarded Michael's labouring back among the carnations, and without any connection of ideas I seemed to see Miss Sally Knox, with her golden-red hair and slight figure, standing on the terrace beside her kinsman.

"Michael! Do ye know where's Misther Flurry?" squalled a voice from the garden gate, the untrammelled voice of the female domestic at large among her fellows. "The tay's wet, and there's a man over with a message from Aussolas. He was tellin' me the owld hairo beyant is givin' out invitations——"

A stricken silence fell, induced, no doubt, by hasty danger signals from Michael.

"Who's 'the old hero beyant?'" I asked, as we turned toward the house.

"My grandmother," said Flurry, permitting himself a smile that had about as much sociability in it as skim milk; "she's giving a tenants' dance at Aussolas. She gave one about five years ago, and I declare you might as well get the influenza into the country, or a mission at the chapel. There won't be a servant in the place will be able to answer their name for a week after it, what with toothache and headache, and blathering in the kitchen!"

We had tea in the drawing-room, a solemnity which I could not but be aware was due to the presence of a new carpet, a new wall-paper, and a new piano. Flurry made no comment on these things, but something told me that I was expected to do so, and I did.

"I'd sell you the lot to-morrow for half what I gave for them," said my host, eyeing them with morose respect as he poured out his third cup of tea.

I have all my life been handicapped by not having the courage of my curiosity. Those who have the nerve to ask direct questions on matters that do not concern them seldom fail to extract direct answers, but in my lack of this enviable gift I went home in the dark as to what had befallen my landlord, and fully aware of how my wife would despise me for my shortcomings. Philippa always says that she never asks questions, but she seems none the less to get a lot of answers.

On my own avenue I met Miss Sally Knox riding away from the house on her white cob; she had found no one at home, and she would not turn back with me, but she did not seem to be in any hurry to ride away. I told her that I had just been over to see her relative, Mr. Knox, who had informed me that he meant to give up the hounds, a fact in which she seemed only conventionally interested. She looked pale, and her eyelids were slightly pink; I checked myself on the verge of asking her if she had hay-fever, and inquired instead if she had heard of the tenants' dance at Aussolas. She did not answer at first, but rubbed her cane up and down the cob's clipped toothbrush of a mane. Then she said:

"Major Yeates—look here—there's a most awful row at home!"

I expressed incoherent regret, and wished to my heart that Philippa had been there to cope with the situation.

"It began when mamma found out about Flurry's racing Sultan, and then came our dance——"

Miss Sally stopped; I nodded, remembering certain episodes of Lady Knox's dance.

"And—mamma says—she says——"

I waited respectfully to hear what mamma had said; the cob fidgeted under the attentions of the horseflies, and nearly trod on my toe.

"Well, the end of it is," she said with a gulp, "she said such things to Flurry that he can't come near the house again, and I'm to go over to England to Aunt Dora, next week. Will you tell Philippa I came to say good-bye to her? I don't think I can get over here again."

Miss Sally was a sufficiently old friend of mine for me to take her hand and press it in a fatherly manner, but for the life of me I could not think of anything to say, unless I expressed my sympathy with her mother's point of view about detrimentals, which was obviously not the thing to do.

Philippa accorded to my news the rare tribute of speechless attention, and then was despicable enough to say that she had foreseen the whole affair from the beginning.

"From the day that she refused him in the ice-house, I suppose," said I sarcastically.

"That *was* the beginning," replied Philippa.

"Well," I went on judicially, "whenever it began, it was high time for it to end. She can do a good deal better than Flurry."

Philippa became rather red in the face.

"I call that a thoroughly commonplace thing to say," she said. "I dare say he has not many ideas beyond horses, but no more has she, and he really does come and borrow books from me——"

"Whitaker's Almanack," I murmured.

"Well, I don't care, I like him very much, and I know what

you're going to say, and you're wrong, and I'll tell you why——"

Here Mrs. Cadogan came into the room, her cap at rather more than its usual warlike angle over her scarlet forehead, and in her hand a kitchen plate, on which a note was ceremoniously laid forth.

"But this is for you, Mrs. Cadogan," said Philippa, as she looked at it.

"Ma'am," returned Mrs. Cadogan with immense dignity, "I have no learning, and from what the young man's afther telling me that brought it from Aussolas, I'd sooner yerself read it for me than thim gerrls."

My wife opened the envelope, and drew forth a gilt-edged sheet of pink paper.

"Miss Margaret Nolan presents her compliments to Mrs. Cadogan," she read, "and I have the pleasure of telling you that the servants of Aussolas is inviting you and Mr. Peter Cadogan, Miss Mulrooney, and Miss Gallagher"—Philippa's voice quavered perilously—"to a dance on next Wednesday. Dancing to begin at seven o'clock, and to go on till five.— Yours affectionately, MAGGIE NOLAN."

"How affectionate she is!" snorted Mrs. Cadogan; "them's Dublin manners, I dare say!"

"P.S.," continued Philippa; "steward, Mr. Denis O'Loughlin; stewardess, Mrs. Mahony."

"Thoughtful provision," I remarked; "I suppose Mrs. Mahony's duties will begin after supper."

"Well, Mrs. Cadogan," said Philippa, quelling me with a glance, "I suppose you'd all like to go?"

"As for dancin'," said Mrs. Cadogan, with her eyes fixed on a level with the curtain-pole, "I thank God I'm a widow, and the only dancin' I'll do is to dance to my grave."

"Well, perhaps Julia, and Annie, and Peter——" suggested Philippa, considerably overawed.

"I'm not one of them that holds with loud mockery and harangues," continued Mrs. Cadogan, "but if I had any wish for dhrawing down talk I could tell you, ma'am, that the like o' them has their share of dances without going to Aussolas! Wasn't it only last Sunday week I wint follyin' the turkey that's layin' out in the plantation, and the whole o' thim hysted their sails and back with them to their lovers at the gate-house, and the kitchenmaid having a Jew-harp to be playing for them!"

"That was very wrong," said the truckling Philippa. "I hope you spoke to the kitchenmaid about it."

"Is it spake to thim?" rejoined Mrs. Cadogan. "No, but what I done was to dhrag the kitchenmaid round the passages by the hair o' the head!"

"Well, after that, I think you might let her go to Aussolas," said I venturously.

The end of it was that every one in and about the house went to Aussolas on the following Wednesday, including Mrs. Cadogan. Philippa had gone over to stay at the Shutes, ostensibly to arrange about a jumble sale, the real object being (as a matter of history) to inspect the Scotch young lady before whom Bernard Shute had dumped his affections in his customary manner. Being alone, with every prospect of a bad dinner, I accepted with gratitude an invitation to dine and sleep at Aussolas and see the dance; it is only on very special occasions that I have the heart to remind Philippa that she had neither part nor lot in what occurred—it is too serious a matter for trivial gloryings.

Mrs. Knox had asked me to dine at six o'clock, which meant that I arrived, in blazing sunlight and evening clothes, punctually at that hour, and that at seven o'clock I was still sitting in the library, reading heavily-bound classics, while my hostess held loud conversations down staircases with Denis O'Loughlin, the red-bearded Robinson Crusoe who combined in himself the offices of coachman, butler, and, to the best of my belief, valet to the lady of the house. The door opened at last, and Denis, looking as furtive as his prototype after he had sighted the footprint, put in his head and beckoned to me.

"The misthress says will ye go to dinner without her," he

said very confidentially; "sure she's greatly vexed ye should be waitin' on her. 'Twas the kitchen chimney cot fire, and faith she's afther giving Biddy Mahony the sack, on the head of it! Though, indeed, 'tis little we'd regard a chimney on fire here any other day."

*The meal was hurled on to the table
by Crusoe*

Mrs. Knox's woolly dog was the sole occupant of the dining-room when I entered it; he was sitting on his mistress's chair, with all the air of outrage peculiar to a small and self-important dog when routine has been interfered with. It was difficult to discover what had caused the delay, the meal, not excepting the soup, being a cold collation; it was heavily flavoured with soot, and was hurled on to the table by Crusoe in spasmodic bursts, contemporaneous, no doubt, with Biddy Mahony's fits of hysterics in the kitchen. Its most memorable feature was a noble lake trout, which appeared in two jagged pieces, a matter lightly alluded to by Denis as the result of "a little argument" between himself and Biddy as to the dish on which it was to be served. Further conversation elicited the interesting fact that the combatants had pulled the trout in two before the matter was settled. A brief glance at my attendant's hands decided me to let the woolly dog justify his existence by consuming my portion for me, when Crusoe left the room.

Old Mrs. Knox remained invisible till the end of dinner, when she appeared in the purple velvet bonnet that she was reputed to have worn since the famine, and a dun-coloured woollen shawl fastened by a splendid diamond brooch, that flashed rainbow fire against the last shafts of sunset. There was a fire in the old lady's eye, too, the light that I had sometimes seen in Flurry's in moments of crisis.

"I have no apologies to offer that are worth hearing," she said, "but I have come to drink a glass of port wine with you, if you will so far honour me, and then we must go out and see the ball. My grandson is late, as usual."

She crumbled a biscuit with a brown and preoccupied hand; her claw-like fingers carried a crowded sparkle of diamonds upwards as she raised her glass to her lips.

The twilight was falling when we left the room and made our way downstairs. I followed the little figure in the purple bonnet through dark regions of passages and doorways, where strange lumber lay about; there was a rusty suit of armour, an upturned punt, mouldering pictures, and finally, by a door that opened into the yard, a lady's bicycle, white with the dust of travel. I supposed this latter to have been imported from Dublin by the fashionable Miss Maggie Nolan, but on the other hand it was well within the bounds of possibility that it belonged to old Mrs. Knox. The coach-house at Aussolas was on a par with the rest of the establishment, being vast, dilapidated, and of unknown age. Its three double doors were wide open, and the guests overflowed through them into the cobble-stoned yard; above their heads the tin reflectors of paraffin lamps glared at us from among the Christmas decorations of holly and ivy that festooned the walls. The voices of a fiddle and a concertina, combined, were uttering a polka with shrill and hideous fluency, to which the scraping and stamping of hobnailed boots made a ponderous bass accompaniment.

Mrs. Knox's donkey-chair had been placed in a commanding position at the top of the room, and she made her way slowly to it, shaking hands with all varieties of tenants and saying right things without showing any symptom of that flustered boredom that I have myself exhibited when I went round the men's messes on Christmas Day. She took her seat in the donkey-chair, with the white dog in her lap, and looked with her hawk's eyes round the array of faces that hemmed in the space where the dancers were solemnly bobbing and hopping.

"Will you tell me who that tomfool is, Denis?" she said, pointing to a young lady in a ball dress who was circling in conscious magnificence and somewhat painful incongruity in the arms of Mr. Peter Cadogan.

"That's the lady's-maid from Castle Knox, yer honour, ma'am," replied Denis, with something remarkably like a wink at Mrs. Knox.

"When did the Castle Knox servants come?" asked the old lady, very sharply.

"The same time yer honour left the table, and——Pillilew! What's this?"

There was a clatter of galloping hoofs in the courtyard, as of a troop of cavalry, and out of the heart of it Flurry's voice shouting to Denis to drive out the colts and shut the gates before they had the people killed. I noticed that the colour had risen to Mrs. Knox's face, and I put it down to anxiety about her young horses. I may admit that when I heard Flurry's voice, and saw him collaring his grandmother's guests and pushing them out of the way as he came into the coach-house, I rather feared that he was in the condition so often defined to me at Petty Sessions as "not dhrunk, but having dhrink taken." His face was white, his eyes glittered, there was a general air of exaltation about him that suggested the solace of the pangs of love according to the most ancient convention.

"Hullo!" he said, swaggering up to the orchestra, "what's this humbugging thing they're playing? A polka, is it? Drop that, John Casey, and play a jig."

John Casey ceased abjectly.

"What'll I play, Masther Flurry?"

"What the devil do I care? Here, Yeates, put a name on it! You're a sort of musicianer yourself!"

I know the names of three or four Irish jigs; but on this occasion my memory clung exclusively to one, I suppose because it was the one I felt to be peculiarly inappropriate.

"Oh, well, 'Haste to the Wedding,'" I said, looking away.

Flurry gave a shout of laughter.

"That's it!" he exclaimed. "Play it up, John! Give us 'Haste to the Wedding.' That's Major Yeates's fancy!"

Decidedly Flurry was drunk.

"What's wrong with you all that you aren't dancing?" he continued, striding up the middle of the room. "Maybe you don't know how. Here, I'll soon get one that'll show you!"

He advanced upon his grandmother, snatched her out of the donkey-chair, and, amid roars of applause, led her out, while the fiddle squealed its way through the inimitable twists of the tune, and the concertina surged and panted after it. Whatever Mrs. Knox may have thought of her grandson's behaviour, she was evidently going to make the best of it. She took her station opposite to him, in the purple bonnet, the dun-coloured shawl, and the diamonds, she picked up her skirt at each side, affording a view of narrow feet in elastic-sided cloth boots, and for three repeats of the tune she stood up to her grandson, and footed it on the coach-house floor. What the cloth boots did

I could not exactly follow; they were, as well as I could see, extremely scientific, while there was hardly so much as a nod from the plumes of the bonnet. Flurry was also scientific, but his dancing did not alter my opinion that he was drunk; in fact, I thought he was making rather an exhibition of himself. They say that that jig was twenty pounds in Mrs. Knox's pocket at the next rent day; but though this statement is open to doubt, I believe that if she and Flurry had taken the hat round there and then she would have got in the best part of her arrears.

After this the company settled down to business. The dances lasted a sweltering half-hour, old women and young dancing with equal and tireless zest. At the end of each the gentlemen abandoned their partners without ceremony or comment, and went out to smoke, while the ladies retired to the laundry, where families of teapots stewed on the long bars of the fire, and Mrs. Mahony cut up mighty "barm-bracks," and the tea-drinking was illimitable.

At ten o'clock Mrs. Knox withdrew from the revel; she said that she was tired, but I have seldom seen any one look more wide awake. I thought that I might unobtrusively follow her example, but I was intercepted by Flurry.

"Yeates," he said seriously, "I'll take it as a kindness if you'll see this thing out with me. We must keep them pretty sober, and get them out of this by daylight. I—I have to get home early."

I at once took back my opinion that Flurry was drunk; I almost wished he had been, as I could then have deserted him without a pang. As it was, I addressed myself heavily to the night's enjoyment. Wan with heat, but conscientiously cheerful, I danced with Miss Maggie Nolan, with the Castle Knox lady's-maid, with my own kitchenmaid, who fell into wild giggles of terror whenever I spoke to her, with Mrs. Cadogan, who had apparently postponed the interesting feat of dancing to her grave, and did what she could to dance me into mine. I am bound to admit that though an ex-soldier and a major, and therefore equipped with a ready-made character for gallantry,

Mrs. Cadogan was the only one of my partners with whom I conversed with any comfort.

At intervals I smoked cigarettes in the yard, seated on the old mounting-block by the gate, and overheard much conversation about the price of pigs in Skebawn; at intervals I plunged again into the coach-house, and led forth a perspiring wall-flower into the scrimmage of a polka, or shuffled meaninglessly opposite to her in the long double line of dancers who were engaged with serious faces in executing a jig or a reel, I neither knew nor cared which. Flurry remained as undefeated as ever; I could only suppose it was his method of showing that his broken heart had mended.

"It's time to be making the punch, Masther Flurry," said Denis, as the harness-room clock struck twelve; "sure the night's warm, and the men's all gaping for it, the craytures!"

"What'll we make it in?" said Flurry, as we followed him into the laundry.

"The boiler, to be sure," said Crusoe, taking up a stone of sugar, and preparing to shoot it into the laundry copper.

"Stop, you fool, it's full of cockroaches!" shouted Flurry, amid sympathetic squalls from the throng of countrywomen. "Go get a bath!"

"Sure yerself knows there's but one bath in it," retorted Denis, "and that's within in the Major's room. Faith, the tinker got his own share yesther-day with the same bath, sthriving to quinch the holes, and they as thick in it as the stars in the sky, and 'tis weeping still, afther all he done!"

"Well, then, here goes for the cockroaches!" said Flurry. "What doesn't sicken will fatten! Give me the kettle, and come on, you Kitty Collins, and be skimming them off!"

There were no complaints of the punch when the brew was completed, and the dance thundered on with a heavier stamping and a louder hilarity than before. The night wore on; I squeezed through the unyielding pack of frieze coats and shawls in the doorway, and with feet that momently swelled in my pumps I limped over the cobble-stones to smoke my eighth cigarette on the mounting-block. It was a dark, hot night. The old castle loomed above me in piled-up roofs and gables, and high up in it somewhere a window sent a shaft of light into the sleeping leaves of a walnut-tree that overhung the gateway. At the bars of the gate two young horses peered in at the medley of noise and people; away in an outhouse a cock crew hoarsely. The gaiety in the coach-house increased momently, till, amid shrieks and bursts of laughter, Miss Maggie Nolan fled coquettishly from it with a long yell, like a train coming out of a tunnel, pursued by the fascinating Peter Cadogan brandishing a twig of mountain ash, in imitation of mistletoe. The young horses stampeded in horror, and immediately a voice proceeded from the lighted window above, Mrs. Knox's voice, demanding what the noise was, and announcing that if she heard any more of it she would have the place cleared.

An awful silence fell, to which the young horses' fleeing hoofs lent the final touch of consternation. Then I heard the irrepressible Maggie Nolan say: "Oh God! Merry-come-sad!" which I take to be a reflection on the mutability of all earthly happiness.

Mrs. Knox remained for a moment at the window, and it struck me as remarkable that at 2.30 A.M. she should still have on her bonnet. I thought I heard her speak to some one in the room, and there followed a laugh, a laugh that was not a servant's, and was puzzlingly familiar. I gave it up, and presently dropped into a cheerless doze.

With the dawn there came a period when even Flurry showed signs of failing. He came and sat down beside me with a yawn; it struck me that there was more impatience and nervousness than fatigue in the yawn.

"I think I'll turn them all out of this after the next dance is over," he said; "I've a lot to do, and I can't stay here."

I grunted in drowsy approval. It must have been a few minutes later that I felt Flurry grip my shoulder.

"Yeates!" he said, "look up at the roof. Do you see anything up there by the kitchen chimney?"

He was pointing at a heavy stack of chimneys in a tower that stood up against the grey and pink of the morning sky. At the angle where one of them joined the roof smoke was oozing busily out, and, as I stared, a little wisp of flame stole through.

The next thing that I distinctly remember is being in the van of a rush through the kitchen passages, every one shouting "Water! Water!" and not knowing where to find it, then up several flights of the narrowest and darkest stairs it has ever been my fate to ascend, with a bucket of water that I snatched from a woman, spilling as I ran. At the top of the stairs came a ladder leading to a trap-door, and up in the dark loft above was the roar and the wavering glare of flames.

"My God! That's sthrong fire!" shouted Denis, tumbling down the ladder with a brace of empty buckets; "we'll never save it! The lake won't quinch it!"

The flames were squirting out through the bricks of the chimney, through the timbers, through the slates; it was barely possible to get through the trap-door, and the booming and crackling strengthened every instant.

"A chain to the lake!" gasped Flurry, coughing in the stifling heat as he slashed the water at the blazing rafters; "the well's no good! Go on, Yeates!"

The organising of a double chain out of the mob that thronged and shouted and jammed in the passages and yard was no mean feat of generalship; but it got done somehow. Mrs. Cadogan and Biddy Mahony rose magnificently to the occasion, cursing, thumping, shoving; and stable buckets, coal buckets, milk pails, and kettles were unearthed and sent swinging down the grass slope to the lake that lay in glittering unconcern in the morning sunshine. Men, women, and children worked in a way that only Irish people can work on an emergency. All their cleverness, all their good-heartedness, and all their love of a ruction came to the front; the screaming and the exhortations were incessant, but so were also the buckets that flew from hand to hand up to the loft. I hardly know how long we were at it, but there came a time when I looked up from the yard and saw that the billows of reddened smoke from the top of the tower were dying down, and I bethought me of old Mrs. Knox.

I found her at the door of her room, engaged in tying up a bundle of old clothes in a sheet; she looked as white as a corpse, but she was not in any way quelled by the situation.

"I'd be obliged to you all the same, Major Yeates, to throw this over the balusters," she said, as I advanced with the news that the fire had been got under. "'Pon my honour, I don't know when I've been as vexed as I've been this night, what with one thing and another! 'Tis a monstrous thing to use a guest as we've used you, but what could we do? I threw all the silver out of the dining-room window myself, and the poor peahen that had her nest there was hurt by an entrée dish, and half her eggs were——"

There was a curious sound not unlike a titter in Mrs. Knox's room.

"However, we can't make omelettes without breaking eggs—as they say—" she went on rather hurriedly: "I declare I don't know what I'm saying! My old head is confused——"

Here Mrs. Knox went abruptly into her room and shut the door. Obviously there was nothing further to do for my hostess, and I fought my way up the dripping back staircase to the loft. The flames had ceased, the supply of buckets had been stopped, and Flurry, standing on a ponderous crossbeam, was poking his head and shoulders out into the sunlight through the hole that had been burned in the roof. Denis and others were pouring water over charred beams, the atmosphere was still stifling, everything was black, everything dripped with inky water. Flurry descended from his beam and stretched himself, looking like a drowned chimney-sweep.

"We've made a night of it, Yeates, haven't we?" he said, "but we've bested it anyhow. We were done for only for you!" There was more emotion about him than the occasion seemed to warrant, and his eyes had a Christy Minstrel brightness, not wholly to be attributed to the dirt of his face. "What's the time?—I must get home."

The time, incredible as it seemed, was half-past six. I could almost have sworn that Flurry changed colour when I said so.

"I must be off," he said; "I had no idea it was so late."

"Why, what's the hurry?" I asked.

He stared at me, laughed foolishly, and fell to giving directions to Denis. Five minutes afterwards he drove out of the yard and away at a canter down the long stretch of avenue that skirted the lake, with a troop of young horses flying on either hand. He whirled his whip round his head and shouted at them, and was lost to sight in a clump of trees. It is a vision of him that remains with me, and it always carries with it the bitter smell of wet charred wood.

Reaction had begun to set in among the volunteers. The chain took to sitting in the kitchen, cups of tea began mysteriously to circulate, and personal narratives of the fire were already foreshadowing the amazing legends that have since gathered round the night's adventure. I left to Denis the task of clearing the house, and went up to change my wet clothes, with a feeling that I had not been to bed for a year. The ghost of a waiter who had drowned himself in a boghole would have presented a cheerier aspect than I, as I surveyed myself in the prehistoric mirror in my room, with the sunshine falling on my unshorn face and begrimed shirt-front.

I made my toilet at considerable length, and, it being now nearly eight o'clock, went downstairs to look for something to eat. I had left the house humming with people; I found it silent as Pompeii. The sheeted bundles containing Mrs. Knox's wardrobe were lying about the hall; a couple of ancestors who in the first alarm had been dragged from the walls were leaning drunkenly against the bundles; last night's dessert was still on the dining-room table. I went out on to the hall-door steps, and saw the entrée-dishes in a glittering heap in a nasturtium bed, and realised that there was no breakfast for me this side of lunch at Shreelane.

There was a sound of wheels on the avenue, and a brougham came into view, driving fast up the long open stretch by the lake. It was the Castle Knox brougham, driven by Norris, whom I had last seen drunk at the athletic sports, and as it drew up at the door I saw Lady Knox inside.

"It's all right, the fire's out," I said, advancing genially and full of reassurance.

"What fire?" said Lady Knox, regarding me with an iron countenance.

I explained.

"Well, as the house isn't burned down," said Lady Knox, cutting short my details, "perhaps you would kindly find out if I could see Mrs. Knox."

Lady Knox's face was many shades redder than usual. I began to understand that something awful had happened, or would happen, and I wished myself safe at Shreelane, with the bedclothes over my head.

"If 'tis for the misthress you're looking, me lady," said Denis's voice behind me, in tones of the utmost respect, "she went out to the kitchen garden a while ago to get a blasht o' the fresh air afther the night. Maybe your ladyship would sit inside in the library till I call her?"

Lady Knox eyed Crusoe suspiciously.

"Thank you, I'll fetch her myself," she said.

"Oh, sure, that's too throuble——" began Denis.

"Stay where you are!" said Lady Knox, in a voice like the slam of a door.

"Bedad, I'm best plased she went," whispered Denis, as Lady Knox set forth alone down the shrubbery walk.

"But *is* Mrs. Knox in the garden?" said I.

"The Lord preserve your innocence, sir!" replied Denis, with seeming irrelevance.

At this moment I became aware of the incredible fact that Sally Knox was silently descending the stairs; she stopped short as she got into the hall, and looked almost wildly at me and Denis. Was I looking at her wraith? There was again a sound of wheels on the gravel; she went to the hall door, outside which was now drawn up Mrs. Knox's donkey-carriage, as well as Lady Knox's brougham, and, as if overcome by this imposing spectacle, she turned back and put her hands over her face.

"She's gone round to the garden, asthore," said Denis in a hoarse whisper; "go in the donkey-carriage. 'Twill be all right!" He seized her by the arm, pushed her down the steps and into the little carriage, pulled up the hood over her to its furthest stretch, snatched the whip out of the hand of the broadly-grinning Norris, and with terrific objurgations lashed the donkey into a gallop. The donkey-boy grasped the position, whatever it might be; he took up the running on the other side, and the donkey-carriage swung away down the avenue, with all its incongruous air of hooded and rowdy invalidism.

I have never disguised the fact that I am a coward, and therefore when, at this dynamitical moment, I caught a glimpse of Lady Knox's hat over a laurustinus, as she returned at high speed from the garden, I slunk into the house and faded away round the dining-room door.

"This minute I seen the misthress going down through the plantation beyond," said the voice of Crusoe outside the window, "and I'm after sending Johnny Regan to her with the little carriage, not to put any more delay on yer ladyship. Sure you can see him making all the haste he can. Maybe you'd sit inside in the library till she comes."

Silence followed. I peered cautiously round the window curtain. Lady Knox was looking defiantly at the donkey-carriage as it reeled at top speed into the shades of the plantation, strenuously pursued by the woolly dog. Norris was regarding his horses' ears in expressionless respectability. Denis was picking up the entrée-dishes with decorous solicitude. Lady Knox turned and came into the house; she passed the dining-room door with an ominous step, and went on into the library.

It seemed to me that now or never was the moment to retire

quietly to my room, put my things into my portmanteau, and——

Denis rushed into the room with the entrée-dishes piled up to his chin.

"She's diddled!" he whispered, crashing them down on the table. He came at me with his hand out. "Three cheers for Masther Flurry and Miss Sally," he hissed, wringing my hand up and down, "and 'twas yerself called for 'Haste to the Weddin'' last night, long life to ye! The Lord save us! There's the misthress going into the library!"

Through the half-open door I saw old Mrs. Knox approach the library from the staircase with a dignified slowness; she had on a wedding garment, a long white burnous, in which she might easily have been mistaken for a small, stout clergyman. She waved back Crusoe, the door closed upon her, and the battle of giants was entered upon. I sat down—it was all I was able for—and remained for a full minute in stupefied contemplation of the entrée-dishes.

Perhaps of all conclusions to a situation so portentous, that which occurred was the least possible. Twenty minutes after Mrs. Knox met her antagonist I was summoned from strapping my portmanteau to face the appalling duty of escorting the combatants, in Lady Knox's brougham, to the church outside the back gate, to which Miss Sally had preceded them in the donkey-carriage. I pulled myself together, went downstairs, and found that the millennium had suddenly set in. It had apparently dawned with the news that Aussolas and all things therein were bequeathed to Flurry by his grandmother, and had established itself finally upon the considerations that the marriage was past praying for, and that the diamonds were intended for Miss Sally.

We fetched the bride and bridegroom from the church; we fetched old Eustace Hamilton, who married them; we dug out the champagne from the cellar; we even found rice and threw it.

The hired carriage that had been ordered to take the runaways across country to a distant station was driven by Slipper. He was shaved; he wore an old livery coat and a new pot hat; he was wondrous sober. On the following morning he was found asleep on a heap of stones ten miles away; somewhere in the neighbourhood one of the horses was grazing in

Even found rice and threw it

a field with a certain amount of harness hanging about it. The carriage and the remaining horse were discovered in a roadside ditch, two miles farther on; one of the carriage doors had been torn off, and in the interior the hens of the vicinity were conducting an exhaustive search after the rice that lurked in the cushions.

THE END

ABOUT THE AUTHORS

EDITH ŒNONE SOMERVILLE AND MARTIN ROSS (Violet Martin) were second cousins born in 1858 and 1862, respectively, to distant branches of a prominent Anglo-Irish Ascendancy family. They lived together at the Somerville home in County Cork for most of their adult lives, traveling frequently to Europe and collaborating on numerous books and articles. Their most famous novel, *The Real Charlotte*, was published in 1894. They are probably best remembered, however, for the series of hilarious stories centered on the character of Major Sinclair Yeates, Resident Magistrate: *Some Experiences of an Irish R.M.* (1899); *Further Experiences of an Irish R.M.* (1908); and *In Mr. Knox's Country* (1915).